Special thank you to all the karate students I know and love.
Those who helped me along my martial arts journey and have stuck
with me long after.
Special shout out to Sensei Charles Fink for the extra encouragement
and feedback! Ousss!
To my great kids who are all black belts. It was a rocky road, but I'm
so proud of all of you!

I0654198

DEATH OF A JADED SAMURAI

1st Edition, 2014, Gemma Halliday Publishing

2nd Edition, 2014, Gemma Halliday Publishing

3rd Edition, 2018, BWL Publishing

CHAPTER 1

"Not again," Gilda muttered as her cell phone vibrated next to her plate, making the ice in her half-full water glass dance. Her stomach churned, as it had all week. She couldn't even eat without that man needing something.

Across the table, Marion Yearly, her best friend and crying towel, scowled as she flicked toast crumbs off the blue tablecloth. "Just turn the stupid thing off. If your boss needs you that badly, he'll find you. Otherwise, he'll have to wait. He knows we're at The Cove Restaurant. We have brunch here every Friday. Maybe you should invite him to join us."

Of course she'd answer Mick's text. She always did, then regretted speaking to her boss on her own time.

"Like he'd want to hang out with his receptionist all day when he sees me half the night." Her face burned. "That didn't come out right. I meant during classes."

Their weekly brunch was far from a peaceful one. Gilda's phone had buzzed at least ten times since they were seated. Three times alone since her Belgian waffle and crispy bacon arrived two minutes ago.

As the phone buzzed again, Marion grimaced. "What does his majesty want this time?"

"He can't find the file for the school's lease. Or the latest inventory list. Or the latest student class lists."

"Or you," Marion said, sopping up runny egg yolk with a triangle of buttered toast. "Tell him to wait until you get there." It's only another hour anyway."

Gilda tossed a wistful glance at her food, her appetite waning as she reached for her phone. If she didn't text him back right away, he'd send ten more messages before she took her next mouthful. "I would, but he's going away for the long weekend and won't be there when I show up. If I answer now, he might leave me alone for a while."

"Even better. You'll have all weekend to find them. He'll just have to be patient for a change. You so have a life and can't keep dropping everything just because the sensei wants something."

Marion, dark-haired and raven-eyed, was taller than Gilda by a full foot and twice as wide. she was built more like an NFL quarterback than a 9-1-1 operator. Of course, Gilda doubted there was a stereotype for 9-1-1 operators anyway.

"I know where they are," Gilda told her. "Give me a second."

"*In the file drawer,*" She typed. "*Lease under Yoshida Lease. Inventory under Inventory. Student lists in the computer database.*"

Once she set the phone aside and blew out a heavy breath, she barely had enough time to cut off a bite of waffle and bring it halfway to her mouth before her phone vibrated again. Her stomach sank. Cripes, at this rate, she'd never get to eat before her doctor's appointment. While her stomach didn't hurt as much as it had lately, she realized her pain was likely from stress caused by Sensei Mick Williams.

Marion grabbed Gilda's phone and sat on it. "That's it. The only time you and I can get together lately is Friday mornings because Mick always needs something. Honey, if I didn't know better, I'd think you two were married."

Gilda flushed and picked at her waffle, not wanting to make a scene. Worse than being married, they were boss and secretary, which he seemed to take as the same thing as husband and wife. Somewhere over the past two years, the line had become blurred. The black belts teased her about being his third arm.

When she started working at Yoshida Martial Arts two years earlier, she'd only see Sensei Mick in passing. She once overheard him tell one of the instructors she was bright and competent enough to figure things out on her own. So, she had. Lately, however, she couldn't seem to breathe without him hovering over her instructing her on how to take each breath.

Yoshida Martial Arts ran as smooth as a straight ribbon of highway and boasted a profit every month. Both of which had made the school's namesake, Shihan Yoshida, sit up and take notice. Was Mick nervous because Yoshida had become prone to showing up at odd times and nosing around? He seemed to constantly undermine Mick's position as manager and sensei, teacher. Male posturing was one thing she'd never understand, no matter how much she saw it at the school.

"Hello?" Marion leaned forward and waved a piece of toast in front of Gilda's face. "For the record, you got two more texts while you were daydreaming. My butt's shimmying so much I feel like a belly dancer."

Gilda snorted then laughed. "I can put it in my purse if it's annoying you."

"Nope. You need to relax and eat your breakfast." A small grin lit Marion's face. "Besides, I'm kind of enjoying this."

Not so sure she wanted the phone back anyway Gilda shook her head. "I think you need a real boyfriend. We both do."

With Marion sitting on her phone, they enjoyed the rest of brunch. Occasionally, Marion flinched. "Ooh, another text from your sensei."

"He's going to think I'm avoiding him." Gilda swiped one last gob of whipped cream with her finger and brought it toward her mouth.

"You are. Stop being a pushover. At least until after brunch,"

"I will."

Marion waved her knife. "Look, you've stuck up for yourself before so stop sticking your head in the sand and lay down some boundaries with that man. Your time is your time. You don't see me answering nine-one-one calls over breakfast, do you?"

Gilda chuckled. "You'd probably get fired if you did."

When a tall, blond man stopped next to their table, Gilda froze, her finger still covered in whipped cream. Detective Jason Thayer was the former boyfriend she'd dumped two years ago in such a dramatic fashion the story made the newspapers for an entire week. Thayer had thrived on his sudden notoriety and got a lot of dates because of the exposure. Gilda cowered in her house for weeks before Marion was able to drag her out and helped her get a job in the karate school in the hope she'd get a backbone.

"Good morning, ladies," Thayer said.

"Good morning, Detective," Marion said, batting her eyes. "Are you here to arrest the kitchen staff for beating the eggs or just to harass Gilda?"

Thayer twisted his face into a grimace before turning to Gilda. She sat motionless while the whipped cream blob slid down her finger. "I'd be happy to lick that off for you, but I have an image to uphold."

"Yeah, you wouldn't want to improve on that now, would you? What do you want, Thayer?" Gilda muttered, pushed her plate away, fighting the urge to flick the goo at his jacket. She wiped her finger on her napkin. No point in giving him more ideas.

He shrugged. "I just stopped by to say hello."

Marion rolled her eyes. "You want to stick with that or tell her the truth?"

"The one where he says he loves me and would die for me, or the one where he cheats on me with any woman who'll have him?" Gilda asked.

Thayer's face darkened and said, "I'm only trying to be sociable."

"I overheard him tell a couple officers he's this close to taking you back," Marion told her, holding her index finger and thumb a quarter inch apart.

What kind of man refused to take no for an answer even after two years? Gilda shut her eyes and inhaled slowly. *I am not going to make a scene.*

"What I said was—"

Detective John Fabio, Thayer's partner, clapped a hand on his left shoulder. "Just ask her out already, so she can deck you and get it over with. We have work to do."

Thayer growled. "If you guys don't mind, I'd like to do this alone."

"I don't mind at all. I was just leaving." Gilda stood and grabbed her purse. She marched up to the cashier to pay for their food. This week it was her turn. A convenient excuse to escape.

Marion joined her, shoving Gilda's phone into her back pocket. "You might want this before I get too attached."

"Who does Thayer think he is?" Gilda asked, reaching for a mint. Needing something to crunch, she took three.

"One of Sandstone Cove's finest. He certainly does look the part, even if he needs an attitude adjustment."

When Gilda's phone buzzed, she gritted her teeth and muttered, "Not again."

"There's another one who looks the part," Marion said.

"Mick?" She left her change as a generous tip, then pushed the front door open. "What do you mean he looks the part?"

Marion popped a mint into her mouth. "Handsome and authoritative, but from the stories I've heard—"

"I don't want to hear any more. It's bad enough the parents at the school keep spreading rumors. I don't need to hear them from my best friend since I have to work with those guys."

"Even if I know they're all true?" Marion asked.

"Especially if."

"Oh, Gilda, Gilda, Gilda. You live in such a secluded little world." Marion draped an arm across her shoulders as they walked toward the doctor's office. "Someday you'll be grateful for me looking out for you. I have to get to work. You be careful, okay? We'll find you a guy who isn't such a jerk, you wait and see."

Ten minutes early for her appointment, Gilda had enough time to catch up on all of Mick's "urgent" texts while her stomach gurgled as it had for over a week. Her gaze darted to the clock for the fifth time in the past minute. Eleven thirty. Normally she never had to wait long for Doctor Ryan Graham to appear in the doorway. He'd delivered Gilda as a baby and had been her doctor ever since.

She tapped her foot against the leg of the chair. The karate school held classes every day at noon. If Doc didn't show up soon, she'd miss class. Not that she was concerned. Mick could handle anything that came up while she was busy.

Still...

After sitting on the hard plastic chair for half an hour, Gilda texted Mick to say she wouldn't be in the lunch hour class. When he didn't text back within seconds, she remembered Walter Levy, the school's senior black belt, was teaching class that day. Mick planned to be halfway to Toronto to attend a family function.

She punched in the school's phone number, not surprised when the answering machine picked up. If she said she'd be there by one, she could grab a peppermint tea at Café Beanz on her way, then clean up before the kids' classes started at four.

"Gilda?" Doc called her into his office.

She left a hasty message, then turned off her phone and followed him. The last thing she needed was more stress from Mick Williams at the moment.

CHAPTER 2

At one o'clock, Gilda set her paper cup on the ground by the brick wall and dug out her key. One more afternoon of work before the karate school closed for the long weekend. After training at seven that night, she'd be free to go home, change into her bathing suit and head to the beach for a dip. Doc Graham's orders were to relax, exercise, and eat more fiber, and she fully intended to do all three.

As she stuck her key in the lock, she realized the door was already open.

Either Walter was still inside, or he'd gone off in a rush. The back of her neck tingled as she called out, "Hello? Anyone here?"

Her stomach clenched as she walked through the small room which served as a hazardous containment room for wet boots all winter to the second set of doors that led to the lobby. No answer. No lights on. No movement.

"Walter? Mick?" she said, peering around the corner toward the dojo, or training hall.

Still nothing.

Gilda flicked on the lights. The lobby was empty. Something—or someone—lay on the mats in the dojo. Knowing the blackbelts, probably meditating after a rough class. She turned on the lights that illuminated the dojo and change area.

"Sorry for the disruption, but I have work to do," she said, then paused and gasped.

Someone forgot to tell Walter Levy samurai didn't commit *seppuku* with a sword. They carried a much smaller knife to kill themselves with. He lay still on the mats with a long, gently curved blade stood upright from his chest. Even from where Gilda stood, she knew he was dead. There was no earthly way it was by his own hand. The katana blade was longer than his arms.

Someone had to...

Her vision swam as she realized his murderer could still be in the school.

Heart racing, she dove between the two chairs behind the reception desk, knocking her head against the one Walter had brought only two weeks earlier, Eyes hot with tears, Gilda struggled to catch her breath as she pulled out her phone to call 9-1-1.

"Nine-one-one. What's your emergency?" a woman asked.

"Somebody stabbed Walter. I think he's dead," she whispered, hoping the killer was long gone.

The woman sucked in a sharp breath, but remained professional, as though she'd received this type of call a thousand times before. "What is your name and location, ma'am?"

"Marion," she said. "It's Gilda. I'm at the karate school."

"Gilda? Sorry, but you sound weird." Tapping sounded through the phone. "What's going on? Was there a fight?"

She peered over the counter and through the open dojo door to make sure she hadn't imagined things. No such luck. Walter Levy still lay on the mats. A black foam blocker next to him made his salt and pepper hair seem whiter than usual.

"Someone killed Walter, one of the black belts."

"Are you sure he's dead?"

Taking one more glance, Gilda nodded. "Yeah. I'm positive. How long before the police arrive?"

"Stay on the line. I'll get them over there right away. Did you touch anything?"

"No, but I—"

"Did you notice any signs of a break in?"

"The door was unlocked, but—"

"Is there anyone in the building?"

Her heart stuttered. She hadn't thought to look, just hide. "Nobody answered when I yelled. None of the other instructors will be here for an hour. I should call Mick before he leaves town."

That sounded wrong, but Marion knew what she meant, even if whoever listened to the recording later didn't.

"Just stay out of the school," Marion said. "The police are on the way."

"Um. I'm under my desk."

There was a brief silence before Marion told her, "You get out of there before I come and drag you out by your ankles." She paused, then added gently, "Don't worry, ma'am, someone will be there shortly."

No doubt the story of Walter's demise would ignite the small town long before the police or her boss arrived. Her suspicions were confirmed when Marion hung up without another word, rather than keeping her on the line until help arrived.

Gilda sighed and hung up, as she steeled herself for another glance at the corpse as she left the building. Body. Body somehow seemed less final. Less dead. Bodies could still be alive.

Halfway to the door, she remembered Mick. Crap. She needed to call him.

With her gaze still on Walter, Gilda pulled up Mick's name and hit the phone icon. She coiled a strand of her light brown hair around her right index finger as she walked to the door. When he answered, she took a deep breath, fighting to keep her voice even.

"Mick? We have a problem at the school. You need to come back."

Noise outside the school made it hard to hear him. "Can't...on road...near—"

Her breath caught in the back of her throat and came out a strangled gasp. "I don't care where you are going. Get back to the school now. Walter's dead."

The front door burst open in front of her. Thayer scowled. "Gilda? What are you doing in here? Don't move until we do a sweep."

She muttered then disconnected and wiped away a tear. Since her father had been an officer for nearly thirty years, she knew the police would ask if she'd noticed signs of a break-in or saw an intruder. Anything that might help.

Once Thayer gave the "all clear", a couple more cops came in. Gilda stood in the middle of the ten-by-ten-foot lobby. No possible evidence in sight. Nothing except dirt tracked in from the students and a trace of mud from the rain shower that morning. Anybody could've tracked it in before class.

Jason Thayer, every bit as handsome as he was in ten years ago in high school when they first met, told her to sit and wait. "The M.E. and forensics are on their way. You're not leaving until we talk."

"I've said everything I'm going to say to you."

"About Walter," he said.

Reluctantly, she sat. She'd prefer to be interrogated by Attila the Hun over an ex-boyfriend who repeatedly cheated on her.

Detective Fabio, his partner, patted her shoulder and handed her a wrapped mint. "Sorry for your loss. How are you doing, kid?"

"Good. Shaken."

"That's normal. Eat the candy. You'll probably go into shock soon," Fabio said. He resembled a stone gargoyle more than the hunk on the cover of a book. He was bald with cauliflower ears, bulging eyes and a tree stump neck. When he walked away toward the crime scene, his limp was more pronounced than usual as he took charge of the crime scenes inside the dojo and the change rooms.

In the doorway of the dojo, Gilda spied a spot of blood. Actually, two spots. One of the kids had a nosebleed last night. Did they stand in that doorway, or had they gone through the student entrance in back? This door was for the instructors and, in an official capacity only, her. When she came to train, she used the student entrance near the change rooms. When she had to interrupt classes, she used the instructor entrance.

"What the hell's going on?" Mick shouted to signal his arrival. "I was past Ponderer's Point when you called. What's so bloody important it can't wait until after the long weekend?"

Careful not to contaminate anything, Gilda lunged in front of him before he could enter the dojo. "You can't go in there."

"Yes, I can. It's my dojo." He swiped a stray dark curl off his forehead. "What are the cops doing here? Someone giving you problems again?"

"I told you..." When her voice cracked, she cleared her throat. "Walter's dead."

Mick flinched. His gaze met hers as his face paled. "That's not possible. I just saw him an hour ago." He paused, then asked, "Are you sure?"

"Pretty sure." She hadn't checked for a pulse, but death seemed a safe assumption.

Six inches taller and fifty pounds heavier than Gilda, Mick picked her up and set her aside like she was a foam blocker. He paused in the doorway in mid-bow.

Blood had reddened Walter's white karate uniform, his expensive, custom tailored *gi*. Urine and feces perfumed the air. Bruises she hadn't noticed earlier darkened his face.

Thayer walked toward them. "Why don't you two step into Mick's office while we take care of things?"

"Good idea." She touched Mick's arm, more to support her spaghetti knees than to comfort him. "Are you okay?"

Still in mid-bow, he cleared his throat and coughed. When he spoke, his voice was low and gravelly, "Does anyone else know?"

"Marion was the nine-one-one operator."

He snorted. "Great, I'm glad she remembered to call the sorry excuse for police before telling everyone else in town. Did you touch anything when you got here?"

"Just the door and the light switches." She swallowed hard to keep the few bites of waffle she'd eaten earlier from vacating her stomach.

Mick faced her, his jaw tight. "Did you search the building?"

She shook her head.

"Gilda, if the killer was somewhere in the building, you could've been killed. Don't you get that?"

"I called the police first," she told him.

His fingers dug into her upper arms. "The killer could've heard you."

Her concern had been for Walter, not her own safety. "I'm pretty sure no one else was here."

"Pretty sure? That's not the same as a hundred percent sure, is it? Don't do that to me again. I can't afford to...Honestly, sometimes you're so naïve." He released his grip on her without finishing his sentence and bowed his head, running a tanned hand through his hair. "I'll be in my office."

"Wait. You can't leave me alone with—" When his door closed behind him, she blew out a sigh. "I guess you can."

That thought stopped her cold. Why didn't Mick bother to look around? Had he fought with and murdered Walter before leaving for Toronto? A guilty man would've kept driving and not looked back. That the two of them fought seemed likely. They'd argued about a lot of things over the past two years. Usually about the way Walter taught classes and how he wanted a share of the school.

Gilda paced the lobby while hugging her stomach. Mick seemed more worked up about her safety than Walter's. What was that all about? Shock. That was all. His reaction didn't mean any more than that.

Already sidetracked, she followed Fabio to the back hallway. Someone had used the sink, which was speckled with pink water. A wet piece of paper towel, tinged with diluted blood, lay on the floor. Farther down the hall, freckles of blood decorated the white tile. She hated the starkness of the white. It was a pain to keep clean, but it did show blood droplets beautifully.

Like morbid modern art.

She crept past the washrooms, around the blood spots, and into the change area. Black curtains from the stalls lay on the floor, torn off the rods across the doorways. Blood splattered the walls, the floors, the benches...everything. Who had Walter fought with to cause so much damage?

Gilda turned and inched toward the door with hope of escaping.

Thayer leaned against her desk while he spoke on the phone. Once he hung up, his gaze met hers. "I hope you don't plan to leave yet. I need the names of your instructors, staff and students."

"It'll take a while," she told him. "This thing's slow on a good day."

She sat behind her desk and stared at the screen, unable to remember the password. Her hands shook. Her mouth went as dry as sunbaked earth. She closed her eyes and scrubbed her face. Her eyes burned with unshed tears. Shock had set in.

"Take your time," Thayer said, pulling out a notebook and flashing Gilda a sympathetic smile.

It miffed her that he'd kept his quarterback body in such impeccable shape, while she'd turned to chocolate chunk cookies and caramel swirl ice cream. Her karate gi covered the bulge around her waist, but her yoga pants didn't. Thank heavens for baggy shirts and hoodies.

"Marion said you found the body, is that right?" Thayer asked.

Gilda choked back a sob. She cleared her throat again, wishing she could curl up in a corner under a fluffy blanket and cry. "Walter? When I came in, I saw him lying there..."

"Did you touch him? Maybe check him for vital signs or anything that might contaminate the scene?"

"No. He looked pretty dead from here."

Thayer snorted. "Are you an expert on bodies?"

"Oh, come on," Mick barked as he emerged from his office. "She already said she didn't touch anything. Cut her some slack."

"I asked her a question."

Mick narrowed his eyes. "And she answered."

"I've only seen them on television," she whispered, vowing to never watch another crime show. Suddenly her cushy chair was more uncomfortable than before.

"Did you search to see if anyone else was in the building before you called for help?" Thayer asked.

"No," she said, although the thought had sort of crossed her mind. "I yelled, then saw Walter and panicked."

"You weren't worried for your own safety? Seems to me that's the first thing an innocent person would think about."

Even after breaking up two years ago, Thayer was as arrogant as ever. Still assured she'd take him back once she came to her senses. After two minutes of interrogation, she wanted to poke him in the eye with a pencil.

"Are you implying that Gilda killed Walter?" Mick shouted. "Are you crazy? The girl won't even kill a spider, and she hates spiders."

Thayer groaned. "I'm a cop. I need to find out what happened."

Gilda squeezed her eyes shut, then told him, "The door was open when I got here. Walter normally locks it when he trains after class, so no one disturbs him. Since it was open, I figured Sensei Mick came in to grab something before he left town and forgot to lock it."

He raised one eyebrow and met Mick's gaze. "Were you here?"

Mick folded his arms across his chest and shifted his weight, scowling at Gilda before he replied, "Earlier. Like Gilda said, I popped in to pick up a couple of things while Walter taught class. Then I left for Toronto. Gilda called when she found Walter."

"How far away were you?" Thayer turned to Mick.

"Just past Ponderer's Point."

"That's less than a half hour away. What were you doing between class and packing?" Thayer grimaced.

"I took a shower and grabbed my stuff for the weekend." Mick's face reddened. "Anything else?"

"As a matter of fact, yeah." Thayer puffed up like an angry rooster. "Did anybody else see you shower or pack?"

"You're insane. I have things to do." Mick growled, then returned to his office.

"Don't leave town," Thayer called out before turning his focus back on Gilda. "He doesn't like me, does he?"

She shook her head. "Not many people do."

"Did Mick or any of the others have a grudge against Walter?"

Gilda hesitated. Not normally. Lately things hadn't run as smoothly as usual. She'd blamed it on the heatwave they'd been having "Nothing serious. No."

Thayer lowered his voice. "If it makes things easier, I've heard rumors from a few parents. I know there's division between the instructors about how to run this place. There's talk of a couple of them leaving to start their own schools."

Since he already knew part of the story, technically it wasn't gossip. Was it? Gilda wasn't willing to take the chance. Mick and the others were her friends. Her family.

"You'll have to ask the black belts," she told him. "I don't know."

"Oh, don't worry. I plan to do just that. First, I need that list and a chat with Mick." Thayer frowned when Fabio entered the room and leaned on the counter next to him.

"Bad news, people. The M.E. was in a car accident." Fabio said. "His office gave the okay for Doc Graham to look at the body before the remove it."

Thayer snorted. "Doc's a local family physician, not a medical examiner."

"I'm aware of that," Fabio said. "Would you rather wait around for an extra four or five hours until they send someone else out from Windsor? Didn't think so." He turned to Gilda. "Did you go down the hallway?"

She winced, recalling the chaos in the back room. "It looks like there was a scuffle back there."

"Why would you say that?" Thayer asked.

"The curtains are torn down and there's blood everywhere," Fabio said.

"I swear, I didn't touch anything," Gilda told them. "One of our students had a nose bleed last night. I didn't get a chance to clean up before I left. Mick and a couple other black belts stayed late, so I went home."

Thayer narrowed his eyes. He probably thought she was guilty just from the way she was babbling. "If the body's in the gym—"

"The dojo," she corrected.

"The dojo. I thought you said you hadn't searched the building. What made you check back there?"

"Curiosity. I wanted to make sure no one else was...hurt." There was so much blood. I thought there might've been a fight or something."

"Good guess," Fabio said. "I don't suppose you know who stayed to train last night?"

Mick reappeared from his office, disheveled and upset. He shot Fabio a hard look, then focused on her. "I'm meeting the others at the coffee shop."

She assumed "the others" were the black belts.

"That's not a good idea," Thayer said. "We'll need to interview them. For now, we need to ask you a few questions. Take a seat."

"Café Beanz?" Gilda asked.

Mick's abrupt change of plans was nothing new, she guessed he had some sort of attention disorder. Nothing short of Thayer drawing a gun and handcuffing him to a door would keep Mick in the building. She'd learned to adapt.

"Yeah. The police won't let them in here. Stick around until they're done, but don't lock up, I can't find my keys. Thanks. Fabio. Thayer. I'll be in touch." Mick left without awaiting an answer.

Thayer sputtered as he reached for his cuffs, but Fabio shook his head and said, "He'll be back."

Of course, Gilda would stay. She didn't have a life outside of the school. Not for two years ago when she caught Thayer in a compromising position with a young, blonde barista from Café Beanz. Mick's current destination.

"Is he always like that?" Thayer asked.

Gilda smirked as she turned on the desktop computer. "Impatient and in a rush? He's been like that longer than I've known him."

"I don't think the caffeine and sugar he lives on helps." Fabio chuckled. "Since he's gone, you can tell us who stayed late last night."

She typed in her passwords automatically. "Mick, Walter, and Razi Mauli, another one of our black belts. There's a black belt grading in November. Razi and Walter wanted to grade for their sandan."

"Third level?" Fabio raised his eyebrows. "Impressive."

"We need to bring him back here for questioning," Thayer said, tapping his fingers on the counter.

Fabio turned back to the crime scene. "He'll be back. His keys are on the floor under his desk."

Gilda had never thought to hide Mick's keys to get his undivided attention for ten whole minutes. Tying him to a chair and gagging him.

"Is everything okay?" Thayer almost sounded like he cared, but she knew his tone was purely professional. An act for his colleagues. He must be up for another promotion.

"I'll print a list of our students."

Unfortunately, time didn't wound all heels.

After the breakup, where Thayer had hit the gym and thrived socially, Gilda became withdrawn and hid behind her desk, her garden, and reading mystery novels. All while eating chocolate chunk ice cream. Working for Mick was the catalyst she'd needed to bring her out of the shell she'd hidden in. The same shell she wished she could crawl back into now.

"Students and instructors." Thayer peered down at her. "You know you don't have to work in a place like this. There are jobs elsewhere."

"Jealous as always. You still hate me being around all the testosterone and chiseled jaws." Gilda nearly burst out laughing. Aside from Mick and Razi Mauli, no one even came close to that description. "I happen to like working here. If it wasn't for me, everyone would kill each other, and..." She stopped, then covered her mouth with both hands before adding, "I didn't mean it like that."

Thayer appeared amused. "I'm going to chat with Fabio, then you and I are going to discuss what you just said." He paused. "I'll bet you're the one who killed Walter. I wouldn't put it past you to stab a man in the heart."

"Me?" Her face and temper were on the verge of bursting into flame. "Not a chance. I'd just throw him into a fifty-pound bag of coffee beans and leave him lying half naked on the floor with a cheap floozy and a mild concussion."

Thayer bowed his head as everyone else in the building burst into laughter. "I told you. That was a misunderstanding. You overreacted and embarrassed me in front of the whole town."

"Hey, your fling of the week talked to the reporters, not me."

"I doubt that," he mumbled.

Once he stormed away, Gilda tried to focus. The school had almost a hundred students, including her. She doubted any of them had reason to kill Walter. Her gut told her the perpetrator was on the shorter instructor list. Sensei Mick, Walter Levy, Xavier Wyndham, Razi Mauli and Erik Cadell were all instructors and black belts.

Shuddering, she contemplated drawing a line through Walter's name, to save the police—in this case Thayer and Fabio—the trouble. In the end, she couldn't bring herself to do it.

She drew in a deep bracing breath and printed two copies of each list, then brought one copy of each to Thayer. "Do you need anything else? Coffee? Tea? An attitude adjustment?"

"Yeah. What time do you normally start work?"

"Eleven-thirty. We have classes every weekday at noon. Today I had brunch with Marion. You're my witness to that. Then I had a doctor's appointment that ran late. I called the school to say I'd be here by one. Oh, I also grabbed a tea at Café Beanz before I came to work."

Which was still sitting outside because she forgot about it when she discovered the door unlocked."

"Fascinating," Thayer said, perusing the lists. "Who answered the phone?"

"When?" she asked.

He scowled. "When you called to say you'd be late."

"No one. Class had started, so I left a message. Mick normally checks the machine when he's here."

Great. Now she'd made Mick look guilty for listening to her message.

"I don't know if anyone actually heard it."

Anyone who was in the school within ten feet of the phone could have. Especially someone who had a motive and needed an opportunity to kill Walter Levy.

CHAPTER 3

U nable to leave, Gilda rambled around the front lobby gnawing on her fingernails. No one nail in particular; they were all fair game. The police were gone, their evidence and half the school was bagged and tagged.

Who'd want Walter dead? He was a quiet, middle-aged, unassuming man. Sure, he'd made his share of mistakes, everyone had, but what had he done to make someone want to kill him?

Marion had called several times to make sure Gilda was okay. She'd even offered to bring over dinner, but nothing sounded remotely edible.

Doc Graham, who'd taken over in the Medical Examiner's absence, hadn't looked happy to be there. Surrounded by the faint aroma of pipe tobacco, he gave her a one-armed hug and told her to call if she needed a friend, the name of a therapist, or anti-depressants.

She'd finally managed to convince Thayer and Fabio she was be fine to wait alone for the cleaning crew. She promised not to touch anything. No one was likely to hurt her, especially since she had a half dozen black belts on speed dial. Although, that hadn't helped Walter any.

Mick strode through the front door and looked around. "Where is everyone?"

"They just left. Didn't you see the parade? Walter caught a lift with the guys from the morgue, and the police are on the hunt for a killer. I've been texting you all afternoon. Where were you?"

She sounded cross but no longer cared. How dare he leave her alone to deal with the police and a hundred parent's calls? This was his school. His business. He was part owner and supposed to run the day-to-day operations, not her.

"Your buddy, Thayer, grabbed me in the coffee shop and locked me in a room the size of a shoe box," he said. "My cell phone was detained by some lab guy, who now has the numbers of you and every other woman in town. Anyway, I meant our students. Is anyone coming to class tonight?"

Gilda stared. "Someone murdered Walter, and you're worried about class attendance? We need to clean up and replace mats before we can even *have* a class. The cleanup crew is coming, and they need someone to lock up behind them."

"They took our mats?" he asked, before peering into the dojo and swearing. "Why would they do that?"

"It's called evidence. The blood is a biohazard. The mats have to be specially dealt with. Everything else went to the lab. At least, I don't have to clean up alone."

Mick let out a long breath. His fingers drummed his left thigh, more nervous than he tried to let on. If he started to pace, she'd know to keep her distance. "Did you post a sign to say we're closed?"

"On the front door. You walked right past it. I also changed the message on the answering machine and posted messages on our social media pages."

"Okay."

No concern. No compassion. Just commands. Demands. Ugh, why had she ever idolized the man? In tough situations, he folded and ran for the nearest coffee shop. Just like Thayer. She brushed that thought aside.

"Did you call the students who normally come tonight?"

Was he serious? "Three. The rest called here to find out when the funeral is and to make sure everyone else was okay."

"No doubt Marion already told everyone what happened."

Gilda shrugged. "So, what if she did? Her help saved me hours of work."

He wandered into the dojo and knelt near the entrance. There were only half the pale green tatami mats inside as normal. "If we call right away, our supplier might be able to ship new ones here by Tuesday."

"I called," she told him. "First of all, they don't have any in stock. Secondly, they want cash up front. Your credit is in question. Oh, and as of five o'clock, they closed for the long weekend."

"Since when do we have bad credit?" he asked. "We've always paid them up front."

"Why don't you call them Tuesday and straighten things out? They won't talk to me anymore. They want to talk directly to you."

Mick rolled his eyes. "You're overreacting. Things aren't that bad. You can straighten it out just as well as I can."

"Trust me, I tried."

He muttered beneath his breath for a minute, then headed for the change area.

Gilda stopped him. "I wouldn't go back there if I were you."

Seconds later, he yelled, "What the bloody hell happened back here?"

"Nice choice of words. Offhand, I'd say a fight," she said, peering around him. "A nasty one."

He frowned. "Good guess, Sherlock. Now tell me who Walter fought with."

"I wish I could." She didn't want to let on she suspected all the remaining black belts. Him, Erik, Razi, and Xavier. Under the circumstances, she was wise to keep her mouth shut until the police could prove who killed Walter, since all four of them were capable of killing her with the flick of a pinkie.

"Where are the rest of the curtains?" Mick asked.

Only two black curtains remained on the floor. The others were in police custody. She grinned at the thought of curtains being under arrest rather than examined for evidence. Her eyes welled up again and she couldn't hold back her giggle.

"Thayer took them in for interrogation."

"Very funny. We need to replace them before we can reopen." He knelt to examine a spot of blood already smeared by the forensics crew's swabs. "We also need to mop the floors and whatever's left of the mats."

"Like I said, Fabio called the biohazard team to come in. We shouldn't even be back here. I only stayed until I could get hold of you."

Mick kicked a bench, which dented the wall and sent more debris raining onto the tiles. Something fell from beneath the bench onto the floor.

"Why did this have to happen now?" he asked. "Yoshida arrives for training on Tuesday. There's no way I can replace everything and clean this place before then. Not with the long weekend. Gilda, you need to put in some overtime. We'll have to pull up all the mats and get some cheap ones at the hardware store."

She put her hands on her hips. "And how am I supposed to get a load of mats here? I don't have a car. Besides, it's the long weekend. The school's closed, and I'm supposed to catch a bus to Fort Erie tonight."

"Yeah? Well, I was due in Toronto an hour ago." He opened a utility closet to get the mop and bucket. "We don't have time to wait for a cleaning crew. We can get rid of the rest of the blood before it starts to smell."

Gilda stared. "We're not supposed to touch anything."

"Well, we can't just leave it like this." While he walked around the corner to get floor cleaner, she studied the bare patches on the dojo floor to assess how many new mats they needed. She glanced back to the bench Mick kicked. What had fallen from the bench?

When she moved the bench aside, a man's ring embossed with a clenched fist on the front lay on the tile. The goju-ryu karate symbol. On the underside of the bench, a broken piece of masking tape clung to the wood by one end. She'd seen the ring before but couldn't recall whose it was. Why would anyone hide it in the school of all places?

Gilda took pictures of both the ring and the tape. At a loss for what to do next, she picked it up with a piece of toilet paper and stuck it in her pocket. She'd keep it safe until she could give it to Fabio. Odd how, after all their careful searching, both the police and forensics crew missed it.

Something else seemed out of place in the change room that she couldn't quite put her finger on. The scale was fine. The bench was back against the now-dented wall. Something seemed amiss that only her subconscious mind picked up.

"I got the cleaner. Let me know how long it takes, so I can adjust your paycheck," Mick said, setting a bottle near the bucket and mop.

"Oh no you don't." Gilda wheeled around with her fists clenched. "I'm not staying. Either do it yourself or stay and wait for the cleaning crew. I've been here all day and I'm leaving."

He took a step back and held up both hands. "Whoa. You okay?"

Her eyes welled with tears as she shouted, "No, I'm not okay! I found Walter's body, faced the police alone, and now you expect me to clean up the mess. I'm done."

She shoved past him on her way to the lobby and let the tears flow.

Mick caught her before she reached for her handbag. "Wait. Gilda, I'm sorry."

She stopped sure she'd heard wrong.

He pulled her into his arms and held her close. His hug seemed awkward at first, but his warmth comforted her. Finally, she lay her head against his chest as he told her, "You're right. I ran out when I should've made sure things—you—were okay. Instead, I left to meet the instructors to ensure they wouldn't quit, or we'd have to close by Tuesday."

"Quit?" Breathless, she tilted her head and bumped his chin. She'd be out of a job. "Why would everyone quit?"

"You've been here long enough to know there are issues. Razi and Walter have never seen eye to eye. Since Razi's not a citizen, he's afraid the police will go after him. Xavier had that argument with Walter last week, and Erik..." He hesitated. "Erik wanted to teach some of Walter's classes."

"Great. I'm working with a band of murderers." She flared her nostrils more out of fear than anger. When she tried to pull away, he kept his arms around her. "What did you have against Walter?"

"Nothing."

Something. She shoved him away. "Seriously? Walter's dead and, for all I know, you killed him."

Mick walked around her desk. "Walter wanted to start his own school, but I didn't think he was ready. He needed more money up-front and more interaction with the students, which is why I let him teach so many classes."

"That was months ago. He threw my flower vase at your office door and left glass all over the lobby twenty minutes before classes started." She'd picked up every shard of glass to make sure no one got cut and ended up cutting her fingers in three places.

"Yeah, then Walter held a secret meeting to try and get the others on his side." Mick dropped onto her comfy chair. "They filled me in later. I was upset, but not mad enough to kill him. Not literally, anyway."

She folded her arms across her waist as a shiver raced through her. In his defense, Mick had bandaged her bleeding fingers that time. He'd even held a wet cloth to her hand to stop the bleeding and pushed a stray hair out of her mouth. Something so insignificant, yet so intimate at the same time. Until his girlfriend, Chloe Del Garda, walked in.

"Yoshida was furious Walter had dared to question your decision."

"And yet a month later, he wanted to hand Walter a school on a silver platter."

"He did? What changed?" she asked.

Mick smirked. "You're not taking the case are you, Sherlock? You're smart and you already know the most about this place. You should be able to tell me whodunit, then we can reopen Tuesday with no problem."

He hadn't answered her question.

"I thought everyone was leaving town for the weekend."

"Not anymore. Your buddy Thayer told us to all stick around while he questions us. Didn't he tell you the same thing?"

More proof the whole town knew Gilda Wright had no life. Her face overheated until she was sure she was redder than the sparring gloves he gave her for Christmas.

"No. Thayer doesn't think I'm capable of anything that requires brain power or physical prowess."

Mick chuckled. "Doesn't sound like he knows you very well. You could kick his butt with both hands tied behind your back. Is he still after you to get back together?"

"Yeah. Some detective. You'd think after two years he'd take the hint."

"He probably realizes you were the best thing that ever happened to him."

"I doubt that. Most of the time, he treated me more like a criminal than anything."

He toyed with Gilda's favorite slim silver pen, a gift from her father shortly before he died in the line of fire. A twenty-seven-year member of the Ontario Provincial Police. Sandstone Cove had named Wright Park in his honor. She didn't want him touching her pen and itched to snatch it away but refrained. She'd have to take it home when she left.

Someone banged on the front door at the same time the phone rang. Both she and Mick jumped, not sure which way to turn. Mick reached for the phone.

"I'll get the door," Gilda grumbled as her heart raced.

"Yoshida Martial Arts." Mick answered the phone then lowered his voice. "What do you want? You're not welcome here. I don't care if you have questions. Don't call here." He slammed the phone onto the desk.

Gilda paused with one hand on the door lock. Her heart drummed so fast she grew dizzy. Mick had never kicked anyone out of the school that she knew of. Who and why now? She'd have to check the caller ID later. Maybe getting rid of him was a good idea. Then she could snoop.

"You okay, lady?" A man in white asked from the other side of the door and flashed an identification card.

"I'm good." Her breaths came short and shallow. Walter's sudden death—murder—had made her afraid of every little bump in the building.

When Mick disappeared into his office, she showed the cleaners the dojo and the change room. "The police took the rest. Mick can let you out later."

He patted her arm. "Thanks. My boys and I will take care of everything. You go get some rest and don't worry about a thing."

"Thank you." She leaned against a clean section of the wall and closed her eyes.

When she opened them, she finally realized what was different about the change room. Normally, a rust-colored scroll listing the kanji of the Four Possessions of the Samurai hung at the far end of the room. HILT. Honor, Integrity, Loyalty, and Time.

The scroll was gone.

Gilda chose to keep her revelation private for now and gathered her things to go home. She not only hated the smells of cleaner and copper but the color red. She let out a sigh that betrayed the tears lurking beneath it.

"Hey, Gilda, can you stay a bit longer? I need to run out and..." Mick stopped when he saw her. "Oh, hell. Come here."

He draped his arms around her and gave her another hug. He smelled of something other than floor cleaner and blood. Something familiar and comforting she hadn't noticed earlier. Stale coffee from Café Beanz.

"Go home, Sherlock," he said. "I'll let these guys out, then check on things tomorrow. Go home and rest. It's been a long day."

"But I need to—"

"No, you've done more than enough. I'll take care of things tonight." He ushered her out of the karate school, leaving her no opportunity to check caller ID, and locked the door behind her.

She stood alone on the sidewalk, her eyes burning with tears and fatigue. She'd bring the tissue wrapped ring to Fabio in the morning when she could think clearly.

After Gilda left the school, she stumbled across the street to Happy Harvey's Hangover Hut. A glorified, tiki-infested liquor and convenience store, Happy's wasn't the place to go if you had a hangover, more like if you were in desperate search of one. Happy—no one ever called him Harvey—was a seventy-year-old man who became disillusioned with retirement. He'd been friends with her parents forever and was still Gilda's good friend.

Right now, she needed a friend more than she needed a bottle. She pulled on the door. Locked. She peered through the glass before she noticed the "Closed for staff meeting" sign on the door.

Disappointed, she wandered the few blocks home, her thoughts as disheveled as her hair. She locked the front door. Alone at last, she lost control of her emotions and collapsed onto the couch for a good cry.

Not that she was Walter Levy's biggest fan, but her imagination led her into frightening scenarios. She spent most of the night staring at the ceiling and pacing, her thoughts following her around the living room to haunt her.

Had one of her coworkers, or even her boss, murdered Walter? Who had called the school so late? It had to be someone who knew Mick would be there.

The question at the top of her list was: What was Mick Williams hiding?

CHAPTER 4

Saturday morning brought calm and grief, but also tweaked Gilda's baser nosy side. She sat at her kitchen table and examined the ring she'd found in before making a to-do list for the day. Within the hour, she'd not only forgotten them all, but abandoned the list to pace the room.

When the doorbell rang at eight, her heart stuttered. Catching a glimpse of her reflection in the mirror behind the door, she cringed. Her eyes were puffy from crying half the night, her skin was pale and blotchy, and her hair clung to her face from sweat and tears. She opened the door hoping she didn't terrify whoever was on the other side.

Xavier Wyndham, second degree black belt and one of their senior instructors, stood on her front step with a cup of coffee in each hand. A former professional bodybuilder and fitness instructor, he would turn fifty next month. Gravity and a lack of serious training had softened him, but not much.

"You okay, Gilda?" he asked. "I heard you found Walter yesterday. That must've been rough. I wanted to check on you sooner, but Thayer corralled us all into itty bitty rooms at the station most of the night."

Her voice came out gravelly and low. "Better than I look, or sound."

"Glad to hear it. I brought you coffee. Extra sugar and cream to combat shock and fatigue." Xavier handed her the cup with a white mark on the black lid.

"You didn't have to do that, but thanks."

While she was dressed for a morning run, she was far from ready. Along with the penchant for drinking coffee, she'd picked up some good habits while working at the school. Her karate skills had sharpened considerably after starting to run, and she'd lost a few ice cream pounds. Caffeine and sugar might help her to focus. At the very least, they'd improve her run time once she forced her tired body out the door.

"I wanted to bring donuts, but I'm cutting weight for that big tournament next month and didn't want to tempt myself." Xavier patted his paunch and looked sheepish. "I want to compete in an easier weight category. The guys I usually fight are monsters."

"Me, too," Gilda told him, then managed a tired smile. "Trying to lose a couple pounds, I mean. Running helps."

"I only run after ice cream trucks." He sat on the top step with a heavy sigh. "Hard to believe someone killed Walter. He was a good guy. Whoever did that must've been pretty strong or found a way to incapacitate him. Like poison or a knock to the head. Personally, I'd prefer something subtle like poison. What about you?"

Why would he talk that way? Did he poison her coffee?

Dumb thought. Walter's sudden death had made her suspicious of everyone. Besides, Xavier always brought her coffee. He and Mick were the only two instructors who gave her a second glance, let alone brought her coffee or treats, especially when they needed her to do extra work. Walter usually brought fresh herbs from his garden.

Gilda blinked back a fresh batch of tears.

"You sure you're okay?" Xavier asked.

"I couldn't sleep."

She had thought about inviting him inside, but not after his talk about poison. Instead, she joined him on the top step. The sun seeped into her pores and warmed her. Inside, she quivered, still able to picture Walter when she closed her eyes.

Xavier patted her shoulder. "You did all the right things, kiddo."

"I didn't do anything," she told him.

Gilda sipped her coffee. Perfect, as usual, with a faint hint of almonds. Amaretto or cyanide? She normally loved the flavor. Today her stomach gurgled from stress and fear. Gut instinct told her not to drink it or she'd be sick whether it was poisoned or not. She could reheat it once her stomach settled.

"All I did was go to work, find a body, and not have a total meltdown until I got home last night."

"Some people would've locked the door and left him for someone else to find."

That thought hadn't occurred to her. Would Xavier have shown up, then left?

She doubted it. At one time, Xavier owned his own martial arts school. He gave it up to pursue a high-ranking job selling martial arts gear. The same company Mick bought their gear from. Xavier had nothing to gain by poisoning her or killing Walter. As far as she knew, anyway.

"Mick said Walter took a katana to the chest," Xavier said. "The autopsy would be more difficult if Walter was poisoned."

Again, with the poison.

"Why is that?" she asked.

"There are as many tests as there poisons. Labs can't test for all of them."

Gilda pretended to sip her coffee, her suspicion of his involvement growing. Then her gaze fell on the dented right front fender of his car. Xavier pampered his Mazda. It was his pride and joy, and he washed and polished it weekly. Any scratches or dents had to be new, or she would've heard him rant about stupid drivers.

"What happened to your car?" she asked at the same time as he said, "We should close the school for a few days."

"Yes." She even answered him at the same time when he replied, "An accident."

"Were you hurt?" Was it her imagination he hid his left hand slightly behind him? She brushed off the thought.

He shook his head. "Nah, I'm fine. How long are we closing for?"

The diversion irked Gilda, but she didn't let on. "Until after the funeral. I'll send everyone an e-mail once I know more."

"Have you...?" Xavier hesitated. "Have you noticed any discrepancies in the books? Money missing? Supplies not in inventory?"

"Do you think someone's been stealing from the school?" she asked.

"Just thinking aloud. There must be a motive for Walter's death. Maybe he caught someone stealing."

Gilda frowned. "Is that what the meeting at Café Beanz was about?"

"It was just a thought."

"I know a couple of the guys want to start their own schools, but I don't believe anyone would stoop to steal from Mick and Shihan Yoshida." Gilda had the impression he was trying to justify Walter's murder out of grief. Or remorse. Xavier seemed to know a lot of ways to kill someone. She shivered, glad she hadn't invited him into her house. She clutched her coffee cup so tight the paper dented. "Mick would've noticed."

"Maybe. If he wasn't so preoccupied with Chloe and his new business."

"What new business?" she asked.

"Well, not his exactly," Xavier said. "He and a bartender friend are flipping houses. I hear they bought a place on Oakland Drive last week. It's already half-gutted and some cute blonde from the gym is doing the decorating."

Why hadn't Mick told her about his house-flipping business? That was probably why he was more distracted than usual. Chloe wasn't a cute blonde, more like a sour brunette. Was he cheating on her on top of everything else?

Xavier glanced at his watch. "I told Walter's wife I'd stop by. The kids are coming today."

"Sure." Gilda brought the cup to her lips, her gaze on Xavier as he walked to his car, then waved over his shoulder. She had no idea he'd become chummy with Jade Levy. In the past, he'd walk on the other side of the room to avoid the Dragon Lady, as he called her. Him going to see her now seemed strange. Death had an odd way of pulling people together.

She had a sudden thought. "Hey, Xavier, are you missing a ring?"

"Why?" he asked. His face darkened as his step faltered.

Gilda hesitated. "I found one with a symbol on it. You don't happen to know who might've lost one, do you?"

He shook his head. "No. Sorry."

"Okay. Thanks. Just thought I'd ask."

Only once he left, did it occur to her he never asked what symbol was on the ring. Did he already know or was he just distracted?

Gilda placed her coffee cup into a sandwich bag and zipped it shut before she carried it to the police station. She hoped to talk to Fabio and avoid Thayer. Fabio grew up in Toronto and trained at the same school as Mick until Fabio became an OPP officer. Rumor—well, Happy actually—said Fabio settled in Sandstone Cove for the peace and tranquility of a small lakeside town after taking a knife to the back during a drug raid. He'd probably started to second guess that idea after being saddled with Thayer.

Fueled by fear, Gilda's mind bounced from thought to thought. She had enough money tucked aside to leave town and rent a hovel on a beach along the East Coast. For years, she'd thought of vacationing near the ocean. Nova Scotia seemed like a good option. Maybe even somewhere tropical, if she could save on airfare. Anywhere she could sit, read, and pretend she'd never discovered a body—or worked for Mick Williams.

A dark car pulled up to the curb and an older man around sixty peered out the window. Scars marred his face, and his eyes were hidden behind dark sunglasses. "Excuse me, Miss."

Her gurgling stomach and common sense made her take a wary step out of his reach. "Can I help you?"

"I'm Gary," he said. "I knew your dad. He was a good man."

She took another step back. "I know who you are. My dad arrested you."

Gary del Garda, local bookie and gangster as well as Chloe's father, flashed a wide smile and waved a hand. "Bygones. I earned every time he put handcuffs on me. I had a healthy respect for the man behind the badge."

"What can I do for you, Mr. Del Garda?" she asked.

"Gary. Please," he said, putting the car in park. "You work for Mick Williams."

She glanced up and down the street, hoping to have a witness in case he tried anything. Kidnapping topped her list. He could hardly do a drive-by shooting now he'd parked in front of her, could he?

"Relax. All I want is information." Gary pushed his sunglasses to the top of his head to reveal his murky blue eyes. "I'm looking for Mr. Williams, so we can settle a business matter." You wouldn't happen to know where I could find him, do you?"

"No, I don't."

"I've seen you with him in Café Beanz."

Gilda tensed, ready to run. "I work for him. That doesn't mean I know where he is when I'm not with him. I'm not his wife or anything."

He winked and lowered his sunglasses. "Considering he's dating my daughter, that's a good thing." When you do see him, let him know I'm looking for him. We have things to discuss."

"I'll do that." She wiped her sweaty palms on her shorts. Had Mick hired Gary del Garda to kill Walter? Nah, too obvious.

He drove away so slowly she didn't dare move away until the dark car turned the corner and disappeared. Only then did she turn her face toward the sun. She could still taste bitter almonds in the back of her mouth.

A day ago, she would've savored the flavor, unaware of any malice. There was one person she knew who'd believe her suspicions, Doc Graham. Not like he could do much to help.

Still, it couldn't hurt to have the coffee tested. Just in case. Armed with the three-quarters full paper cup, she headed for the police station six blocks over.

Since Fabio was on the phone, she set the plastic bag on Thayer's desk. "I think Xavier Wyndham just tried to poison me. I need you to get this tested."

"You think he tried to poison you with coffee?"

"With cyanide."

"Cyanide?" Thayer didn't bother to hide his amusement. "Honey, if someone slipped you cyanide, you'd have stomach cramps and be hallucinating more than usual."

When Gilda slammed her palms on his desk, the coffee sloshed in the bag. Since Mick and her mother had already stressed her out for the past week, she wouldn't have noticed extra stomach pain anyway. "Don't be such a jerk. There's already been one murder at the school, what's to say there won't be more? Have the coffee tested. It's probably nothing. Worst case, I'll be out a good cup of coffee."

Thayer rolled his eyes. "You're such a drama queen. Stay away from Xavier and let me take care of the rest. I'm the cop, not you."

"Then get off your lazy butt and do something cop-like," she shouted.

A few feet away, Fabio sat at his desk with the phone pressed to his ear. He glanced up and nodded. Whoever he was talking to irritated him to the point his jaw whitened, and he lowered his voice. He held up an index finger to signal he wanted a word with her. Probably to warn her to keep her nose out of the investigation before he got ulcers.

Thayer ran a hand through his thick blond hair, then studied the paper cup before he told her, "For today, I'll humor you. Xavier got this from Café Beanz. I know that for a fact they made amaretto coffee this morning. I got one for Anna at the front desk. Since she's still working, I'm assuming no one added cyanide."

"That's astounding police work, Detective." Gilda snorted. "Wouldn't that be the perfect way to disguise cyanide though?"

"It would be if he'd made it at home, added the poison, then brought it straight to your house in a generic paper cup," he said. "What are the odds he stopped at Café Beanz with cyanide in his pocket and they just happened to have amaretto coffee brewing?"

Slim to none. She didn't need him to tell her that. Apparently, she needed sleep more than she needed a run. She touched the tissue-wrapped ring in her pocket but chose to wait for Fabio.

"Go home, Gilda," Thayer said, handing the plastic bag back. "Even you know we need probably cause to get a search warrant. Unless you get violently ill or drop dead, I don't have probable cause. Only your wild accusations and insanity."

"It's only borderline insanity and you have no proof." She snatched the bag from his hand. The argument sounded better inside her head.

"Neither, my dear, do you," Thayer said.

Fabio flashed a smug smile as he hung up.

"You're not going to do anything, are you?" Gilda sighed.

Thayer snorted. "I am doing something. I'm investigating a murder and took a break for this amusing little intermission. I wish I had as much time to fool around as you."

Deflated, her face heated. She knew was growing redder by the second as she gazed at the white tile floor. Was that a bloodstain or jelly from a donut near her chair? Part of why she'd taken the job at Yoshida's after breaking up with Thayer was to learn self-defense and feel empowered. Even after two years of training, that confidence escaped her now.

"Go home, Gilda," Thayer told her.

"What are you going to tell Walter's widow?" she asked.

"The same thing I'm telling you. Don't leave town. I'll also tell her to stay at least five hundred yards away from you if she values her sanity."

"How dare you?"

Fabio took her by one arm. "Come on, Gilda. I'll walk you out. Thayer, don't arrest anyone before I get back."

Gilda folded her arms across her stomach and left the police station with Fabio and ranted, "That man's a twit. I'd hoped becoming a detective would change that, but nope."

"Nope, he's still a twit." Fabio chuckled as they stepped into the sunshine and paused at the top of the stairs. "You need to leave the detective work to me and Detective Twit. Worry about keeping that boss of yours out of trouble and make sure your students don't desert the school. It won't be easy to focus on training where a murder occurred."

"You're telling me," she said. "My boss keeps happy and out of trouble all on his own. Did you need me to answer more questions?"

"Nah, I have bigger fish to fry than you, honey. Go grab a fresh coffee and relax. Whoever killed Walter could be long gone by now."

Or still in their midst.

"Wait." She dropped the tissue wrapped ring in his palm. "I found this after you guys left the school. It was taped to the underside of a bench that Mick kicked."

"Anger issues, huh?"

"Frustration."

Fabio opened the tissue, then frowned. "I've seen this before. The closed fist is the *goju* karate symbol? Whose is this?"

Gilda shrugged. "I thought it was Walter's, but now I'm not so sure. Why hide it?"

"You're guess is as good as mine," he said. "I'll drop it by the lab and see if we can get some prints. Did you grab the piece of tape?"

"No, sorry." She wanted to smack her forehead. "We could go by the school to see if the cleaners missed it. I took pictures."

"Text them to me. I'll call the cleaners before we do more interrogations." Fabio hesitated. "Give me that cup. I'll get it checked. None of us can be too careful."

"You believe me?"

He scowled. "I need you as a witness, so I'm humoring you. Don't mistake the two."

"I appreciate that."

As Gilda descended the stairs, she didn't look back. She didn't want to know if he tossed her cup into the trash can.

She wandered across the street to the karate school to see just how clean it was and, despite Fabio saying he'd take care of it, to check if the piece of tape was still there. Sticking her key in the lock, she held her breath. For the first time since she'd worked there, she was nervous entering the building alone.

The lights in the school were off, but someone was inside the dojo. Once her eyes adjusted to the dim lighting, she breathed a sigh of relief.

Mick had moved the remaining tatami mats together to form a small practice space he was practicing on. All he wore were the thick, white cotton pants and a heavy layer of sweat. Mick never bothered to wear his gi jacket when he trained alone. His movements were sharper and cleaner than the other black belts. His muscles rippled with each motion, even in the low light.

She watched, mesmerized, as he took down one imaginary opponent after another. He finished his training and bowed, not bothering to look toward her when he pushed his damp hair out of his eyes. "What do you want, Gilda?"

Busted. "I came to check on things."

"There's nothing to check on." He started the new kata, the sequence of movements that mimicked a fight.

Gilda wandered to her desk and frowned at the assorted burger wrappers and leftover paper cups scattered across her desk. "You'd think at some point grown men could learn to clean up after themselves."

Mick gave a loud kiai and carried on as if he hadn't heard her.

She shoved the mess into the trash, then logged in to check e-mails. Sympathy notes from parents. A couple new students who wanted to terminate their memberships and get their money back. An e-mail from Yoshida to remind them he'd arrive for training on Tuesday at five o'clock sharp. Wednesday morning, because of the long weekend, was Walter's funeral.

"I left Yoshida a message to reschedule our training under the circumstances," Mick told her as he walked in. Droplets of sweat splattered the laminate floor in his wake.

Gilda glanced up. "I take it he didn't like the idea."

"What do you mean?"

"He sent an e-mail instructing you to book him a room with a hot tub and a king-sized bed."

"That demanding, egomaniacal, little rodent." Mick swore and punched the wall hard enough to leave a shallow indent. He shut his eyes and pinched the bridge of his nose. "I'll let the black belts know. Can you contact our students?"

"It's Sunday of the long weekend. Most won't be home."

"Improvise. Send an e-mail. Leave a message. Isn't that what you'd normally do?" Mick wiped sweat off his face. "Forget it. You should be somewhere else, too. It's not healthy to hang around here right now. You need some time away after yesterday."

She nodded. "So do you. Besides, Thayer wants us here, remember?"

"In town, not in the school." When the front door opened, Mick didn't bother to look over his shoulder. "Thayer's a jerk. Go enjoy your weekend. I'll deal with that two-faced—"

"I'm a two-faced what?" Thayer asked, strolling up to her desk. "I thought the school was closed."

"We are closed." Mick folded his arms across the well-defined muscles of his chest. "Gilda and I were just leaving. What do you want?"

"Relax, muscle head." Thayer's gaze flicked from Gilda to Mick then back. "I thought I'd see if either of you remembered anything else."

He could've asked before she left the station. "Yeah, I remembered I was going for a run."

"Since when do you run?" he asked.

"Since I dumped you."

Mick's jaw twitched. "Since she started training wanted to get in shape. You have a problem with that?"

Thayer held up both hands. "Nope."

"You want a running buddy?" Mick met her gaze. "I need to get out of here."

Thayer scowled. "What are you? Her bodyguard?"

"Only when you're around," Mick replied. "In case you missed the memo, Thayer, I don't like you much. You have a habit of mistreating my friends."

"Last I heard, she's your employee, not your friend. Gilda's perfectly capable of protecting herself and I've got stitches to prove it." He backed away. "I'll leave, but as long as Walter Levy's killer is still out there, I'll keep getting in your face. and Gilda's."

Neither spoke until Thayer left the building. Once he closed the door, Mick leaned against the desk and blew out a long breath and muttered, "I really don't like that guy."

"Get in line."

"I used to date a girl who worked at Café Beanz. She had a fling with the creep," he said. "The funny part was his girlfriend caught them in the act one night and beat the snot out of him."

"I was his girlfriend, and it wasn't very funny."

Mick grinned. "I know. I still can't believe you gave him a black eye, threw him into a gigantic bag of coffee beans, and left him lying there half-naked a concussion. By the time I found out, it was all over the newspapers, they broke up, and she left town. Last I heard she had two kids and a seventy-year-old sugar daddy."

"A sugar daddy, huh? She might be onto something." Gilda babysat black belts, had a mortgage on a house the size of a throw cushion, and no one at home. "See you later."

Mick ran to his office and returned pulling a shirt over his well-muscled torso. "Hey, wait up. I was serious about tagging along."

There was safety in numbers. Unless he was Walter's killer. Gilda nodded. "Where do you want to go?"

"Surprise me." He locked the door behind them. "I need a change of scenery."

A year and a half ago, she decided to run around the high school track. She got halfway around on her first attempt. The next day she pushed herself to three quarters. After three more tries, she ran one complete lap, then collapsed into the grass. Now she ran five miles through the streets of her hometown. She took him on her usual route, along Main Street to the park, then down the trail by the river. They ran side-by-side, keeping their thoughts to themselves.

Ten thousand people called Sandstone Cove home during the summer. Nestled along the northern shore of Lake Erie, the town boasted sandy beaches and hot, lazy days. By far, the town's biggest selling feature—until Walter's murder—was that no serious crimes had occurred since someone shot a local cop. Gilda's dad.

Apparently, word hadn't gotten out yet that a man was murdered. Most tourists wouldn't really care. It was none of their concern, so they continued to play on the lake, Jet Ski, and steer their boats through the cove.

Gilda's regular run took forty-five minutes. Today, moving at Mick's pace, she cut her time by five minutes. Two blocks from her house, she slowed to a walk. Sweat trickled between her shoulder blades and down the curves of her back as she gasped for breath.

"That was awesome," she told him.

"Yeah, I needed that. Sometimes it's best to stop thinking and run hard. We'll have to go out together again sometime." Mick grinned as he wiped his forehead with the bottom of his shirt. "For a run, I mean. You mind if I grab a glass of water?"

"Sure." She led him inside, then grabbed them each a towel. "Have you talked to Walter's wife yet?"

He slumped onto a chair at the table. "No, but I should call her, considering he was an instructor."

"Are you serious?" Gilda gawked as she set two tall glasses on the counter that divided her kitchen from her tiny dining area. As she took a pitcher from the fridge, she said, "You owe her more than a lousy phone call."

"Like what?"

"Flowers would be a nice start. Maybe a sympathy card from the school."

"Why? I didn't kill him."

As she poured two glasses of water, she contemplated throwing it in his face. "I didn't say you did, but acknowledging Walter's death is the descent thing to do."

Mick got up and leaned on the opposite side of the counter's breakfast bar. His breath cooled the sweat on her bare arm before he drank the entire glass of water at once. "You're right. I'm not good at that kind of stuff. Can you pick out some flowers?"

"Right after I shower and have lunch."

His gaze strayed below her face, another grin flickering. "I'll deal with Yoshida. I'm not sure how many people will show up to train Tuesday, but we'll have a moment of silence before class."

"That's a good idea. I'll add that in the e-mail to the students."

"Make sure you post one of those cards from the funeral on the bulletin board." Mick reached for the pitcher and refilled both their glasses. "I know it seems like I don't care, but he and I were friends a long time and things are a little weird. It'll be strange without him around."

"It'll be hard to replace him. The kids loved Walter. Some of them will have a hard time dealing with the loss."

Mick thought for a moment. "Maybe I should teach the kids' classes for now. Erik and Xavier can cover the adult classes."

"What about Razi?" she asked.

"He'd rather assist then teach." He drank half his second glass of water. "Razi's never struck me as the jealous kind. You know the kind of person who'd kill to get what they wanted. He hates the spotlight."

"Huh. Now who's playing private detective?" Gilda smirked.

Mick winked. "Busted. Tell me, Sherlock, would you eliminate Razi as a suspect?"

She shrugged. "No. He has a background as a soldier, and as much opportunity as anyone. Including you."

"That was a jab. What about you?"

"I have an alibi," she reminded him. "I was at brunch with Marion and both Thayer and Fabio saw us. Then I went at the doctor. I know

Razi and Walter got along on a professional level. Did they get along outside the school?"

"Razi's not real social. He comes to watch MMA fights, but not for long. The guy's a man of mystery." He set his glass on the counter and laid his hand on hers. "Thanks for the drink. I'd better go."

Averting her gaze as her heart raced, Gilda noticed a dark car drive past. "Someone was looking for you earlier."

"Oh yeah? Who's that?" He finished the last of his water.

Gilda let him swallow before she said, "Gary del Garda."

Mick flinched like she'd burned him. "What did he say?"

"Just that he had business to discuss." She narrowed her eyes. "What would he want with you?"

"Probably just a misunderstanding," he said. "Don't worry about it."

Gilda had questions, but she doubted she'd get any answers. "Was your family upset you can't visit this weekend?"

"Actually, my parents wanted to come here to help. I told them I have enough to do without entertaining and they'd only be in the way of the investigation."

Gilda had told her mother the same thing. What she'd omitted to say was that she and the black belts were suspects. That would come out once everyone in Sandstone Cove discovered how Walter Levy died.

She pictured him every time she shut her eyes. The katana. The blood on the tatami mats. The ring. She should've shown it to Mick before giving it to Fabio. Someone would've bragged about a memento like that.

Mick slid his hand around her waist and pulled her into a hug. "You don't look so good. Why don't you take a shower and get some rest?"

Before she could ask about the ring or who he suspected, Mick walked out the door.

Walter Levy was dead. A known bookie was looking for Mick.

What was going on with the black belts at Yoshida Martial Arts that Gilda missed?

CHAPTER 5

F reshly showered and fed, Gilda was too restless to stay indoors, yet too nervous to go to the school. She put on her headphones and strolled along the shoreline littered with garish towels, screaming kids, loud music, and seagulls. Places like Café Beanz were far more crowded than normal. On weekends, she gave up on even getting close to the ice cream shop until late August, which was probably for the best since she wanted to grade for her next karate belt in the fall.

If it wasn't for the tourists, Sandstone Cove would be just another little lakeside town full of deadwood. Instead, the area was renowned for miles of sandy beach, rugged jetties, lush forests, and driftwood that local artisans turned into expensive souvenirs. Water sports, hiking, and camping were mainstays that drew people in year-round.

Yoshida Martial Arts sat along Main Street tucked between Nine Lives Consignment Boutique and the Novel Ideas Bookstore. More kitsch. All combined, it was why Gilda hadn't left Sandstone Cove, even after her dad died and her mom moved to Fort Erie.

She sat on a large tree trunk that had washed ashore in a storm years earlier. Her initials, along with Thayer's, were carved in the wood for all time—or at least until someone cut it up for firewood, or Mother Nature washed it back into the lake.

Gilda was in love with Thayer once. On a shallow, fleeting level, she still cared. Her thoughts ambled from Thayer to Mick, then stalled. Most days Mick acted like an annoying older brother. Some days, ones like today, the attachment seemed deeper. More intense. Those occasional moments of innocent intimacy, like him touching her hand in her kitchen, suggested he felt the same way.

Then he'd run out and hook up with a girlfriend.

Mick kept a wealth of information locked in his office. He always said they were personal papers, nothing for Gilda to be concerned with. Now she wondered. Just when she thought she knew everything about the school, including the black belts and Mick, she found out about Walter's past and Erik's plans for a school. What had they all kept from her? Possibly something that got Walter killed.

She ignored her phone when it vibrated in her pocket. Mick would be upset she wasn't at his beck and call. He could deal with the police and students for a few hours. Her hands hadn't stopped shaking since she'd discovered Walter's corpse.

She blinked back an onslaught of tears as her phone rang again. Reluctantly, she checked the screen. A text from her mother, two missed calls from Marion, and one from Thayer. Not a peep from Mick. Why did that disappoint her so much?

Her mother wanted her to "come home", even though she'd never lived in Fort Erie, only Sandstone Cove. Thayer warned her not to leave town or else.

The "or else" made her laugh out loud. Who did he think he was? Sure, he'd proposed marriage. They'd even set a date. She had the dress, the caterer, the church, and the hall. He had the girl from Café Beanz, a honey in Fort Erie, and, according to Fabio, another one who worked in Happy Harvey's Hangover Hut.

Restless, Gilda walked up Main Street. She passed Yoshida's, Café Beanz, and the Victorian-style brick front of the hospital, toward the pricier part of town. Ponderer's Point was a finger of rocky beach dotted with mansions, condos, and summer cottages easily four times the size of Gilda's house. An off shoot of Sandstone Cove, at the far end of the point sprawled a sturdy pier where yachts docked and seagulls squawked, seemingly without stopping to take a breath.

She climbed toward her favorite place to sit near the squat white lighthouse and daydream. The dreams were more like stories she told herself to pass the time. A handsome lighthouse keeper would come to her rescue and sweep her off her feet. Or a wealthy playboy on a blinding white yacht. Or a sexy karate teacher...

Gilda shook her head and sat on a granite boulder. It didn't matter who the leading man was, the story always ended the same. She'd refuse him until he convinced her he was worthy. After some Herculean feat, she'd fall into both his arms and his bed.

Who was she kidding? It would never happen.

Maybe her mother was right. She needed a boyfriend, not the steamy novels Marion loaned her. She'd only started reading crime novels after breaking up with Thayer.

Today, however, she pulled her knees to her chest in need of an escape. No leading man or bodice-ripping endings. Just a hollow pain in the pit of her stomach. Grief, she'd heard, pulled people and communities together, yet she felt more alone than ever. The sky, bleached from the heat, seemed to close in on her. Suffocating her. Daring her to take a deep breath that could be her last.

"Those are a lot of big sighs for a little girl." Doc, tall and white-haired, picked his way over the rocks toward her. He wore tan Bermuda shorts and a straight-back-from-Hawaii flamingo print shirt with well-worn Birkenstocks. "It sounds like the world's caving in on you."

Gilda had first met Doc the day she was born, having been one of his first deliveries. He'd guided her through measles, broken ankles, acne, and heartbreak. When he lost his wife to cancer earlier in the year, Gilda was the first to deliver an apple-peach cobbler and Shepherd's Pie to his door.

"I can't believe Walter just died yesterday," she told him. "It seems like a week ago."

"Yes, a murder most foul. I'm sorry you were the one to find him," he said, as he sat next to her and lit a pipe. She found the sweet scent of tobacco comforting. For a few blissful minutes, she dismissed all thoughts of second-hand smoke and lung cancer as she pictured her father on the porch with his pipe.

"Yeah." She rested her chin between her knees.

"And I was unlucky enough to get him on my autopsy table." He puffed. The burning tobacco reminded her of her grandfather who smoked a pipe right up until he died at ninety-five. "Seems like we both got the bitter end of the stick this time."

"Was the Medical Examiner badly hurt in that accident?"

"A few broken ribs and a broken collarbone. He'll be off for a few months."

As bile crept up Gilda's throat, she swallowed hard. "Have you seen Walter yet?"

"I did the preliminary this morning and have him prepped," he said. "Normally, I'd send him to the state, but Thayer insisted I take a look.

Not sure what the rush is, but I had to take a break when the widow came to identify the body."

"Why did Jade have to see him? Mick and I identified him at the school."

"She is his next of kin. It's understandable she wanted to see for herself."

"To make sure it was him or to make sure he was dead?" she muttered.

Doc raised a thick, white eyebrow. "Excuse me?"

"Sorry. That was rude." Gilda's face warmed.

"You've always been a perceptive young lady." He patted her hand. "I can always count on you to notice things others can't."

"What did you think after the preliminary exam?" she asked. "I mean, I saw the katana and the mess in the change room, but..."

Doc met her gaze. "And you think there's more to the story."

She met his gaze. "Do you think I'm crazy?"

He took a long drag from his pipe before he said, "I think you have boundless potential as a writer. The actual cause of Walter's death is blatant. You saw the sword. Unfortunately, I can't tell you more than that. Confidentiality issues, that sort of thing."

"I know. Sorry for prying. I just feel awful about everything. Jade must be devastated. Do you think Walter could've been poisoned first so someone smaller could take him down easier?"

"You pity her, but think his widow is guilty?"

Gilda shrugged. "Someone. Not necessarily her."

"You know I can't talk about that. What do you think happened?"

"I think either his attacker was bigger, stronger, and faster, or they drugged him." She scanned the horizon. "If he was drugged and semi-conscious, anyone could've killed him."

Doc took one last drag on his pipe before he knocked it against the boulder. "My job is to determine how he died. Thayer and Fabio worry about whodunnit." He looked Gilda in the eye. "You need to let the rest of us do the detecting."

"What makes you think I'd—?"

"History has a habit of repeating." Doc smiled.

"I honestly saw Mrs. Watson steal drugs from your office. She even admitted to it." Indignant, she slid off the rock, lightly scraping the backs of her legs. She'd never live the incident down for as long as Doc lived.

"Honey, you were ten years old and delirious," he said. "You just woke up after surgery for a ruptured appendix. Mrs. Watson, my nurse, was getting you painkillers."

"I know what I saw, and I know what I heard."

"You also insisted she sprouted shiny wings that looked like soap bubbles and flew out the window to her car."

"Oh yeah."

He hugged her. "I must admit, you almost had me convinced until then. Do us both a favor. Make sure you have more evidence this time. I have to get back to work before Fabio and Thayer show up with more questions. I'll talk to you later."

"Take good care of Walter," she told him, then picked her way over the rocks.

As Doc sauntered over the rocks, leaving the scent of tobacco in his wake, Gilda smile. Walter was in good hands. Doc was diligent and not much got past him. Except Mrs. Watson. Who'd since left nursing to run the Nine Lives Consignment shop with her grandson.

She'd barely reached the sidewalk when she noticed a dark sedan she swore belonged to Gary del Garda. For someone who insisted he wasn't following her, he seemed to stick close to her. What did he want with her?

Gilda made a snap decision to visit Walter's widow to keep from having Gary approach her again. After a stop at the corner store to grab a bouquet of Gerbera daisies, she walked across town to Darlington Court, the town's newest subdivision. She'd order a fancier bouquet on behalf of the karate school later.

While Gilda thought she knew Walter, Jade had always avoided her as much as possible. If nothing else, Walter's widow would keep their large new house, complete with a swimming pool, three car garage, and the luxury cars to fill each slot.

Gilda, in her shorts and snug yoga top, felt sorely underdressed standing on the front step. She hesitated, taking three deep breaths before she rang the doorbell. Rather than a normal ding-dong, the chimes had an airy, Zen-like tone far less jarring than other doorbells.

Jade, drawn and pale, opened the door wearing a pink silk kimono. Her delicate features tensed as she gave a slight bow. "Miss Wright. What can I do for you?"

"I'm sorry for your loss," Gilda told her, handing her the bouquet, which appeared gaudy next to Jade's elegance. "Walter was a good teacher and friend."

Her lips drew into a small tight bow, making her look even more like a geisha. "That is very kind. Walter thought highly of you. You were the one person at the school he could always count on. Please come in."

"He said that?" Gilda asked as she followed Jade across the bamboo floor.

They entered a sunroom decorated with treasures probably brought back from their many trips to Japan. While Walter wasn't Japanese, he'd fully embraced his wife's culture. The low black lacquer table was already set with tea for two. If someone else was here, why hadn't they remained in the sunroom? Perhaps she was expecting company, or someone had just left.

Gilda smiled. "You have a lovely home."

As Jade followed her gaze to the teacups, her cheeks turned pink. "I have had so many visitors that I keep the table set. Excuse me. I will prepare fresh water."

"I shouldn't impose," Gilda said. "I'm sure you have a million things to do.

"It is no bother." She placed the teapot, flowers, and both cups on a bamboo tray, then shuffled down the hallway. Beneath her kimono, she wore tabi socks and woven grass sandals, zoris, that she and Walter brought back from their last trip. He'd also brought Gilda a pair, which she used for decoration, so she didn't ruin them.

Gilda wandered around the room to admire the carvings and paintings amid the lush, tropical plants. Walter had a penchant for growing the most delicate of plants. She hoped Jade had the same green thumb to keep them flourishing.

"My apologies for the wait, Miss Wright," Jade said as her clogs tapped the floor. "I have made Walter's jasmine tea. His personal blend from the garden. He drank it every evening."

"That sounds great, thank you." Gilda sat across from her host, who poured two thimble-sized cups of tea from a hand-painted pot. It would be a brief visit.

Jade wore a stiff smile. "Walter's first-born son, Donald, assures me I have nothing to be concerned about."

"Oh, that's right." Gilda sipped her tea, sweeter than normal jasmine. The tea flowed more easily than their conversation. "I forgot he has older children. Did he have two or three from his first marriage?"

Jade's face tightened further. "He had three children. Two boys and a girl."

Taboo topic. Gilda wanted to kick herself for bringing them up. "It's nice they came to help. You must get along well with them."

"Wonderfully." The word strained through Jade's white teeth. She drank her tea in one gulp, then poured a second cup.

"I'm sorry. I shouldn't be so nosy," Gilda said as she finished her thimbleful of tea and set her cup on the tray to avoid leaving a mark on the table. "I only came to see if there was anything I could do to help."

Jade seemed to regain her composure as she struggled with a small smile. "I was told you have been most helpful with the police and in comforting Walter's students. I appreciate you taking the time to come by. You and Sensei Mick have been good to us over the years."

"I should go. If you need anything..." Gilda glanced around not sure what more she could offer that the widow didn't already have.

She gave a slight bow. "I will call."

Right after donkeys held public office. Gilda realized she'd made a mess of the entire visit. "I am deeply sorry for your loss."

When Jade stood, her kimono didn't hold so much as a crinkle. It fell smooth and perfect like someone ironed it the instant she stood. They walked toward the teak front door, footsteps echoing on the bamboo flooring. As Gilda reached for the doorknob, a door creaked, then slammed upstairs. She jumped back with a gasp.

Jade's eyes widened before she gave a small laugh. "The wind slams the guestroom door. Walter always laughed at me when I would jump."

"Oh. I thought it was one of Walter's kids."

Her face darkened to the color of a baby pink rose. "They choose to stay in a hotel when they visit, so we do not get in each other's way."

Gilda glanced up the staircase to the open hallway, sure she heard a door open slowly. Someone moved inside before the door shut. Quieter this time. A second person was in the Levy home.

A faceless man wearing a yellow robe.

Whatever Jade was up to, she was far from alone while she mourned her husband.

CHAPTER 6

The plants in Gilda's backyard garden welcomed both she and her whirling mind home. They seemed to smile when she watered them, making the intense sadness that had washed over her ease. If Jade had a lover, he could've been jealous enough to kill Walter.

Or maybe Walter discovered her promiscuity, so Jade paid someone to kill him?

Gilda's stomach lurched. She'd seen far too many movies about people who hired hit men to do away with troublesome spouses. While she didn't know anyone in Sandstone Cove capable of such a thing, she imagined someone would—for the right price.

Then she froze while staring at a large, red dahlia. She did know someone. The same someone who had business to discuss with Mick.

Gary del Garda.

She struggled to remember what Walter had told her about his family. Jade was from New York City, the daughter of Japanese immigrants who ran the restaurant where she and Walter met. He'd forgotten to mention until later that she was a high school senior at the time, and he was a married father of three.

If Jade's family still held a grudge, they could've hires a someone to...

Gilda blew off the thought. Walter and Jade had been married fifteen years. If Jade's family wanted him dead, he wouldn't have lasted that long. She focused on watering the plants, letting each tiny drop of water soak her worries into the ground.

"Gilda? Are you here?" Mick called from around the side of her house.

Her worries practically climbed back up her calves to cower behind her knees. "In the backyard."

"I rang the doorbell. I guess you didn't hear it," he said, swearing as he fumbled with the latch on the gate. "Why do you have a Chinese puzzle lock on your gate?"

She turned off the water. "Just lift the latch. What's up?"

"Why do you think something's up? Can't I just visit?" He sat on the steps of the back porch. "You have a really nice yard."

"Thanks. It's peaceful here. Most of the time. You've never come to my house before this week. What do you want?" she asked.

Mick sighed. "I've been locked in Thayer's interrogation room for the past two hours. I needed a friendly face and fresh air. That place reeks worse than the school after a tournament. I wonder if they've even heard of air fresheners. We should send over a case."

She sat on the stone bench near the foot-tall lavender a few feet away from him. "Not that I mind the company, but why not go see Chloe?"

"She's at work." He hesitated. "She doesn't like me stopping by when she's there."

Gilda raised her eyebrows. Chloe was a customer service representative at the bank. It wasn't like she could ban him. "What did Thayer want now?"

"Hair, skin cells, blood. Everything but my first born, which I don't have." Mick basked in the sunshine. "He used the old standby about trying to eliminate people, but when he asked for a semen sample, I left."

"Semen?" Gilda asked.

He shrugged. "Something to do with the change room curtains, which I do not want back, by the way."

"Eww!" She scrunched up her face.

Mick chuckled. "I think I had that look, too."

"Does he want to talk to me?"

"Just me and the black belts. Personally, I think he's out to get all of us. Except you."

"I thought I'd be the biggest target on his hit list."

"Nah, Thayer's got a soft spot for you." He picked a small daisy near his foot. "He doesn't think you're capable of killing someone. Face it, Sherlock, you're just too nice."

"I am not." She folded her arms and sat up straight. With nothing to stop her, she toppled backward into the huge, pink peony.

Mick flew across the grass and caught her by the ankle before she landed in the dirt. When he pulled her upright, their faces ended up inches apart. "Are you okay?"

"Yeah. Thanks for grabbing me." A surge of heat swept through her. "I mean for not letting me fall."

That didn't sound any better.

"My pleasure." He grinned, then sat beside her with, one hand around her waist. "You got new nail polish. I've never seen your toenails pale green before. They look like mint chocolate chip ice cream. My favorite."

Positive her face was rose red, she muttered, "Thanks."

"Actually, ice cream sounds good," he said, moving an inch closer. His grip tightened on her waist. "I might stop for some on my way home."

"It does sound good," she whispered, in need of a cold shower.

Mick cleared his throat and suddenly became all business again. He moved his hands to grip the bench on either side of his legs. "You called everyone to cancel classes tonight, right?"

She focused on a multilayered orange poppy. The heat from his hand seemed to sear her thigh—even from two inches away. "It's Saturday. We don't have classes."

"Is the funeral Tuesday or Wednesday?"

"Yoshida's workshop is Tuesday," she reminded him. "The funeral is Wednesday. Back to normal Thursday." What was wrong with her? Mick had never rattled her so much before.

He hesitated before asking, "Are you okay? I mean, after finding Walter and all."

"I think so. I stopped to see Jade earlier."

He smiled. "Wow. You've been busy today. How's she doing?"

Gilda frowned. "You haven't even gone to see her?"

"I've been busy at the police station. I doubt she'd want to see any of us right now."

"True. She doesn't exactly seem shaken up."

"I guess we all grieve in our own ways," he said.

She thought about the man in the yellow robe. Jade had an interesting method of mourning the loss of her husband. "What did you do today? Besides sitting in an interrogation room."

"After our run, I had breakfast with—" He clamped his mouth shut. "I should go. I'm sure you have stuff to do."

"Yeah." Left out of the loop again. What was going on with him? Time to go fishing. "I heard rumors a couple of the black belts wanted to open their own schools and."

He draped his arm across her shoulders and rested his head against hers. "I hate rumors. They get people in trouble that was never there to begin with. If you need anything, call me. Don't worry about work until after the funeral."

"What about Yoshida's workshop?" she asked.

Mick swore. "Except that. Can you...?"

"I'll make sure everyone knows about the workshop, the funeral, and when classes will resume," she said. "I'll even make sure the school is clean and ready. You need to replace the mats though."

"Consider it taken care of." He gave her shoulders a squeeze as he kissed her cheek. His lips lingered near her ear as he asked, "What would I do without you, Sherlock? You're the best."

Once Mick left, she forgot all about gardening. When a surge of heat tore through her, she splashed her face and armpits with cold water from the hose before returning to the yard. He never answered her question about the black belts. If he did, her brain erased it when he kissed her.

Later that afternoon, she wandered up the street to the school to check for messages and send the required e-mails. She could've called to check the phone messages but was too restless and needed to move.

The lights in the building were on, but the door was locked. Mick must've forgot to turn off the lights when he left. She crossed her fingers and prayed there were no more bodies. This time she'd probably scream, run for home, and never go back.

Inside the dojo, Razi Mauli had his back to her as he scrubbed new tatami mats. The water bucket stood on the wood floor of the lobby. Sweat soaked his short black hair and army green shirt. Rumor around the school was he'd been an Israeli soldier trained in krav maga. He'd done things that would've given Gilda nightmares.

She wished she'd called Marion. If the school reopened in two days and someone found her inside, Marion would kill her. She set down her handbag and scribbled a note to grab air fresheners and disinfectant spray.

"Miss Wright, what are you doing here?" Razi asked.

She jumped and dropped her keys to the laminate floor with a clatter. "I work here. What are you doing?"

He leaned the mop against the wall. "Sensei Mick asked me to replace the mats. The police took more than I thought."

Gilda swallowed hard. "How do you know the police took them?"

"Biohazardous materials," Razi said. He studied her before narrowing his eyes. "Was this a test?"

"I guess so. Sorry."

A genuine, honest-to-goodness smile, something she'd rarely seen before, brightened his face. "You watch far too much television, Miss Wright."

"Probably. Where'd you get the mats so fast?"

"From my basement. Sensei Mick helped set up a dojo in my basement, for my training. I offered to loan them to the school until he can get new ones."

"That's nice of you. Thanks," she told him, leaning against the counter. "Did you know Walter very well?"

"Walter was a simple man with a complicated life," he said. "Some things he did made me laugh. A few made me sad. Several made me wonder if his head was up his posterior."

She'd never heard Razi talk so much. "What kind of things?"

"I do not gossip, Miss Wright." Hence, the reason he rarely spoke.

"Who should I talk to?"

Razi shrugged his broad shoulders, then lifted the bucket. "Anyone who will speak with you, I suppose. Perhaps start with Sensei Mick and work down the list."

"Why Sensei Mick?"

He walked away, silent except for the slosh of the water in the bucket.

"Razi?" She followed him down the hall to the utility room and waited while he emptied the bucket into the large sink and rinsed the mop. Mick had to know more than everyone else. He seemed to know about Walter's potential karate school, even if he wouldn't discuss it with her.

"Did Walter mention he wanted to start his own karate school?"

"Once again, Miss Wright, that is gossip."

"Not if I ask you to tell me." She crossed her fingers and hoped he believed her. "Relaying information when someone needs to know isn't gossip. Running around town telling everyone what you know out of spite, that's gossip."

"Interesting interpretation." Razi put the bucket and mop away, then turned to clean the sink. "And of what use is this information to you?"

Gilda hesitated as the scent of bleach reached her nostrils. "What if his death had something to do with him wanting to leave Yoshida's to open a new school?"

He maintained his silence as he rinsed the sink before wiping it dry. If Razi had murdered Walter, there wouldn't be a speck of blood anywhere. Razi was meticulous. When he finally did speak, he asked, "Do you think it could be dangerous for you to seek his killer?"

"Probably."

He lay a damp hand on her shoulder. "Be careful, Miss Wright. Even the most harmless kitten can pose a danger when angered."

She didn't move until the front door closed and silence settled over the school. Settling behind her desk, she hoped Gary had no idea she was alone. Of everyone involved, he made her the most nervous.

Neither Xavier nor Razi had ever spoken to her as much as in the past twenty-four hours. It struck her as odd, especially for Razi, who rarely spoke at all.

Mick seemed to gravitate closer to her, then pull away. Was he trying to distract her and, if so, from what?

Gilda took care of the small pile of paperwork before she ordered flowers for the Levy family. Once the work was done, she snooped. The call that came while she and Mick cleaned blood off the floors was made from Mick's condo. Her stomach lurched. If Chloe had moved in with him, why did he keep flirting with her?

Chloe Del Garda had signed up for karate a year earlier. Even though Mick had noticed her, he hadn't acted on the attraction until six months ago. Far too soon to cohabitate, in her opinion, but Mick obviously didn't share her view. Of course, while Gilda didn't see eye to eye with him on a lot of things, she respected him enough not to stick her nose into his private life.

She couldn't imagine what would've happened for Mick to ban his girlfriend from the school. Sure, they argued, but he'd never black-listed anyone that she knew of.

Gilda headed toward Mick's office to see what sort of secrets he held there. Halfway to his door, she paused.

The ring.

She hadn't asked anyone except Xavier about it. If it wasn't made locally, she'd have a hard time to find information. On the other hand, she might be able to track it down to give Fabio a hand. At least that was her official reasoning. Unofficially, she had no idea who the ring belonged to, and doubted Fabio would keep her in the loop.

Rather than search Mick's office, she returned to her computer. An hour later, all she had was a throbbing headache. No leads. No photos. She clicked her pen in frustration until a noise pulled her focus away from the website.

A sound. A movement. Probably something small and light, like a rat. She glanced up from the monitor and frowned. Gilda hated rats as much as Mick hated cats.

Staying behind her desk, she stood to do a visual search. The dojo was semi-dark. The lights in the change room were out. She chalked it up to stress before adding the details of Walter's funeral to the website.

Someone was in the dojo.

Whoever it was must've snuck in while she was alone.

Or planned to make Razi victim number three.

Heart racing, Gilda reached for the nearest weapon, a pair of scissors. Despite the two years of karate training, she'd never be able to hold her own against someone intent on killing her. Not that scissors would help against someone with serious weapons training.

She skirted the desk, careful not to knock anything over, as she headed for the dojo. She paused and listened. No footsteps. Nothing.

"Is somebody here?" she asked.

Like an intruder intent on murder would answer.

"Mick? Razi? Who's there?"

Bare feet squeaked on a mat as the figure in the shadows turned on their toes and ran. Gilda caught a glimpse of bare feet, smooth legs, and muscular calves. A man. Turned on their toes. A black belt would turn that precisely. An outsider would likely turn on their heel or the balls of their feet.

She reached to turn on the lights but missed the switch. Armed with the scissors, she gave chase anyway as the shadow man raced for the back exit at a startling speed.

When he opened the door, a brief explosion of sunlight blinded her. His fuzzy shadow was visible for seconds before the door slammed. By the time she entered the back alley everything was silent and still. No barefoot ninjas. No vehicles burning rubber down the alley. Nothing.

Gilda cursed beneath her breath until she'd locked the back door and retreated behind her desk. Who could've broken in and what were they looking for?

Perhaps someone knew about the missing ring.

"Are you still here, Gilda?" a voice called from the front door.

She flinched, tightening her grip on the scissors. If someone walked in with bare feet, there was no telling what she might do. "Yes."

"What's going on?" Mick strolled in sweaty and naked from the waist up. He wore a dusty pair of black sandals.

"I didn't think you'd be here."

He paused in front of her desk. "And I didn't think you'd be armed. Are you okay?"

Hands shaking, she set the scissors on the desk before collapsing onto the chair. "Someone was in the dojo. They ran out the back door, but I didn't see who it was."

He smoothed back his hair with both hands. "I'll look around. What are you still doing here anyway?"

"I came to order flowers for Jade and send an e-mail to all the students," she reminded him. "Razi was here. He washed the mats."

"Lady Macbeth." Mick grinned. "Except I can't picture you as the sort of woman to drive a katana through a man's chest. Verbally maybe, not physically."

She set her pen down. Thayer had said he could picture her stabbing a man through the heart. "Why would you say that?"

"Like I said, you're too nice." He disappeared down the hall. "Sit tight. I'll check things out."

He walked around to the back room and flipped on every light in the building. When he returned, he left them blazing. "I think all you heard was a loose vent cover and Walter's ghost playing games."

She scowled. "That's not funny, Mick. It wasn't a ghost. I saw a man. He turned on his toes, then I grabbed the scissors and chased him out the back door." She peered over her desk to double check. He wore black sandals. Easy to put on in the car if he had snuck in, but he, of all people, had every reason to be there.

"Please stop staring at my feet. You're scaring me." He stepped back. "You don't plan to stab me, do you?"

"No." She returned to her chair, not sure what to do next.

He stalked across the dojo, then peered out the back door before returning to sit beside her. "What do you think he wanted?"

The second chair was Walter's contribution to the school. When things were quiet, he enjoyed sitting next to her to learn everything he could to run his own school.

"Something I found after Walter..." Her eyes burned with tears.

Mick leaned back with his eyebrows raised. "Something you failed to give the police? Sherlock, you astound me. What is it?"

"A ring. Someone had taped it to the bottom of the bench you kicked. I picked it up and gave it to Fabio," she lied as she pulled out her phone to show him the photo. "Is it yours?"

"No, but I've seen one like it." Mick enlarged the image. "Send that to me, so I can ask around."

"Which would be great unless it belongs to the killer."

"Why?

"Then he'd come after us."

Mick forwarded the picture to his phone. "No, he'd come after me. Do you think someone would ask about it if they killed Walter?"

"Why would they hide it in the first place?"

"The tape could've been from something else. Maybe the ring fell off someone's finger and got stuck behind the bench."

Gilda studied the photo of the engraved golden fist. "It's been so hot my fingers keep swelling. I needed to soap my grandma's ring off, so often I just left it at home. How would it slip off someone's finger?"

"Walter lost fifty pounds. He might've worn it on a chain until he got it resized," he said. "Did the police find a chain? It could've broken in the struggle."

"They had no reason to look for one."

Mick grinned, then jumped off the chair. "The drain."

Convinced he'd lost his mind, Gilda followed. When he fell to all fours and leaned his face close to the tiles, she shook her head and asked, "What are you doing?"

He pulled his keys out of his pocket and turned on a pinky-sized flashlight. "Right there. See that?"

Just beneath the grate, something gleamed. She punched his shoulder. "By Jove, Watson. You've solved the case."

Mick scowled. "Don't mock me. Find something to get it out of there."

"I'm busy. You figure it out." Gilda dismissed his treasure hunt and returned to her desk with the suspicion Mick was trying to keep her mind off things. She was positive the ring hadn't fallen from a chain. Someone taped it to the bottom of the bench and Mick jarred it loose during his tantrum.

He stalked past her with a growl, then disappeared into his office. When he reappeared, he carried a hammer and chisel.

Within seconds, he banged on the floor. Gilda covered her eyes. Whatever mess he made he'd expect her to clean up. She imagined shards scattering everywhere but refused to witness the destruction.

After a couple minutes of hammering, Mick let out a triumphant, "Aha." The tools clattered to the floor before he ran around the corner and flung a delicate gold chain with a crud-encrusted pendant on her desk. It needed to be soaked in sanitizer or bagged and given to the police.

"Eww." Gilda recoiled. "Whose is it?"

"Am I supposed to do everything?"

She would've thumped her head on the desk, but the grungy chain was in the way. "Of course not. You've caused enough chaos for one day."

"Don't forget to clean the hallway. I made a bit of a mess,"

Gilda had nothing handy to throw that wouldn't damage the wall if she missed.

Two minutes later, the shower started. Goose bumps strolled up and down her arms. Mick rarely used the showers at the school. Why hadn't he gone home when he only lived a few blocks away?

Chloe.

Having done enough sleuthing for one day, Gilda needed to go home, have a light dinner, and sleep. She turned off the computer and started down the hallway. Having second thoughts, she stopped and childishly stuck her tongue out. For once, Mick Williams could clean up his own mess.

As she reached for her purse, her gaze fell on the chain. Using hand sanitizer and a paper towel, she rubbed the grit from the swirled letters of the pendant to reveal a name.

"Chloe." Gilda stared.

Mick gave his girlfriend the gold necklace for her last birthday. She must've lost it after class.

She slid it onto a clean tissue and thought about bringing it to Fabio, then hesitated and placed it on Mick's desk. Chloe could've lost the necklace weeks ago. Just because it was in the drain didn't automatically make her a murderer.

Gilda smiled as she walked out of the school, leaving both the necklace and the mess for Mick. Hopefully, she'd make it home without running into anyone she'd rather avoid.

CHAPTER 7

Mid-Sunday morning, Thayer sat across from Gilda in Café Beanz and waved to the server for a coffee. Dark, puffy circles shadowed his eyes as he announced, "We have a lot to talk about."

She set aside her breakfast sandwich. Her meager appetite squelched not only by Thayer's presence but the sight of Gary's car out front. "If you want to talk about Walter, I'll come down to the station. If this is personal, forget it."

"How many times do I have to apologize?" he asked. "I'm sorry. I messed up. What more do you want to hear?"

"I've heard everything from you I want to hear." She took the bag out of her tea.

"Then why won't you take me back? We made a really great team."

She hugged her cup. "Experience. Like Happy says, 'A tiger never changes his spots.'"

Thayer shook his head. "Tigers have stripes. Besides, since when did you start taking dating advice from a guy who sells booze?"

Gilda shot him a glare. "The same time you let that barista grind your beans behind the counter."

His bronze face deepened to burnt umber. "That was a one-time thing."

"Yeah. The one time I caught you," she told him, meeting his sour glare. "I know about the other girls, too. The blonde from the quilt shop. The redhead from the ice cream parlor. The Goth girl from Happy's. The yoga teacher from Fort Erie."

He squeezed his eyes shut before he reached for her hand and said, "I'm a changed man, Gilda. Why won't you believe me?"

When the server placed his coffee on the table, he leaned to watch her walk away.

Gilda chuckled. "Yeah, that's blatantly obvious."

He held up both palms. "What? I'm a man who appreciates a woman's natural assets. Is that a crime?"

"Only if you're dating me at the same time. Do whatever you want. You're not my problem anymore, and you never will be." She slid out of the booth, taking her leftover food and coffee.

"I'm serious, Gilda," he said. "We made a great team. Those other women meant nothing. You're the only person who makes me feel good about myself. By the way, that house we looked at came back on the market. If that isn't a sign—"

"I have a house, Thayer. The only thing you and I made well together were headlines. Right after I threw you into a fifty-pound bag of coffee beans and you split your scalp on the grinder."

Chuckles erupted from other patrons. One lady even applauded.

Thayer frowned. "You've always had a bad temper. The barista left me, you know."

"So did I." Gilda handed her sandwich to the server and asked for it to go. "In case you hadn't noticed, I've done better since I kicked you to the curb. I wouldn't take you back even if you begged and bought me a pink Porsche."

She walked away but only got as far as the next booth before he asked, "What about Mick?"

Gilda had a perfectly good explanation for "What about Mick?" She'd practiced it in front of her bathroom mirror every night for a year until she'd convinced herself Mick Williams was off limits. Mick never listened to her. He made her do all the work yet took all the praise. He was only gorgeous on the outside and was more bull-headed than her.

"What about Mick?" Thayer asked again.

"Mick won't date you either." She grinned.

A man sitting at the counter applauded and said, "You tell him."

"I don't need your approval either."

Fabio sat hunched over his coffee. "From your sudden departure, I take it my partner asked questions about Walter you didn't like."

She took her wrapped sandwich from the server. "Nope. All he wants is for me to take him back."

"It's not good to let lust cloud an investigation. Have a seat," he said, then shoved the last of a Danish into his mouth.

"Like I told your lunatic partner, I'll go to the station to answer questions. For now, I have things to do."

Fabio nodded. "The karate school's closed until after the funeral. Besides, you're stuck here for the weekend. What's so pressing?"

"My life. Good-bye, Detective."

He stirred his coffee. "I see. Good-bye, Gilda. Enjoy the rest of your breakfast. Don't choke on your guilt."

Gilda left the café daydreaming about dumping scalding coffee over both their heads.

"Aren't you the social butterfly today?" Gary's question startled her.

She'd forgotten about seeing his car parked out front.

He sat behind the steering wheel with a coffee in one hand and asked, "Thayer and Fabio bothering you? They aren't stupid enough to think you killed Walter, are they?"

"No." She walked around the front of his car.

"Then Thayer must still be trying to win you back." When her mouth dropped open and she turned to face him, he grinned. "Don't look so surprised, I hear a lot of things in my business."

Gilda stood near his window. "What do you want?"

"I was watching them," he said, pointing up the street.

Mick and Chloe stood in front of the school in heated discussion she guessed involved the recovered necklace. Chloe thrust a handful of papers at Mick before she shoved past him. Mick stood in front of the school, staring after the yellow Ferrari as she sped away. As he flipped through the papers, he cursed, kicking the brick wall before he entered the school.

"Now there's a man with things to hide," Gary said.

"Tell it to the police. They're inside." Gilda scuttled to the far side of the street.

She would've felt sorry for Mick, but she figured whatever was going on was his fault anyway. She was in no frame of mind to confront him after seeing Thayer. All she knew was things around Sandstone Cove were getting stranger by the minute and she was stuck in the middle.

* * *

Shortly after five that evening, Mick pushed his way into Gilda's ten-by-ten-foot living room, accompanied by the scent of alcohol. He shut the door behind him, locked it, and faced her. His body appeared tensed, and his hands clenched for a fight.

Gilda's knees quivered as he closed the gap between them, panting like he ran the entire way from his condo. The room suddenly seemed more claustrophobic than cozy.

"What are you doing?" she asked, inching toward the kitchen and afraid she was about to die. If he tried anything, she could defend herself with a frying pan.

"You have to help me, Gilda," he whispered, looking over his shoulder at the front window. "My heart's beating like crazy and I can't breathe. I don't know what to do. I think someone wired my phone and is trying to kill me."

"Wired your phone? What are you...?" she asked, then frowned. "Are you sure someone tapped your phone? Why?"

He yanked the curtains closed. "I never told anyone about the new karate school or the lawsuit against Walter, but Erik knew about both. And they're not the only ones."

Gilda perched on the edge of the couch. "What new school, and what lawsuit against Walter?"

"Trust me. You don't want to know." He dropped onto the flowery couch she'd inherited from her great-aunt. The springs squeaked as Mick sank about four inches lower than she normally did. His foot tapped against the hardwood floor in no particular rhythm. "What's wrong with your couch?"

"It's old. Antique, actually."

"You need a new one."

"You don't pay me enough," she replied.

Mick glanced up to see if she was kidding.

Gilda was completely serious. "What new school and what lawsuit?"

"I can't..."

"Okay, then how would anyone tap your phone?" she asked. "They'd need to have access to it, which isn't likely since you hardly ever let go of it. I have no idea how to bug a phone."

"That's because you don't have a mean bone in your body, babe," he said. "Do you have some coffee or something? I could use a drink that's not alcohol based."

"Water?"

He stood. "Forget it. I'll stop at Café Beanz on the way back."

"Back where?" Her neck tingled.

"The school. I should finish a few things before I meet with Xavier." Mick averted his gaze. "He wants to discuss the instructor's position that suddenly opened up."

Walter's job. Gilda frowned. "That seems kind of ghoulish."

"This isn't how things were supposed to go," he said.

Gilda hugged her stomach. "How were they supposed to go?"

"Walter was supposed to take over the Sandstone Cove school. Razi and I planned to set up a school in Fort Erie that he could run. I wanted time to focus on other things."

"Flipping houses."

He sputtered. "How'd you know?"

"Xavier mentioned it. I was surprised you didn't tell me." She doubted his new occupation had anything to do with Walter's murder anyway.

"I've been busy."

Gilda got up to peek through the curtains. No sign of Gary's car or of Chloe. All that moved in her yard were bees in the flowers. "Who do you think tapped your phone?"

Mick stood so close behind her, the length of his body warmed her back. He leaned over her shoulder, his breath sending a shiver down her arm. "I don't know. Maybe I'm just being paranoid. I probably forgot who I told what."

Likely, but that didn't explain his shaking hands or the sudden concern for his personal safety. So much for, "I'm a samurai. Nothing can hurt me." That theory hadn't helped Walter any. All thoughts of Walter disappeared when Mick's hand rested on her shoulder, and she wanted to melt beneath his warmth.

"I guess that's the problem with secrets," she told him. "Did you call Chloe?"

"No." Mick backed away, leaving a warm spot on her shoulder. He returned to the couch and resumed bouncing his feet on the floor. "I can't."

"What's going on, Mick? Not that I want to pry, but... You're not yourself."

His gaze darted around the room. After professing his love for Chloe repeatedly over the past few months and taking her to Jamaica for a week, it seemed odd he'd barricaded himself inside Gilda's house.

"Everything's fine," he said. "Just fine."

Tired of non-answers, Gilda sighed and went into the kitchen to make a cup of tea.

Mick followed. "Are you making coffee? I could really use a cup."

She plugged in the kettle. "Chamomile tea."

"I hate tea."

"Then don't drink it."

When Gilda took a bag of cookies from the cupboard, he shot across the room and grabbed it from her hands. He paced the kitchen while trying to open the bag with shaking hands. Finally, he wandered back to the living room window and peered through the curtains. The behavior was unusual, even for Mick.

"Are you stoned?" she asked.

"I haven't taken drugs, if that's what you're asking."

"Then either sit down or go home. You're scaring me."

He sat at the table but continued to fidget. "I haven't felt right since lunch. My brain's turned to soup and my whole body keeps vibrating."

"Where did you have lunch? Maybe it's some kind of reaction." She grabbed two mugs. A rain barrel wouldn't hold enough tea to calm him.

"At my place with Chloe. She wanted to talk so we had a late lunch. We needed to settle some things between us." His gaze dropped.

Apparently, they'd already made up after arguing in front of the school that morning. Gilda had no right to be jealous, yet she was. "What did you eat?"

"Antipasto. Cheese. Sangria."

"You do know Sangria is fruit in wine, don't you?"

He frowned. "Chloe said it was grape juice."

"Nobody gets drunk off grape juice." Gilda tried hard not to laugh while adding a teabag to each mug. "Did it taste weird?"

Mick shot her a scowl. "How would I know? I don't drink wine or Sangria."

"Did it taste like almonds?"

"It was sweet, and she force fed me something after every sip."

"Did she drink any?" she asked.

"I didn't notice."

Either Chloe didn't want him flat-out drunk, or she didn't want him to taste whatever she'd laced the sangria with. Why would his girlfriend drug him? If she wanted to kill him, she'd failed miserably. Mick's eyelids drooped and his head bobbed. If Chloe had wanted to incapacitate him long enough to bug—or debug—his phone, she'd done a good job. Mick would fall asleep soon.

So much for his dinner with Xavier.

Gilda unplugged the kettle and led him back to the living room. "Why don't you lie down for a minute? I'll call someone to pick you up."

"Can I stay here? You have a cozy place." His words slurred as he grabbed her around the waist and pulled her close. His gaze locked on hers. "We can protect each other from Chloe and the killer."

"Why do we have to protect each other from Chloe?"

"Because I gave her the necklace. She said she lost it after class. She was mad you cleaned it off while I took a shower." He breathed in her ear. "When I told her to relax, she gave me another drink and asked me a bunch of questions."

"About what?" Gilda pried his hands off her.

"About you and me," he said, wrapping his arms around her once more. "About Walter and Jade and Yoshida. Chloe knows about everyone. She's got scary connections. That's why I need to stay. You're safe."

"You're safe. I'm on Chloe's hit list," she muttered. Besides, the neighbors would talk, and her mother plan their wedding. "That's not an option."

"Please, babe, I need you." He planted a slobbery kiss on her cheek. Dangerously close to her mouth. "You're smart. You're cute. You're sexy."

"I'm flattered, but you're far from sober." She helped him sit on the couch.

As he lay against the cushions, Mick asked, "Do you think Chloe tried to kill me?"

"Ask her when you sober up."

"I caught her sneaking around with Walter before he died."

"What?" Gilda's eyes widened.

"They were in the change room when I went to pick up some gear. They were rolling around on the floor after class. At least they weren't in the dojo."

That gave Mick a motive to kill Walter and Chloe. "Did they hear you?"

"No."

"Were you mad?" she asked.

"I wanted to kill them both," he admitted. "Then I went to see Jade. Big mistake."

"Was she mad?"

"She knew. Walter's had a few girlfriends over the years."

One more reason for Jade to want to kill her husband. Cheaper than a divorce.

Mick grinned. "She took me into the hot tub, then evened the score. The woman's a freaking animal. I could hardly walk to my car when she was done with me." He stopped. "You didn't need to hear that part, did you?"

"Are you people rabbits?" Gilda stood and reached for her phone.

"Lonely. Scared. Confused. Ever since my wife left..." Mick reached for her again. "Come here, babe."

"Oh no." she said, pulling away. "Chloe could have us both killed with the snap of her fingers."

Xavier didn't pick up, but Razi answered on the first ring.

"Nah, she won't kill you." Mick hooked a finger in the hem of her shorts. "She likes you. Everybody likes you. You and me, we make a great team."

Gilda tried to move away, but he clutched the fabric. His hand was hot against her leg. "Yeah. I've heard that before. Razi, can you please come to my house and pick up Sensei Mick. He's drunk."

Mick pulled her off balance. "Come on, baby. Gimme a kiss."

"Why is Sensei Mick at your house again, Miss Wright?" Razi asked. "And why does he want a baby to give him a kiss?"

"Because he's drunk and obnoxious." She shoved Mick's hand off her leg. "I just hope he passes out soon."

"Sensei Mick rarely drinks alcohol."

"Well, he does today."

By the time she hung up, Mick's eyes were closed.

With a sigh, she draped a blanket over him. With a grin, he grabbed her wrist and pulled her on top of him. Despite dreaming of being with him for the past two years, she hoped he'd pass out soon and let her go.

Her mom had warned her to be careful what she wished for. Lesson learned.

"Get some sleep," she whispered. "Razi's coming to pick you up."

"I wanna stay with you." Mick stroked her hair and kissed the top of her head for a long minute before starting to snore.

She sighed, then tried to move away. Strands of her hair were tangled in his fingers. "Ouch! Geez. How'd you do that so fast?"

While Gilda untangled her hair, Mick slept peacefully. She only lost a few strands before going to wait for Razi on the front steps. For a man she thought she knew well, Mick Williams had her confused from spinning head to quivering toe.

She gazed up at the stars with a deep sigh. "Dad, I wish you were here. Maybe you could help me figure out what's going on."

CHAPTER 8

G ilda tossed all the blankets off her bed, felt a chill, then pulled them back on despite the heat. She and huddled beneath them like they offered protection from her thoughts. They didn't.

Razi had arrived hours ago, hauled Mick to his car and took him home. She hadn't heard from either since.

Her thoughts strayed to Walter and who could've killed him.

Mick said he'd left before Walter's class that day. Everyone in the school knew Walter locked the door when he trained alone. He liked the privacy. Either someone in the class or someone who came in later, like Chloe, had killed him.

As far as she knew, no one had stepped forward to say they saw anyone enter or leave the school. The only other way in was through the back door that couldn't be opened from the outside. Not unless someone left it propped open or knocked loudly for someone to open it.

Gilda covered her eyes with one hand. Why hadn't she checked the alley? Since she couldn't sleep anyway, she pulled on black yoga pants and a dark hoodie. With her thoughts moving faster than her legs—or her sense of reasoning—she grabbed a flashlight off the counter. Taking her keys, she peered out the window.

No dark sedans. No yellow Ferraris. Nothing but a yowling tom cat.

As she locked the door and stuck her keys into her pocket, her thoughts tumbled. Who had keys to the school? Walter. Mick. Razi. Yoshida. Did Xavier and Erik have keys? She couldn't recall. They must've to cover classes.

Her pace quickened as her thoughts tripped over each other. She was positive Erik no longer had keys. He'd abused his privileges when he brought friends into the school one night for unauthorized training and a party. Mick suspended Erik from the school for a month.

Xavier had a snit one night. Something to do with Walter. He threw his keys at Mick in a rage. Mick calmly picked up the keys, tossed them in a drawer, then punched a hole in his office wall when Xavier left.

Which brought her back to Walter, who apparently was a ladies' man, although Gilda had never seen that side of him.

But she had seen something.

Her shoulders tensed and her paced slowed as she recalled Walter sparring with a new white belt during the woman's first class. He threw several punches and wild spin kicks, which sent the woman running out of the school. The woman and her lawyer husband threatened to sue. While Mick smoothed things over behind closed doors, there'd been tension between he and Walter—actually, all the black belts and Walter—ever since.

Was that the lawsuit Mick alluded to?

Gilda doubted the couple had changed their minds and walked away. When the woman signed up, she already seemed to know Walter and kept her distance from the start. There had to be more to the story than anyone told her.

With the school in sight, Gilda glanced around for witnesses, then snuck into the back alley and turned on her flashlight. She and crept toward the green fire door at the rear of the school, with one eye on the dumpster that stood between the Italian restaurant and the consignment store next door. Anyone, especially a killer, could use it to hide.

The alley was darker than she expected. Odd. There was a light over the back door of Yoshida's. In fact, Xavier never failed to remind them how he'd personally installed it, so he could find his car when he left late at night. While the light was there, the bulb was broken. The back door itself rippled in the light like someone tried to break in.

Gilda shuddered. No time to be afraid. She didn't trust Thayer or Fabio. Nor did she want to be alone with any of the black belts, including Mick, until she'd found proof of their innocence.

There was no lock for a key. Someone had pried the door to the point they could insert a screwdriver to pop the latch. Too bad she didn't have a screwdriver to test her theory. The warped door, however, did nothing to make her feel safer either inside or outside of the school.

When gravel crunched behind her, the hairs on her arms stood. She aimed the beam in both directions. Her flashlight cast shadows on the gravel, but she saw nothing scarier than a crumpled beer can, and a wad of paper towels. She was hearing things.

Behind the school were four parking spots, two for the staff of the karate school and two for the Nine Lives Consignment Boutique next door. Since Mrs. Watson, nearly eighty, had backed into the building twice in one week, Mick installed a gray post with a wide band of reflective tape in front of the far corner. Scrapes marred the post and the tape. Both were tinged with blue paint from Mrs. Watson's Ford Fairlane. Below the streaks of blue, a silver scrape tore the reflective stripe.

The alley brightened as Thayer growled, "You'd better have a good reason for sneaking around this late."

She spun around, blinded by a flashlight beam aimed directly into her eyes. Her breath stuck in her throat for several seconds before she managed to say, "I work here. I'm allowed to sneak. What're you doing here?"

"Mrs. Watson's grandson lives on the second floor of the consignment store," he said. "He reported a prowler."

"As you can see, I'm not a prowler. You have no probable cause to arrest me."

"I should haul you in on principle alone. Let me guess, you forgot your key and need to find another way inside." Thayer stood so close her stomach clenched. A far cry from her earlier reaction to Mick.

Thayer chuckled. "Admit it, you just can't keep your nose out of my investigation, and you're convinced the murderer came out the back. We already checked that."

Gilda raised her flashlight, careful to aim the beam into his face. "Which means you and Fabio already searched the alley and found the same things I found."

He shielded his eyes, then nudged her flashlight down. The beam travelled down his T-shirt and tight jeans. "Then maybe we should compare notes."

"You never looked back here, did you?"

"Of course we did," he said. "We're trained professionals. What did you find?"

She indicated the post. "Blue scratches from Mrs. Watson's car. One deep scrape with silver paint, which could've come from Xavier's car. His rear bumper had a similar scrape."

"That's it?"

She stood her ground. "What do you have?"

"Not a chance. Give me one more."

"The broken lightbulb over the door."

He nodded. "Could be something. Same with the marks. When was the break in?"

"That's your job. When did anyone call the police about it?"

Thayer shrugged. "As far as I know, no one did."

"What do you have?"

He studied her for a long minute, then pointed across the alley to a sign designating a school parking space. A deep dent warped the metal post. "Looks like someone was in a big hurry. Who drives a silver car besides Xavier?"

"Walter. Razi. Happy. Fabio. Pretty much half of Sandstone Cove."

Thayer scowled. "Only the karate black belts are actually on our suspect list."

"Maybe you should expand your list," Gilda suggested. "What about Chloe, Jade, and Gary? They all stood to gain with Walter dead, especially Jade. Chloe might've done it to get back at Mick. As for Gary..."

He rubbed a hand over his face and groaned. "Don't even go there. You know we could work together amicably. Maybe even be friends again."

Gilda started to walk away. "After two years of me pushing you away, you still don't get it, do you?"

Behind them, a metal garbage can toppled to the ground with a crash, making Gilda shriek. Thayer drew his weapon seconds before a calico cat raced down the alley.

"Where'd that thing come from?" he asked.

Gilda shone her flashlight toward the consignment store. A weathered wooden staircase led to the apartment above the store. From there, anyone could climb over the railing and onto the karate school roof. Anyone unafraid of heights, which let her out.

"It's the grandson's cat," she told him.

Thayer narrowed his eyes. "That's a steep jump, even for a cat. What's up there?"

"The roof." And the air conditioner and vent for the building.

Thayer started up the stairs, then reconsidered when the light in the small apartment over the consignment store turned on. "Is there another entrance to the school up there?"

"As far as I know, it's just the air conditioner."

She gazed up the stairs, across to the roof, and down to the cracked asphalt in the alley. If he went away, she could go find out. Someone agile could run out the back door, climb the stairs, and run across the rooftops to the grocery store at the end of the block. With all the tourists armed with beach toys, shopping bags, and souvenirs, they could disappear into the crowd.

A barefoot ninja. She shuddered and shook her head.

"Gilda?" Thayer asked, waving a hand in front of her face. "Did you have an idea or a stroke?"

She pushed past him. "Neither. I'm tired and I'm going home."

"I don't think so, honey." He reached for his handcuffs, but stopped when he realize he wore civilian clothes. "If you know something, tell me now, or I'll lock you up."

Her mouth dropped open. "For what?"

Thayer put his hands on his hips. "Mostly for your own protection, but also for impeding an investigation."

"I showed you the post and the dents in the door, didn't I?"

"I suppose."

She scowled. "And I told you about the roof."

Thayer huffed. "True. Then, do me a favor. Go home, stay out of trouble, and don't leave town."

She didn't make any promises, but she did go home with no plans to leave town. Two out of three wasn't bad. Was it?

CHAPTER 9

G ilda jammed her hands beneath her armpits to keep them from shaking. Doc's request for her to meet him at the morgue Tuesday morning puzzled her, especially since Thayer and Fabio already sat on two plastic chairs outside his office. Thayer glanced up first. He definitely wasn't happy to see her.

Fabio put aside his magazine. "Nice to see you, Gilda. I take it Doc called you."

She fought the urge to hyperventilate. "Yeah. He wanted to see me about something."

"Us too." Fabio stretched his legs and scratched at the growth of stubble on his chin. She guessed he hadn't shaved since Walter's murder. "We've been waiting an hour."

"Really? He called me ten minutes ago," she told him, tapping on Doc's office door.

"Are you serious?" Thayer asked, jolting upright. "He made us wait out here for almost an hour, yet he just called you?"

"Yes, I did." Doc appeared in the doorway. "Do you want to debate my motives, or do you want to know why you're here?"

Thayer barged into the room ahead of the others.

Fabio shrugged before following his partner.

"We need to chat," Doc whispered, grabbing Gilda's arm. "Fabio gave me the coffee you thought was poisoned."

"You didn't drink it, did you?" she asked as her eyes widened.

"No, but by the look on his face, I'm sure he'd want me to right now," Doc said. "You were right. There was a trace of cyanide. Not enough to kill you. Just enough to give you bad stomach cramps."

"Which is exactly why I saw you on Friday. I've had cramps for the past couple weeks." She glanced into his office. Thayer sat with his arms folded across his chest, while Fabio toyed with Doc's Newton's cradle. As the metal balls clacked, she asked, "Do you think the two are related? That Xavier wanted me to get sick and keep out of the way for a while."

"It's possible." Doc nudged his glasses up his nose.

"Do you think he killed Walter? Maybe he thinks I did."

"I can't help with Xavier's thought process or motives," Doc's reply was punctuated by curses from Thayer before the metal balls went silent. "But I can help you with them. Shall we?"

Gilda skirted around Thayer and Fabio to sit on the third chair across the heavy pine desk from Doc. All the questions that went through her head when she took her run earlier were lost to nerves.

"I'm aware this is privileged information, and that my duty is to both the police and the victim's family," Doc said.

Thayer shot Gilda a nasty glare. "Then maybe someone who's neither should leave."

Doc cleared his throat. "Gilda has a vested interest in this case. I'd like her to stay."

"I do?" She hoped he'd say it was a crime of passion, or a fight gone bad. She didn't want to think someone intended to murder Walter. "If you say it was an accident or self-defense, I'll back off. I swear."

"I wish I could ease your concerns," he said. "But from what I noted during the autopsy, the katana attack came after the fight."

"Like a brawl or are we talking karate moves like they do in training?" Thayer asked. "Is that why he was so bruised?"

Doc looked amused. "About the bruising, there were several precise, well-placed strikes. A high-ranking student, or a black belt could be that exact."

His words did little to ease Gilda's concerns. "Would the blows have been enough to knock him out?"

"If you're asking about direct hits to the head, the answer is no," Doc said. "Nothing that left a mark or could have incapacitated him."

She closed her eyes. "Could someone have poisoned him."

Thayer twitched. "You did check for poisons, right?"

"We ran toxicology screens for known poisons and found nothing," Doc told them. "But then I—"

"Then maybe the killer could've simply been stronger and faster," Fabio said. "There are a lot of different pressure points martial artists learn to aim for at that level."

"Which is why Gilda is here." Doc turned to face her.

She hesitated. "I'm still learning all that. The only people stronger and faster than Walter in our school are a couple of the black belts."

"Who?" Thayer asked.

"Mick or Razi. Both have extensive martial arts backgrounds. Xavier doesn't have the power, but he's big on poisons. Erik could do some serious damage if he was mad enough." She scowled, unable to stop talking. "I can't see any of them killing Walter."

"Whoever did would have to be familiar with the school and with Walter's schedule," Thayer pointed out. "Like anyone who either attends classes or has kids at the school."

Fabio whistled. "That's a lot of suspects."

"What if you exclude kids and people who couldn't physically carry out the crime?" Doc asked. "Or someone who didn't have access to—"

"Then we're back to our four main suspects," Thayer said.

"Unless the killer had help," Doc said.

"Either from someone who lured Walter to the back room or let the killer into the school." Thayer's gaze met Gilda's when she frowned. "What's wrong with you?"

"There's more, isn't there?" she asked.

Fabio raised one eyebrow. "What makes you say that?"

"Because she's known me for forever," Doc said. "She's right. Walter was poisoned, but with something we don't normally test for. Cobra venom."

Gilda's heart raced. Cobra venom was far more exotic than she expected and not something she knew much about. She was willing to bet Xavier did.

"Cobra venom? That seems like a long shot, doesn't it?" Thayer asked. "I didn't think you'd have the capabilities to test for something so exotic."

"Normally, no, but I was acting on a tip," Doc said as he flipped a pen across the backs of his fingers. "I could never have tested for it except I called in a favor."

Fabio shifted in his seat. "A tip? You mean a phone call or something someone like Gilda said?"

"I received a private message stating that Razi Mauli was recently been overseas visiting family. Also, that Mick was in the Dominican Republic last week, and Walter's wife went to Asia a couple months ago." Doc hesitated. "I wasn't convinced at first. When I did some online research, I learned a couple curious things."

"Like what?" Thayer asked.

Doc's eyes shone. "Cobra venom is a neurotoxin. That means it paralyzes the nerve centers that control breathing and heart rates. Walter would've become slow and drunk, making him vulnerable to attack. Even someone Gilda's size could've attacked and killed him. You gentlemen have work to do."

Direct and dismissive. The detectives took the hint and left. When Thayer paused in the doorway and opened his mouth, Fabio grabbed his collar to drag him away.

Doc's lips tightened into a thin, white line as he faced Gilda. "I suggest you watch your back, my dear."

"You think I'm in danger?"

"If someone's been poisoning you, I'd say so. Keep me in the loop? You have my number, so call if you need backup."

"Backup?" She laughed. "You make me sound like some big-league detective."

"We both know you're more of a Nosy Nelly, but I am concerned," he said, moving around the desk to stand in front of her. "If there's a murderer in your midst and you keep sticking your nose where it doesn't belong, there's a chance someone will try to chop it off your pretty face."

A chill ran through to her core. "Someone doesn't like me asking questions."

"Hence the cyanide. My dear girl, I brought you into this world, and I don't want to bury you next to your father," Doc said. "Promise you'll be careful."

"I promise," she whispered, giving him a hug.

She shuffled out of the hospital, her heart beating somewhere near the pit of her stomach. Doc had a point. Maybe it was best to get on with her life. Why worry about finding a killer when Thayer and Fabio were far more qualified and had better resources?

On her way home, she pushed open the door to Café Beanz. She planned to pick up a coffee and a muffin, then go home to make sure her uniform was clean for the training with Yoshida that evening. His classes were tough, but she'd learned to focus on everything except the pain until she got into a hot Epsom salt bath.

Yoshida. He lived in Toronto and visited so occasionally she hadn't even thought of him as a suspect. He had visited the school a lot more than usual lately. Did that have anything to do with Mick's plan for a new school? If enrollment kept going up, they'd outgrow the old one in a year or two.

Gilda took a deep breath. She'd promised Doc that she'd keep her nose out of things. No more investigating. If she didn't honor her promise, she'd end up under his scalpel in one way or another. She paid for breakfast, then scurried home to get ready for the workshop.

That was when Gary del Garda stepped out of Happy Harvey's Hangover Hut. Their eyes met and he waved before he unlocked his car. While it wasn't obvious he was following her, he kept popping up a lot lately.

Whatever he wanted with her, he was tenacious and should've been a cop alongside her father.

* * *

Later that afternoon, Gilda was startled to find a lone figure standing in the lobby of the martial arts school. A shriek stuck in her throat. She cleared her throat, then bowed and said, "Shihan Yoshida. Sensei Mick didn't mention you were arriving early."

"I neglected to tell him." When Yoshida turned to face her, his eyes narrowed. He was no taller than her, yet his presence seemed to fill the room with tension. "I hear you have spoken with a number of people about Walter Levy's passing, Miss Wright."

She shrank back without moving her feet. "I wanted to know why someone would kill one of our most indispensable black belts."

"Everyone is dispensable. Do you think by asking questions you can solve a man's murder?" He toyed with blocks on her desk that a young student left behind.

"No," she told him, yet that's exactly what she was doing. No wonder Mick called her Sherlock. "I feel like I owe it to his family to help find his killer."

His eyebrows rose as he placed a business card on top of the bottom layer of three blocks and his hard gaze met hers. "Did you kill him?"

She swallowed hard. "No."

Yoshida's face softened as he piled two more blocks on top of the card. "Then you owe them nothing. Keep your mind on your work and your nose in your business. Asking questions and meddling in the affairs of others will not save this school."

Save the school?

She wanted to ask what he meant but his concern seemed more like a threat than a stern piece of advice. "I will. Thank you."

"I will return in time for training. I suggest you not attend." He turned on his toes and, abandoning his block creation, walked out the door.

Once the door closed, Gilda hid behind the desk. Despite the heat, she had a serious chill deep in her bones. A cup of tea would take the edge off, yet she was afraid to set foot outside the building. Too many suspects. Too few answers.

She glanced at the clock. No sign of Mick or the black belts. No classes. No students. No Walter. She sobbed as tears fell on her paperwork and smear the ink.

Yoshida was right.

She didn't kill Walter, nor did she owe his family anything, including peace of mind. The questions, snooping really, were to prove her coworkers weren't murderers.

Why had he told her not to come to train that night? Either he knew something was going to happen—or it was a threat.

"Who's in here?" Mick asked from the front door. It wasn't like him to be paranoid, but this wasn't the first time he'd yelled into the school without setting foot inside. Was he worried about running into the murderer, or just Yoshida?

"Just me."

He peered around the corner and asked, "Are you armed?"

"I have a stapler. Does that count?"

"I can deal with that." Mick leaned on the counter. "Whoa. Are you okay, Sherlock? You look as green as the mats."

"Yeah. A bit rattled. I'm fine."

"What are you doing here then?" he asked.

She sighed. "Mid-month payments. Tidying up before the workshop. I don't want to fall behind while we're closed."

"That always makes me sick," he said. "Anything else I should know?"

"Yoshida was here. He just left."

The muscles in his face tensed. "What did he want?"

"I don't know, but he was sure surprised to see me." She paused, then added, "The door was locked. I used my key to get in."

"What did he say?" Mick asked, disappearing around the corner to his office.

Gilda bit her lower lip.

When she didn't reply, he peered around the corner. "Gilda? What's going on? Are you sure you're okay?"

"Fine." She shuffled her paperwork.

"Uh-huh. Did he check out the dojo?"

Her throat tightened. "He stood where you are now, peeked through the doorway, then left. Oh, and he warned me not to train tonight."

Mick frowned. "What were his exact words?"

"He suggested I not attend." She hugged her stomach. "He also told me to stop meddling in the affairs of others, since it won't save this school. What did he mean?"

Mick ran a hand through his thick hair. "Go home, Gilda."

"But I—"

"Go home and don't come back until after Walter's funeral."

"I have to—"

His jaw hardened. "You don't have to do anything. Take the night off. Hang out with Marion. Go to a movie. Just don't show up here."

She didn't bother to open her mouth. After a moment, her shoulders sagged. "Are you serious?"

He turned away. "I'll see you tomorrow."

Gilda tidied her desk before wandering outside in a daze. The questions popped up at a rate that matched her pace. Only once she was in her garden did she give herself the luxury of sorting through them. Her biggest question was what was Mick up to and why did both he and Yoshida tell her not to show up for the workshop that night?

Frustrated, she yanked out weeds for half an hour before the phone rang.

"Okay, what's going on?" Marion asked.

She sat on the back step and tried to sound nonchalant. "What are you talking about? I'm home working in my garden."

"Oh, I don't know. First, I overheard Thayer tell someone he ran into you at the morgue, then Mick called me. Keep in mind, that man has never, ever called me before. I don't even know where he got my number. Anyway, he suggested I keep you busy tonight. He even offered me bribe money. What in heaven's name have you done?"

There must be something going on if Mick was trying that hard to keep her away from the school.

Gilda sighed. "I haven't done anything. I swear."

"Well, your boss seems to think I need to keep you busy tonight. He suggested we go to dinner and a movie." The sounds in the background suggested Marion was still in the dispatch office. "What do you say? My treat. Well, Mick's treat. I'll stop at home and change, then we can have dinner and a couple glasses of wine at—"

She was still stuck on one detail. "Mick put you up to this?"

"Not totally. You are my best friend, you know," Marion said. "What's wrong? Did I miss something?"

"No, but I have. There's a training class with Yoshida tonight. Both Mick and Yoshida told me not to show up."

"Holy crap. Is your karate that bad?"

"Funny, girl. I think there's something going on that I've missed. I suspect if I do go tonight, I could find out more."

"No. No. No. See, honey, that's where you and I differ. If someone like Mick told me to stay away, I'd listen. No maybes about it. If Yoshida says it... Hang on a sec, will you?" Her next words were muffled, "Get lost, Thayer. No, I'm not talking to Gilda. I'm talking to my boyfriend."

"Yeah? What's his name?" Thayer asked in the background.

"Tiny. Do you want to mess with a guy named Tiny? I didn't think so."

Gilda laughed, then told Marion, "I have to get ready. I'll talk to you later."

"Don't you dare hang up on me, Tiny," Marion shouted, then lowered her voice. "Honey, do you have brain damage? Listen to Mick. Forget training. Meet me at my place and we'll grab dinner and a lot of wine on Mick's tab."

"Marion, I have to—"

"Do you want to end up like Walter?" she asked.

Gilda got up to pace the garden path. "No, but what if Walter discovered something the killer didn't want him to know? What if someone else dies?"

"And what if that someone is you?" Marion groaned. "Girl, you're gonna give me gray hair. Whatever happens, you're gonna end up in the middle and get killed no matter what I say. You're just like your father. I mean that in a good way. Most of the time."

"There will be other students there."

"And what if they're all involved?" she asked.

Gilda sat on the stone bench and shook her head. She hadn't thought that far ahead. All she could do was wash up, grab a snack, and show up for the workshop despite the warnings. What was the worst that could happen?

CHAPTER 10

When Gilda walked into the school Tuesday evening, she walked around the corner and ran straight into Yoshida. Something flickered across his face when he saw her. Fear? Anger? Whatever it was, the emotion dissipated as fast as it appeared.

"Miss Wright." He gave a slight bow, the lines in his face suddenly etched even deeper. His head was freshly shaven. He pulled the knot in his obi even tighter.

Ready for battle.

"Shihan Yoshida." She bowed, then set her pink sports bag on the floor. "I'm not sure how many students will attend tonight."

"Ah, yes. The death and pending funeral of Mr. Levy."

He usually didn't bother to remember names. Not of their students or instructors. Today he seemed to make a special effort. She scurried to the change rooms, put on her gi, and tied on her green belt. Attending the workshop was more than a chance to learn more about Walter and his murder. If she wanted to grade for her blue belt in the fall, she needed the extra practice. Focusing on training her body would give her worried mind a temporary break.

She hoped.

Since Razi had replaced the missing mats, the training hall looked more like it had before Walter's murder. She lined up with the other students, ten in all, not including Mick and Yoshida who stood in front of the class. Mick shot her a glare but wasted no time. The highest-ranking brown belt began the opening ceremony by calling the rei, or bowing in ceremony. After they'd bowed in, everyone stood.

Beads of sweat quivered on Gilda's upper lip, despite not even warming up yet. Tension hung as heavy and humid as storm clouds.

Yoshida nodded to Mick, who faced the students. Three black belts, two brown belts, a blue belt, two green belts, an orange belt, and a yellow belt made up the class. All adults, to Gilda's relief.

"Thank you for coming," Mick said, toying with his belt. "We've lost one of our most distinguished black belts, which has affected us all."

At the far end of the line, Erik snorted.

Yoshida's face twisted until he resembled a demonic kabuki theatre mask she'd seen in a shop in downtown Toronto. "Do you have an objection?"

Gilda cringed and wished Erik would keep his mouth closed, train hard, then go home. Unfortunately, he didn't think the same way.

"Walter was far from a distinguished black belt," he said. "He left his family to marry a high school kid and harassed teenage girls all around town. Mick never should've left him in charge of the kids' classes. The guy was a menace who should've had supervision."

Gilda's eyes widened. As she glanced toward the senior belts, she realized every student gawked at Mick. Some, like her, shifted uncomfortably.

Mick reddened before he stepped forward. "We're here to train, not to bad mouth our fellow students."

"Whatever," Erik spoke louder as though primed for a fight. "The guy was a scumbag. The only reason you let him stay was because he paid you big bucks to be a silent partner."

Gilda gasped. Was this what he and Yoshida were afraid they would find out?

When her gaze met Mick's, his face hardened, and he turned away. The visible cords in Mick's neck betrayed his tension. "I think you should leave before you say something you'll regret."

Erik asked. "Seriously? You're kicking me out?"

"Only for tonight," Mick explained, as sweat trickled down the side of his face. "You and I can talk tomorrow to straighten things out. For now, I'd like you to calm down."

"Of course," Erik said with a bow, then smirked. "How dare I bad mouth your replacement. Did you tell Gilda what's going on or are you afraid she and everyone else will see you for the jerk you really are?"

Changes? Replacement? Gilda pressed her lips shut but kept her ears tuned to the mutterings around her. Razi's eyebrows twitched upward when he met her gaze. He seemed just as confused as her.

Yoshida lunged forward until he stood toe to toe and nose to nose with Erik. "That is enough. You will wait in my office. I will deal with you later."

In a show of defiance, Erik glared at Mick, then turned his back, disrespecting not only his fellow students, but his teachers. He didn't bother to bow at the door. Rather than change or go to the office to wait, he grabbed his duffle bag and left the school.

My office, Yoshida had said, although it wasn't his office. It was Mick's. A slip of the tongue, or was there something more going on?

Gilda and the others didn't have long to fret. The instant Erik left—taking his gear and leaving the tension—Yoshida's face hardened to stone. Feet shoulder-distance apart, hands clasped behind his back, and nostrils flared, he barked out orders for the warm-up. For half an hour, they ran and did the hardest, most nauseating series of drills Gilda had ever pushed through. She guessed torturing his students was the only way Yoshida could let off steam.

She breathed in through her nose, out through her mouth, and fought hard not to succumb to the alternating urge to either throw up or collapse in a simpering heap. Furtive glances passed between the students as they ran laps, then dropped to the mats to do ten push-ups, ten sit-ups, and ten leg raises before running again.

No one talked. No one groaned. No one dared.

Even Mick seemed so focused he didn't acknowledge her presence. When Xavier finally groaned, Yoshida added one more set of twenty push-ups, then instructed them to line up.

"You all stink," Yoshida growled. "I hope your karate is not as bad as your warm-up. Stop being lazy. Show me intensity. Show me guts."

Any more running and Gilda would show everyone her guts.

A half hour of working on katas came next, followed by stances. Yoshida made them hold each stance, particularly shiko dachi, or sumo stance, until Gilda's thighs burned, her arms grew too heavy to lift, and her throat burned from swallowing bile.

Mick clapped a hand to her shoulder, nearly knocking her over. "Go drink some water."

"I'm good." Her voice was raspy.

"You're white and about to puke. Get a drink before you're completely dehydrated. That goes for all of you. Take a break."

Yoshida's eyes narrowed. "No drinks. No breaks. They will train until I let them leave. They have much to learn."

"They need water and a chance to catch their breaths," Mick said, his voice commanding. Stern enough to make Yoshida take a step back and the students straighten their posture. "Five minutes water break, then we'll work on kumite."

Gilda gave an inward groan. Sparring was her least favorite part of class on a good day, especially with Yoshida instructing. She backed out of the dojo, bowed, and hoped water would help her queasy stomach.

Down the hallway, someone retched in one of the bathrooms. Another student darted outside for fresh air.

Before she reached for her sparring gloves and mouth guard to return to class, she took a few deep breaths. Across the room, Yoshida organized gloves, blockers, and any other gear within reach. He was either nervous, obsessive, or both.

"You okay?" Mick paused next to her.

She flinched. "Mostly."

He whispered, "This is your last chance to leave. What's he doing?"

"Rearranging our gear. Apparently, nothing meets with his approval today."

"This could turn into an interesting class," he said.

"What do you mean could?"

"Don't say I didn't warn you, Sherlock," Mick said, then entered the dojo and called for everyone to line up. "Take a partner. We'll spar for two minutes then change partners. Keep going until you've sparred everyone in the room."

Gilda's stomach cramped when Yoshida grinned. An even number of students included Yoshida, who put on his gloves and kept his beady-eyed gaze focused on Mick. Things were about to get ugly.

Razi paired up with her first and asked, "Are you okay?"

"No talking," Yoshida barked.

She nodded and pushed in her mouth guard. Razi took it easy on her. He sparred, but not as hard as he could go. She once saw him knock Xavier back six feet onto his butt. If he ever hit her full strength, she'd probably go right through the cement brick wall.

When they changed partners, the lone yellow belt in the room grabbed Gilda. "Is Yoshida always like this? Everyone said he's tough, but—"

"No talking," Yoshida snapped.

Gilda shook her head.

They fought one another until the only people she hadn't sparred with were Mick and Yoshida. Before Mick could get across the room, Yoshida stopped before her and bowed. She bowed in return before he jumped into his sparring stance with a loud kiai, and put on an intimidating scowl. He called hajime to start two minutes of torture for her indiscretion of showing up.

Gilda had watched intense gradings before. She'd even seen Yoshida "teach" Walter a lesson when he aggressively sparred the white belt who then left the school in tears. This Yoshida's face twisted into the frightening kabuki mask. She expected to see smoke curl out of his nostrils like a dragon.

He lunged without warning. Completely caught off guard, she was too slow to block. The edge of his glove caught her lower lip. The taste of blood and sweat met the tip of her tongue. Yoshida was playing for keeps. When he moved in again, she blocked his punch, but caught his kick in her upper thigh. Pain radiated up and down her leg. The bruise would be as dark and angry as his eyes.

"That's enough," Mick told him.

The demon mask didn't crack. Gilda's bravery, however, wouldn't hold out much longer. Her survival instincts kicked in. On his third strike, she blocked both punches, then the kick that followed. She managed to throw a kick to his groin, which made his cheek flinch and intensified his anger. Fear made her jump out of his reach. This was no time for pride.

Fury twisted Yoshida's face. He flew at her with his hands and feet a blur. She took several hits to her face before her breath stuck in her throat, clogging her airway. She began to hyperventilate. As she fought for breath, all she could do was turtle into a heap on the mat, while trying to cover her face and ribs.

"Yame." Mick yelled for everyone to stop.

The blows rained down onto her head and back. His kicks battered her legs. Suddenly, the blows stopped as someone shielded her to ward off fists, feet, and everything else Yoshida threw. No matter which way the older man moved, they blocked his access to her shaking body.

As Razi pulled her toward the wall, away from the fight, tears mingled with the blood and sweat on her face and soaked her uniform. Her hands shook and her chin trembled. She touched her swollen lip and came away with watery pink blood.

The other students watched as Mick and Yoshida circled one another. Xavier jumped forward to intervene. Mick shouted for him to stay back, but Yoshida punched him in the face. Xavier crumpled to the floor as blood gushed from his nose.

Razi cautioned the others to stay out of the away. No one moved.

A cut on Mick's cheek seeped red. One of Yoshida's eyes grew red and puffy. Neither man backed down. Try as he might, Yoshida was unable to get past Mick's defenses. When he stopped throwing punches and lowered his arms, Mick did the same.

Yoshida flared his nostrils as he growled. "You are not a man of honor. You disrespect me in front of my students."

"No respect intended, Shihan. I'm protecting my students," Mick told him.

"They would not need protection if they could fight." He pointed to Gilda. "That one is weak and lazy. She will never be a black belt."

Gilda wiped her face with her sleeve. It came away pink with blood.

Mick shook his head. "She's a worthy student. You had no reason to harm her, or to fight with such disrespect in a training exercise."

Yoshida suddenly noticed the silence around them and shouted, "Who told you to stop? Sparring stances on. Hajime."

"Put your gloves away. Class is done," Mick instructed.

"This class is not done. I am not finished," Yoshida shouted.

Mick unstrapped his gloves and threw them against the far wall. "Yes, it is. Our emotions have gotten the best of us all."

Yoshida stood in the middle of the dojo with his gloved hands dangling by his sides while Mick told everyone to go home. Gilda, Razi, and Xavier lingered and looked. Each looked to their sensei as he wiped the back of his hand across the gash on his cheek.

Mick bowed to them, careful to keep one eye on Yoshida. "I'm fine. Go home. Shihan Yoshida and I have things to discuss."

Gilda paused in the doorway. "Are you sure you—?"

"I'm sure."

She backed out of the doorway. Even though Yoshida was in full monster mode, she understood. The two men needed to settle things between them.

"Are you okay?" Xavier held a tissue to his nose as he put his other arm across her shoulders. "You took a few good hits."

Gilda coughed, still struggling to catch her breath. Her heart raced and her body shook. Her voice sounded like she'd eaten sandpaper when she told him, "Your nose looks broken."

"It wouldn't be the first time someone busted my nose. I'll survive. You should go to the hospital."

After a fast trip the washroom to throw up, she found an empty change stall and hid behind the new blue curtain to swallow the tears that threatened to dissolve her into a pile of goo. She could have a good cry later while she soaked in Epsom salts. Her uniform was so wet she needed to peel the fabric off her arms and legs an inch at a time. Every muscle in her body burned. Her throat ached, raw from a blend of emotion, vomit, and the brutality of the class.

Xavier approached her again when she left from her stall, but was interrupted as the three other women in the class stopped to give her hugs on their way out. He gave her a quick hug and walked away saying, "I'll see you tomorrow."

Walter's funeral.

Fresh tears filled her eyes as she nodded.

Razi waited until everyone else left before he spoke, "I apologize, Miss Wright. That was not something any student should have to endure. I doubt Sensei Mick expected Shihan Yoshida to go that far. No one did."

"He's never done that with anyone else, has he?" She peered into the dojo, but Mick and Yoshida were already behind the closed door of Mick's office. Their voices were loud, yet muffled.

"Not that I am aware," he said. "It seems the aim of this workshop was to spar with you and Sensei Mick the entire time."

"Why? I've never done anything to him."

Razi shrugged. "Perhaps he is mentally unstable. What Sensei Mick would call bat-shit crazy."

She couldn't help but smile at his choice of words before she checked her face in the mirror. Her lower lip was fat and puffy but had stopped bleeding. The brow over her left eye tinged with purple, blue, and green.

"Go home, Miss Wright." Razi nudged her with his elbow. "I will and look out for our sensei. Please, ask Xavier to take you home. You should not be alone."

She hoisted her duffle bag to her shoulder and blew out a breath. With Razi on guard, Yoshida wouldn't get away with doing anything to Mick.

Unless he killed them both. In which case, aches and bruises would be the least of her concerns.

Xavier was gone by the time she stepped onto the sidewalk and received alarmed glances from tourists passing by. Shaken and barely able to see through her tears—or her puffy eyes, she'd have to get home under her own steam.

"Whoa. Did you get the number of the horse and buggy that hit you?" Gary asked, cigarette smoke curling around his head. He flicked the butt into the gutter and walked over for a closer look.

She tried to laugh but even her cheeks hurt. "I don't have the energy to deal with you. I'm going home to soak."

"You're in no shape to walk anywhere, especially alone," Gary said. "Let me give you a ride."

"It's only a few blocks. I'll get there on my own." She stumbled away, the weight of her duffle bag throwing her off balance.

He shook his head. "Stubborn little mule. You're so much like your father. I'm won't to try anything funny. I swear on your daddy's grave. My only concern is to get you home safe."

Gilda hesitated. If she sat down now, her muscles would seize, and she might not be able to stand again for days.

"You could call for a police escort, if it makes you feel any better. I'll even loan you my phone," he said, taking a phone out of his pocket.

She rolled her eyes, unable to speak due to pain and a surge of emotion.

He pocketed the phone, then grasped the handles of her duffle bag. "Come on, honey. If your old man ever saw my Chloe as beat up as you, he would've made sure she got home safe, no matter whose kid she was. I owe him that much. Of course, he also would've arrested the so-and-so who hurt her, but that part's out of my league."

She let him toss her bag into the backseat. When he opened the car door, he helped ease her weary body onto the passenger seat. She had no fight left anymore. All she wanted was to go home, sit in a warm bath and cry.

"Who did this to you?" he asked, pulling into the steady beach traffic. If you say Mick, I'll fix him good."

She sniffled. "Mick stopped it."

"Now I am surprised. It must've been that Yoshida character," Gary said. "I hate to point this out, but no teacher should ever do that to a student. Somebody needs to teach him a thing or two about respect."

As Gilda touched her swollen lip, she agreed.

"You want me to arrange a little payback? I can get a guy who's so quiet and fast even Yoshida won't know what hit him."

Smiling hurt. "You're thoughtful. In a weird way. No, thank you."

"So, you're just gonna lick your wounds and pretend it never happened, huh?"

"Yup."

"You won't even stand up for yourself."

"No point."

Gary made a U-turn to pull the car directly in front of her house. Before she could shift to open the door, he ran around the car. He helped her out, then grabbed her bag. "Let's get you in and settled. Have you got ice for those bruises?"

"Not much," she said.

He stared. "How much do you think you need?"

"Enough to fill my bathtub." She let him unlock her front door.

"You may want to think on a tad smaller scale to avoid hypothermia." Gary led her to the couch and helped her get comfortable, then strolled into the kitchen to rifle through the freezer. "There's enough here for a good start. I'll make you a couple ice packs, then get more for later."

Gilda limped to the kitchen and leaned in the doorway. As much as Gary scared her silly, she admired how he'd dropped everything—even if it was stalking Mick—to take care of her. "I can to this. You have better things to do."

"Yeah, I can see that. It's no bother. Sit and relax. I'll get what you need." He poured ice cubes into a couple large plastic bags and zipped them closed. "You got painkillers? You'll going to need them."

"Top cupboard to the left of the fridge." She ambled into the living room and slouched on the couch with her ice pack and a cold bottle of water. Her body ached from head to sole and she began to shiver.

"Take a couple now. Before the shock wears off," Gary said, handing her the bottle, then draped a plush blanket over her legs, and turned on the television. "I'm going to Happy's for ice. You need anything else? Whiskey? Wine? A good hit man? I know guys."

This time she managed a rough laugh, hoping he was making a warped joke. "I'm good. Go home, I'll..." She waved a hand at a loss for words. Cry. Fall apart. Lose her mind. There were too many to choose from.

"Get comfy, baby girl, I'll be right back." He pulled the door closed.

Gilda reached for her phone on the coffee table and lost her balance. She toppled off the couch, landing on her sore wrist. Not a graceful move, but less embarrassing with Gary gone. Sitting up slowly, she hoped she hadn't caused further injuries, then speed dialed her mom.

"Gilda, how are you? I'd hoped to see you on the long weekend. Did you find something fun to do? You didn't hang out with that boss of yours, did you? How are Marion and your friend Walter? He's such a sweet man." Her mom's questions came like rapid fire that sent Gilda reeling against the couch.

"Walter's dead, Mom," she said, choking back tears. "I told you that."

Stunned silence.

Taking advantage of the opportunity, she asked, "Do you know Gary del Garda?"

Still nothing.

"Are you there?"

A rush of breath came over the phone. "How do you know Gary?"

Without wanting to alarm her mom, she said, "He seems to be looking out for me. I'm not so sure I like the attention."

"Why is he stalking you?"

"He's not stalking me. I run into him sometimes," Gilda assured her.

"Keep your distance from that man. He's dangerous."

There was a knock at the door before the dangerous man in question called out, "Hey, Gilda. I've got your stuff."

"Gotta go. Call you later." What would her neighbors think if they heard a known criminal yell at her door about having her stuff. She tucked the phone beneath the couch cushion. "Come on in."

Gary puffed, as if he ran rather than drove the few blocks to Happy Harvey's and back. "Why are you on the floor? You were on the couch when I left. Should I take you to the hospital?"

"Wow. You sound just like my mother." She faked a laugh. "I lost my balance trying to reach the phone."

"A bag of ice." He crossed the room in two large steps and set a large paper bag on the coffee table. In the other hand he clutched two pink roses from the plastic vase on Happy's front counter. "A bottle of wine, a couple apples, and microwave lasagna. I thought you might be hungry. I'm a great cook, but I doubt you'd want me messing around in your kitchen."

She reached for the small ice pack next to her on the floor. "Thanks."

Gary helped her back onto the couch, then took everything into the kitchen. Five minutes later, he returned with a fresh ice pack and the heated lasagna on a plate with a side salad. A couple minutes later, he brought her a glass of white wine and the two roses in a vase.

Despite the pain, Gilda smiled. "You're the best butler I've ever had."

His face paled. "What did you call me?"

"A butler. What did you think I said?"

"Nothing. Eat, rest, and build your strength. Walter's funeral's tomorrow. Lock the door behind me in case that spineless little rat wasn't finished."

Gilda narrowed her eyes before she asked, "Why would you call him a rat?"

"Figure of speech. I'll check on you tomorrow." He left before she could thank him.

There were a number of people she could call to find out more about Gary, including Marion. Unfortunately, as she gazed at the lasagna, wine, and roses, she was overcome by tears.

In no shape to speak to any of them, she hobbled across the room to lock the door before settling on the couch. Thankful for soft food and water, she ate, took more painkillers, and dozed off to I Love Lucy reruns.

CHAPTER 11

G ilda stared at the dingy ceiling as she lay on the couch the next morning. Once she felt stronger and had time, she'd paint every room in the house. She hurt in places she'd only read about in medical magazines in Doc's office.

Walter's funeral was in five hours, which was probably how long it would take her to get upright and force her weary body into clothes.

She thought about scrambling eggs for breakfast, but standing hurt too many body parts. Toast with peanut butter and jam was easy to make, even though her jaw ached as she chewed. If she ached this bad today, she could wait for tomorrow's recovery pain.

According to Erik, Walter was supposed to replace Mick at the school. If Yoshida wanted to open more schools, why not let Walter run a new one instead? She and Mick had an interesting thing going on in Sandstone Cove.

With the school. That was all.

When she tried to reach back to rub a stiff muscle in her back, her hand cramped. "What was that man thinking? I'm no black belt."

She continued to curse Yoshida on her shuffle to the shower. After trying to wash off the previous night and failing miserably, she'd nearly finished covering the lighter bruises on her face with foundation before the doorbell rang. She waddled to the door aching to flop on the couch and ignore whoever it was.

Erik stood on her doorstep, his hair rumpled and his expression cold. "What did they say after I left last night?"

No "How are you? You look awful." Not even a cup of coffee to bribe her for information.

Gilda had half a mind to slam the door in his face but didn't have the strength. The other half reminded her he was stronger, faster, and could knock her door down with a single punch.

She joined him outside in the sunshine. The warmth soothed her weary body and battered face. Gary's car was nowhere in sight. "No one said anything. Yoshida just pushed us until we dropped."

While it was mostly true, he didn't look convinced. "What about after?"

"Mick sent us all home." She limped to the porch swing. "I came home and took painkillers before my body seized up." And cried until her head ached.

He studied her a moment, then asked, "Who did the damage to your face?"

"Yoshida."

He swore. "Mick let you spar that jerk. I'm glad I left. He would've killed me.

"Mick tried to stop him, but..."

"Why would he go after you?"

She shrugged. "Maybe he doesn't like nosy people."

Erik snorted, then rubbed his face with both hands. "He must've heard about you playing detective. You got any coffee?"

"No, I just got up." A mourning dove cooed on the roof across the street. "Where did you go after you left last night?"

"What do you care? Are you Gilda Wright, super sleuth or something?"

She huffed, then shot him a glare. "Why did you come to talk to me?"

He opened his mouth, probably to chastise her, then looked away. "For the record, all I wanted was the chance to teach classes and learn to run my own school. I know I'd do a good job."

Gilda's neck prickled. "So why didn't you?"

"Yoshida thought I was too immature," Erik said. His face reddened as his blond hair tousled by the breeze. "He convinced Mick my technique and personality weren't up to his standards and that I'd only screw things up. Guess I proved him right, didn't I?"

"What are you going to do now?"

"No idea," he admitted. "I shouldn't have come here. I figured with all the problems lately, if anyone had answers it would be you. You don't need to be dragged into things."

She wanted to blurt, "I already am, so spit it out," but bit her puffy lower lip to keep the words inside. Erik would leave and never tell her anything.

"I know it's on the tip of your tongue to ask, but I didn't kill Walter. I have an alibi."

"You do?" she asked, surprised he felt the need to offer one.

He bowed his head and muttered, "I was with Chloe."

"Mick's Chloe?" Her eyes grew wide.

Erik nodded. "We ran into each other and had a couple drinks. She said she and Mick were having problems and she...needed someone. if you know what I mean."

More fuel to stoke the fire. "Walter was killed around midday. Right after class."

"Yup, I know. I got fired from my job Friday morning then went for a liquid lunch. Chloe was talking to some guy when I walked in. Something about her dad and a gambling debt Mick was upset about. I told her I needed money to start my own school, so I could move on."

Gilda sucked in a sharp breath. "You wanted to compete with Mick?"

"Are you kidding me? He and Yoshida would kick my butt. I'm moving in with my folks in Niagara while I figure things out. I need the money for start-up and equipment."

"How much money would it take? For curiosity's sake."

"More than enough to go to a loan shark or his daughter for," Erik said, then stood. "I'm sure it doesn't surprise you. I'll bet you've heard worse lately."

She really wanted to hear more, but didn't want to meddle. "Yeah, I've heard enough to make my hair go straight."

"And to make you give up the notion of catching a murderer, I hope. You don't want to be next name on the list. See you around." Erik walked out of her yard and across the street to his silver sports car. A Miata with a scrape on the rear fender.

Was his comment a threat or a warning? Maybe Erik was part of the reason Gary was suddenly becoming buddy-buddy with her. Mick owed Gary money. If Gary did loan Erik money, getting close to Gilda could be one way to keep an eye on both his investments.

Once Erik left, she struggled to her feet, groaning from the aches in her muscles. She needed coffee, breakfast, and to tell Fabio about the scrape on Erik's car. She also needed to skip her run. She'd never be able to pull off her sweaty shorts to shower later. A few days off would do her good.

One thought struck Gilda on her half-hearted walk to the coffee shop. Who else in Sandstone Cove knew Walter met his wife when she was a schoolgirl? If any of the parents found out, they wouldn't bother with theatrics. They'd run straight for their lawyers. No second chances. Many would've labelled him a pedophile with no chance of explanation.

No one at the café questioned her bruises when she ordered a large coffee and a cinnamon bun the size of her battered face. They knew where she worked and how hard she trained. It seemed bruises following a visit from Yoshida were common. She ambled home with her head bowed, hoping to discourage anyone from talking to her.

Locking the front door to keep out the world, Gilda sat in the back garden and tried to focus on the flowers and birds. She managed to eat half the cinnamon bun, despite the ache in her jaw. At least she didn't need to use a straw. Pureed cinnamon bun didn't sound as desirable as a soft, warm one did.

Walter loved cinnamon buns, but Jade insisted white flour and sugar were taboo. He'd buy the largest one he could and share it with Gilda.

Tears filled her eyes as she finished the bun, then cradled her coffee in both hands. She shuffled barefoot through the garden to do a walking meditation. Peace. Each blade of grass caressed her bare feet. Each flower reached out. Each sunbeam warmed her hair. The fragrant air...

Who was she kidding?

Nothing about limping through the little garden with a hot cup in her hands and anxiety in her stomach was remotely peaceful. Maybe she'd do better with an indoor meditation and a nap. Gilda went inside and lit a candle. She turned on her favorite meditation and sat on a cushion. She pushed all thoughts out of her head to focus.

One by one, the images from the training session faced. T knots in her shoulders and neck loosened.

Peace. Blissful, mindless peace. As she slowed her breathing, her shoulders softened. Zen. She released a long breath that took a third of her stress with it into the atmosphere.

Until someone oblivious to her hard-sought tranquility banged on the front door.

She jumped and let out a loud groan.

"Gilda, honey, you in there?" Marion asked.

Crap, Gilda forgot to call her last night.

"Are you okay? Mick told me you got a little banged up. Open up. I've got arnica and fruit."

Gilda considered ignoring her, but Marion was crafty. She'd peer into every window and jiggle the door handles. Sooner or later, she'd grab the spare key. If Gilda didn't open the door to fill her in on the details, she'd never get any peace.

Tension reclaimed her upper body as she blew out the candle.

Marion held an enormous basket covered in red cellophane and tied with a floppy blue bow in both hands. She peered over her dark sunglasses as her eyes grew wide. "Oh. Wow. That must've been some class. We all told you not to go, but—"

"But you're not about to say I told you so, right?"

"Show's how well you know me." Marion pushed past her. "I told you so. That's quite the fat lip, girl. Did Erik do that?"

"Why would you say that?" Gilda asked.

Marion gave her a one-armed hug. "Everyone knows he's a hot head. Anyway, I bumped into Sensei Mick earlier who looks almost as bad as you. He said you were having a hard time with Walter's death, and I should leave you alone today, which I took as code for meaning you needed a friend."

"I appreciate that."

"I know this isn't much," she said, handing Gilda the crackling basket. A few of the parents pitched in. We thought it might cheer you up."

"That was thoughtful, thanks." She glanced at the assortment of fruits and chocolates, then handed it back. "Walter's family might need this more than me."

Marion pushed it back. "Oh no, honey, this one's for you. See, it's got all your favorites, and a few of mine. Besides, I already stopped there to drop off a basket and a gift certificate, but no one was home. They're either at the funeral home or shopping for black clothes."

"Maybe." A brief panic attack threatened. Did Gilda even own anything black aside from workout clothes? "Does this mean you're not coming to the funeral?"

"I can't get away from work since Walter wasn't a relative or any-thing." Marion toyed with her sunglasses. "Mick doesn't look so good. I mean, he's a stud like always, but he looks like he needs a long vacation."

Gilda set the basket on the coffee table next to her candle. "Weird. He and Chloe just got back from Jamaica a while ago, then I saw them arguing in front of the school."

Odd. Did Mick and Chloe's fight have to do with the debt Chloe mentioned to Erik?

"Aw, gee. That's too bad. Do you think he's back on the market yet?"

"Even if he was—"

"Yeah. I'm not his type. Hey, can I get a glass of water?

She wiped her forehead, releasing the damp bangs plastered to her skin. I've been doing errands and still have to get to work."

Gilda limped to the kitchen, set the basket on the table, and poured Marion a glass of cold water. "You're right, I've never seen Mick so frazzled."

"Yeah, I think he's going gray, especially after you showed up last night."

"I went there to train. He's involved in things that have nothing to do with me."

"Sure, you did," she said, before guzzling half the glass before giving Gilda a hug. "Whatever you say. Call me after the funeral. I want to know everything that happens, and I do mean everything. You know I'm peeved you didn't call me last night, right?"

"Yes, I know," Gilda admitted. "I was a mess after everything... Gary was nice enough to give me a ride home."

"Gary del Garda drove you home. Why didn't one of the black belts?"

She sighed. "Mick stayed to deal with Yoshida. Razi stayed to make sure things didn't get out of control. Erik left before class started. Xavier...just left. Thank you for the basket. I'll bring it to the school to share with the others."

"Don't you dare. This is for you to enjoy. Just save the truffles for movie night."

"You bet." She guessed that was part of Marion's plan all along. She set aside a box of chocolates to thank Gary for his help.

Once Marion left, she locked the door and brushed all thoughts of Gary under a mental rug. In the silence, she felt more alone than ever. A wave of suffocating emotion swept over her. She relit the candle and sat on the cushion to finish her meditation. Even after ten minutes, her Zen-like state remained out of reach as her monkey mind did somersaults.

Mick. Razi, Xavier. Erik. Walter. Yoshida.

Why did it surprise her that none of the black belts were what they seemed?

CHAPTER 12

Gilda wore her black shift dress for Walter's funeral since it was the one dress in her closet she could pull on with her muscles so sore. Her mother's mantra, "every girl needs to own a little black dress," always came back to haunt her. Years of living on her own still hadn't silenced the echo of her mother's fashion advice.

Given the choice, Gilda preferred the pastel blue suit and black silk blouse. Her show of defiance was to add a colorful lace shawl to the boring black dress. "Take that, Mom."

She slipped into her favorite black flats to appease her screaming calves and shuffled down the hall. Everyone she knew would be at the funeral, including the remaining black belts, and she had a zillion questions, the biggest being "Which one of you idiots killed Walter and what were you thinking?"

As she reached for the black clutch on the counter, someone rapped on her front door. Who couldn't wait long enough to see her at Dunn's Funeral Home in ten minutes? Okay, twenty judging by the speed she shuffled toward door.

"Hey, Sherlock," Mick said. He wore black shoes, black fitted slacks, black dress shirt open at the collar and a dark bruise on his face from the cut he got the night before at the workshop. He looked like a long piece of bruised licorice.

Gilda ignored the flutter in her chest and asked, "What do you want?"

Despite the bluish hues on his face, the corner of his mouth twitched. "After last night, the least I could do is escort you to the funeral home. I never should've let things with Yoshida get that far. You deserve a black belt for that."

"How thoughtful." And self-serving. "Isn't your girlfriend going with you?"

"Chloe couldn't get time off and I didn't want to walk into the funeral home alone." He glanced over his shoulder as a car drove away. "Why was Gary parked in front of your house?"

"He saw me last night and took pity. I guess he was keeping an eye on me." She followed him out and locked the door, even though she'd never felt the need to do so before. "Why the escort? Were you worried I wouldn't show up?"

"When Thayer said you thought Xavier tried to poison you, I got worried."

For Fabio to tell Thayer, he either was convinced, or the lab found something.

"I thought you two hated each other. How come he's suddenly telling you my life story?" she asked.

"Because he heard what happened in class last night," Mick told her. "He also found out Xavier brought me coffee that morning and wanted to know if I got sick."

"And did you?"

"I never drank it," he said. "I got busy, then dumped it because it was cold. Did you drink yours?"

"I pretended to. I brought it to the police after he left." Gilda hugged her arms to her stomach. "Normally, I wouldn't think twice, but he kept talking about poisons and I wasn't sure what to think."

"Clever girl. Impulsive and suspicious, but clever. We should go. We don't want to be late."

Thoughts tumbled like puppies in Gilda's head. She couldn't make sense of it all, especially after precious few hours of sleep. What would Xavier have to gain by poisoning her? Unless he had something to hide. Or, as Mick suggested, she was ready to suspect the worst of her friends.

The funeral home was already filled to capacity when they arrived. Gary nodded to her, then turned to chat with Mrs. Watson, who owned the consignment store next to the school. The three strangers near the casket had to be Walter's kids from his first marriage.

Mick led her toward Xavier, Erik, Razi, and Yoshida, whose gaze seemed focused on something across the room. Yoshida took a quick glance at Gilda and frowned. Wasn't she the right shades of black or blue for his liking?

Erik's eyes grew wide. "Geez, Mick, you look as bad as Gilda. It's about time you two showed up. We thought you'd leave us here alone."

"I wanted to make sure Gilda got here," Mick said. "Excuse me while I go pay my respects."

Yoshida's face darkened. "She is not here to cause trouble, is she?"

No more than you. Gilda bit the inside of her cheek to keep her mouth shut. The last thing she wanted was another bout with Yoshida, particularly in public.

"You never know. You'd better keep an eye on her," Mick told him on his way to talk to Jade.

Yoshida turned away and headed toward the casket.

Razi stood with his feet shoulder width apart, eyes scanning the room as he asked, "How are you, Miss Wright?"

"Alive and kicking." Probably the wrong thing to say under the circumstances.

"Amen to that," Erik muttered. He walked past Mick, then exited the room.

Yoshida followed at a distance.

Gilda started to go after them.

"Miss Wright." Jade Levy blocked her path. She'd foregone the geisha look for a business-like, tailored black suit and a touch of make-up to lighten any dark circles beneath her eyes.

Xavier and Razi offered their condolences before approaching the casket.

"I hear you have been asking questions about my husband's killer," Jade said.

Her face warmed. "Walter was a friend. I just want to help."

The widow stiffened. "Please do us both a favor and leave things alone. You do not want to get in over your head."

"Is that a threat?" Gilda gave a nervous laugh.

"I am not a killer. Please stay away from the ones I love. It is most unpleasant when bad things happen to good people." She brushed something off Gilda's shoulder.

Lint? Black widow spider? Gilda shivered, not used to so much paranoia. "What do you plan to do now that Walter's...?"

"If the police approve, I will go to New York with my family, then decide what I will do next," Jade said. "I do not wish to cause further trouble here."

The fine hairs on Gilda's arms rose. What kind of trouble was she referring to? "I'm sure a change of scenery will help."

Jade grasped her wrist and whispered, "I know you are trying to help, Miss Wright, but none of the people you deal with are what they seem. You could be in danger."

"But Mick—"

"Especially Mick. Be careful. You have no idea what kind of devil those men are involved with." Jade left the scent of jasmine in her wake as she went to greet an elderly couple at the door.

Gilda stood alone. A devil? Did she mean Yoshida or Gary?

Mick nudged her lower jaw. "Trying out for a job as a fly catcher?"

"No, I—" She paused before glancing toward Razi and Xavier near the casket. "I'm going to say good-bye."

He grasped her arm. "Are you okay? What did Jade say?"

"Nothing. I'm in pain and hate funerals," she said.

"Not many people enjoy them, especially the guy in the box." Mick steered her to the casket. Was he afraid she'd make a dash for the French doors? No worries there. Even Mrs. Watson could've run faster than her. "Notice anything odd?"

She touched her fingers to her lips to keep from crying. His hair had never looked tidier. "About Walter? He's dead and not wearing a gi?"

"Try harder."

"Give me a hint."

"His jacket. Breast pocket," Mick murmured against her hair.

The pocket of Walter's suit bulged with a white napkin folded with double points. Nestled beside it was a piece of dark fabric rolled into a scroll. "What is it?"

"Pretend to cry," he said.

"Why?"

He nudged her ribs with his elbow, digging into a large bruise. "Just pretend to cry."

She didn't need to pretend. Tears welled in her eyes from the pain. When her gaze fell on Walter's heavily made-up face, she forgot about Mick and whatever he was about to pull. Reality crashed in. Walter was dead. They'd never share a cinnamon bun again.

"Are you okay, Sherlock?" Mick put one arm around her as he pulled the dark fabric from Walter's pocket and scrunched it in his hand.

She dabbed at her eyes. "No, I'm not okay. That hurt."

The minister cleared his throat. "Please be seated. The service is about to begin."

Mick hushed Gilda when she tried to ask questions. He led her to a seat, stuffed the fabric scroll in her purse, then rested his hands in his lap.

An accomplice to his crime, she found it hard to concentrate. Her thoughts focused on the swatch of cloth than the minister's words. The material seemed familiar. She itched to find a quiet spot to check it out. How had Mick even noticed it?

While everyone else drove out to the cemetery, Gilda stepped into the sunlight not sure which direction to point her shoes. Her hands shook and her legs were weak.

Mick placed a hand on her lower back. "Come on. You need caffeine and a large dose of sugar."

"Are you a doctor?" Gilda asked, still sniffling.

"Just a concerned friend."

"Since when?" she asked. "You know we could both go to jail for tampering with evidence."

"Unless it's not evidence. I felt bad for letting you down and I wanted to help."

"You didn't believe a man with a sword in his chest was murdered?"

"No, I didn't believe someone I knew could kill him. Idle threats are one thing, but to follow through takes something I can't fathom."

"That makes two of us."

Mick opened the door to Café Beanz, led her to a corner booth, then ordered them each a coffee and a slice of peach pie. "All right, fork it over, Sherlock."

Gilda pulled out the roll of rust-colored fabric and spread it on the table. In small block letters on one edge of the cloth, someone had painstakingly written "first, not last." A shudder ran through her. That sounded a lot like a threat.

"It's the first kanji from the missing scroll," she said softly. "Whoever killed Walter must've taken it. Why would they put it in his casket?"

Mick crumpled the cloth into his hand like a used napkin as the curvy, blonde server arrived with their coffees.

"Be right back with that pie," she said with a wink.

"No rush." He smiled. Once she left, he leaned on the table. "No one outside of the school would've known it was there, or what it meant."

Gilda agreed. "Now what do we do?"

When he handed the piece of cloth to her, his fingers brushed hers. "You'd better hang onto this since you're the local P.I."

"Since when?" she asked.

"You notice things other people don't. For example, that the scroll was missing. And you saw the dent in Xavier's fender. I'm not sure if you trust me or not, but we need to stick together on this."

She took a deep breath, then nodded. "That means you have to trust me, too. Why didn't you tell me about Walter and Jade's history? Or that Erik wanted to leave the school. Or Xavier—"

Mick drew a hasty line with one finger across his mouth.

She frowned, then looked over her shoulder.

Xavier strolled toward them, his suit rumpled and tie askew. His face was red and his left eye puffy. Angry, red knuckle marks discolored his flesh. He ordered a coffee, then sat next to Gilda and said, "I see you guys didn't go to the cemetery either."

"I needed to sit." She moved closer to the window when the stench of whiskey reached her.

Mick shot her a warning glare. "I wanted to make sure she was okay. I thought she might pass out when she saw Walter."

Considering she'd spent more time with Walter's body than he had, she was curious what he was up to.

Xavier patted her knee beneath the table, his hand lingering a couple seconds longer than she was comfortable with. "It's okay, honey. For the record, I don't even want to go to my own funeral."

"Amen to that," Mick said. "I saw you talking to Erik when we left. Was he the one who roughed you up?"

"I tripped and fell." He turned a deeper shade of crimson. "Erik caught me."

Mick smirked. "More like his knuckles caught you. You'll need a better cover story than that."

Gilda's doubts nearly scuttled away when her pie, warm and dripping with melting ice cream, arrived. She was sure Erik made it appear that he'd helped Xavier to his feet. He was fast and sneaky. His speed and agility gave him an edge in tournaments. It also made him a likely killer.

"That looks good." Xavier called to the server for a slice of pie.

"Eat up. This stuff's guaranteed to shake off anything life throws at you." Mick nudged her plate closer, then picked up his fork and asked Xavier, "What did Erik want?"

When his coffee and pie arrived, Xavier scooped in three teaspoons of sugar. "He asked what happened to the sword that killed Walter."

Gilda paused with a forkful of peach less than an inch from her mouth. "He what?"

"What does he want with it? It's a murder weapon. Bad karma," Mick said.

"I'm not sure. He sounded like he really wanted it, probably for..." He cast a nervous glance from Mick to Gilda.

"I know about his new business," Gilda told him. "Is that why he wants the sword? For a decoration in his karate school?"

Across the table, Mick cocked his head, a bead of vanilla ice cream on the corner of his mouth. "Who told you?"

"Thayer and Erik." Xavier sat back when the server brought his peach pie with ice cream. Before touching the coffee, he dug into the pie like a starving man.

Mick moved slower. At first, Gilda thought he was savoring each bite, then she realized his eyes had glazed over in thought. She hoped he'd fill her in once Xavier left.

Five minutes later, Mick pulled out his wallet and threw a ten-dollar bill on the table. "I've gotta go. Walk Gilda home will you, Xavier? I'll check on her later."

Gilda huffed. She didn't like being referred to in third person while still sitting there. Where was he off to in such a hurry that he didn't he take her along? So much for sticking together.

Xavier moved to the other side of the table, giving her some space. "What's with him?"

"Maybe he's going to see Chloe."

He sipped his coffee and made a face. She thought he'd probably poured in too much sugar, yet he added one more spoonful. "Last I heard, they broke up. Personally, I think she's a spoiled brat. No one else likes her either."

Apparently, Walter and Erik did.

"She's not so bad." Gilda shrugged.

Xavier snorted. "Have you noticed Gary del Garda hanging around the school lately? I think he's spying on Mick to make sure he treats her right."

She sipped her coffee without comment.

"Good thing he's friends with you. You're the only one who knows where Mick is. I don't think he calls her half as much as he calls you. If I didn't know better, I'd think there was something going on between you guys."

She shook her head. "Hardly. I guarantee every phone call we have is about the school. Trying to keep track of Mick is like catching steam. Half the time, I have no idea where he is, or what he's up to."

Xavier crossed his forearms on the table, ready to listen.

Gilda finished her coffee, then managed to lose him after they left by ducking into Happy Harvey's Hangover Hut. All she needed was a few minutes of peace.

What she got instead was a head-on collision with Jade Levy in the doorway. "Oh no. I'm so sorry. I wasn't watching where I was going. Are you okay?"

Jade hugged a paper bag to her chest. Bottles tinkled. "I am okay, thank you."

"Is the burial over already?" Could she be any more tactless? It had to be the pain pills talking.

"I forgot to pick up the champagne to toast Walter's life. I do hope you will join us."

"Is your friend going to be there?"

She frowned. "Which friend?"

Too late to turn back now. Gilda had bulldozed into dangerous territory. "The one who was upstairs when I stopped by the other day. Your house guest."

Jade's face paled beneath the fluorescent lights. "You must be mistaken. There was no one at my house."

Happy, as if sensing the sudden awkwardness, moved around the counter and edged closer, straightening bottles on the shelves as he cast furtive glances at Gilda. Hopefully, he'd have her back if things got ugly.

The words slipped out even though her brain screamed for her to shut up. "I thought I saw a man in a yellow bathrobe."

"You were hallucinating. I would never cheat on my husband. He was my world." Jade shoved past Gilda, knocking her into a stack of beer cases then fled out the front door to a waiting silver sports car. With stars of pain shooting across her vision, Gilda couldn't see who was driving.

Happy grabbed her arm to steady her. "You okay, *amiga*?"

She gasped at the surge of pain. "I will be."

"Not know what you said, but she look...how you say? *Culpado*," he said. "She come here many times. She married?"

"Widowed. Walter was her husband. The instructor murdered on Friday." She kept her gaze on the door in case Xavier found her. "She's guilty of something. I just don't know what."

Happy walked back to the counter then handed her a bag of ice. "Not as good as *um saco de ervilhas,* but it works."

"Not as good as what?"

"*De ervilhas*. Little *verde* vegetable. How you say it?"

Verde. Green. "Peas. A bag of peas. I don't have any."

Happy placed the bag and a small bottle of wine in a paper bag. "Good. You take these. Both numb pain."

Gilda pushed the bag away. "I'm not in pain."

"Take anyway. You walk like *um pinguim* and look like... what's it? Frankenstein monster. Bad karate?"

"Is that obvious?" She set the bag on the counter. "What's *um pinguim*?"

Happy pressed his arms along the side of his body and waddled across the floor.

She laughed, cracking open her cut lip. "A penguin. I didn't think it would be that obvious."

"It better not be Sensei Mick who hurt you." He shook a thick, calloused finger. "I no sell him good scotch again."

"Not Mick. Shihan Yoshida."

Happy's expression darkened as he said, "Watch out for that one. He is a devil."

"Mick?"

"Yoshida." Happy cast a glare out the window toward the school. "You do not do what he says, he make life miserable. Nothing good for that one. Go home, *amiga*. Heal and stay away from the devils."

Hadn't Jade said the same thing?

CHAPTER 13

"What a crazy, stupid week." Gilda filled another small bag with ice and clutched it to her aching face before sprawling on the couch. As soon as she closed her eyes and drifted off to sleep, her phone rang.

"Meet me at the school," Mick said.

She wiped drool off her cheek. "Right now? Why?"

"Now, Gilda." He hung up without waiting for an answer.

Unwilling to get off the couch, she groaned. Her whole body hurt. She grumbled about giving up karate and finding a new job. Throwing the ice pack in the freezer, she grabbed a water bottle and shuffled to the karate school. The door was unlocked, and the lights were on. So far, so good. That didn't stop her heart from hammering against her bruised ribs.

"I'm here," She called out. "What do you want?"

Mick, Erik, Xavier, and Razi sat in Mick's office. All four appeared somber, yet there was tension in the air. They all avoided looking her in the eye.

"This looks like an intervention," she said.

Mick cleared his throat as he motioned to an empty chair. "We're worried about you playing Gilda Wright, P.I."

"Did Jade call? I didn't mean to be rude to her in Happy's, but she makes me nervous, and I tend to say the wrong things."

Concerned glances darted across the room. The men shook their heads in weird, almost pre-rehearsed, unison.

"Actually, Mrs. Watson called," Mick said. "Her grandson saw someone lurking around the karate school the other night and called the cops. I spoke to Thayer."

"I wasn't lurking." She huffed. Skulking maybe. "I wanted to see if there was another way in or out of the school. People saw Mick leave, but never saw anyone come or go until I arrived."

Erik sneered. "Did you find a top-secret entrance, Agent Smart?"

"No, but it looks like someone tried to pry open the back door. Then a cat jumped out of nowhere and..." She hesitated. "Is there an opening to a vent up there?"

Mick flinched. "Not that I know of. The door's old news. Some kids tried to break in. I fixed the worst of the damage, but fire doors are expensive to fix."

Xavier took her hand. He still reeked of whiskey. "Look, honey, no one wants you to get hurt. Leave the detective work to that sorry excuse for a cop."

"Who?" she asked.

"Thayer." Mick studied the desktop. "Has he interviewed you guys yet?"

Razi nodded. "Yes."

"Unfortunately," Erik said, rolling his eyes. "The guy has rocks for brains. Good thing he's got a solid partner."

Gilda wasn't about to argue. She held the same opinion.

"Once about Walter. The other about the dent in my bumper," Xavier told them.

She recalled the damage to the pole out back and the chips of silver paint. "Do you always park in back?"

"That's exactly what Thayer asked." Xavier's face reddened. "Hardly ever I told him Erik parks there more than I do."

"You told him that?" Erik roared. "Man, he made it sound like he had a video tape of me smashing into it and taking down half the bloody building."

"He and I saw the same scraped post, and figured someone hit it."

Erik's nostrils flared. "Are you saying I killed Walter, ran out the backdoor, then hit the post before I left?"

"It's possible." Gilda shrugged.

"I didn't hit anything." Erik stood, knocking his chair over backward. "That scrape came from a black car that backed into me at the grocery store. Xavier's scrape came from when he hit something in the back alley. I saw it happen."

Mick held up a hand. "Why don't we all go take a look?"

"Forget it," Erik groaned. "I have better things to do."

"We all do," Mick said. "But accusing each other isn't helping. First, we'll check out the post and help Gilda get over this need to solve a murder without serious help."

"Mental or police?" Erik asked.

Mick didn't answer.

Gilda shook her head. "If you mean I should work with Thayer, forget it. He's a jerk." When the others raised eyebrows, her face burned. "It's no secret we used to date."

"You're not helping yourself, Sherlock. Show us what you found." Mick led them to the alley via the back door.

Gilda pointed to the post near the corner of the building. "That one has a gouge and flecks of silver paint."

"Should we call the cops?" Xavier asked. "I'm sure they can prove by the angle of the gouge, the color of the paint, and the phase of the moon that my car hit that sign when I pulled in, then hit this post right after I killed Walter Levy."

"Sounds right," Erik chuckled. "Case solved."

Gilda hadn't mentioned the sign. "Knock it off."

"Hey," Xavier went on. "If they weigh my car, I'll bet they can even prove I lost three pounds training Tuesday night and had Jimmy Hoffa's body in the trunk. Do you think they can figure out where I buried him?"

Mick stepped between them. "That's enough. We're not here to accuse anyone."

Not without proof and reinforcements. Gilda nodded. "It's all speculation. Not proof."

Razi paused to examine the door, then shrugged off the damage and headed inside without a word.

Erik glanced at his phone. "I gotta go, kids. This was fun. Let's do it again sometime. Maybe bring booze and make it a party."

Xavier glared at Gilda, then stormed down the alley out of sight. She'd suffered a stomachache for over a week before Walter died. It wasn't a stretch to think Xavier tried to poison her in preparation for Walter's demise.

"I know he's mad, but what if I'm right?" she whispered.

Mick draped an arm across her shoulders. He smelled like coffee. "Then you'd better sleep with one eye open."

"Great." She returned inside the school.

Razi stood next to her desk shifting his weight from foot to foot.

Marion paced and spun a half turn at each end of the lobby while gnawing on her thumbnail. When she saw Gilda, she caught her in a hug, then dragged her across the room. "I should've said something sooner. Now I don't know what to do."

"About what?"

"The day Walter died?" Marion asked. "I think I saw his killer."

Gilda shook her head. "But you were in the office when I called nine-one-one."

Marion clutched Gilda's shoulders. "I mean before that. When I was on my way to work. I drove past the school and saw Mick come out. I had to stare. I mean, what's not to like, right?"

"What else did you see?" Mick asked.

Marion blushed. "I followed him for two blocks before I realized I was going the wrong way, so I turned around. That's when I saw the killer go into the school."

Mick lunged toward her. "Who was it?"

"Walter's wife," Marion said.

Gilda frowned. "Jade? That would make her the last person to see her husband alive. But she's so little. Is she strong enough to do something like that?"

"Oh yeah," Mick said, then his face reddened.

"I do not speak gossip." Razi bowed his head.

Gilda looked from one to the other. "What do you guys know?"

Mick motioned for Marion to leave.

"Oh no. I want to hear what's going on." She folded her arms across her ample chest. "If Gilda's staying, so am I."

"There's enough gossip floating around town," Mick told her. "Go home."

Taller and wider than Mick, Marion scowled. "Make me, little man."

When Razi stepped toward her, Marion squeaked, threw her hands in the air and ran out of the building without saying goodbye. He locked the door behind her.

"Start talking or I'm going home," Gilda growled.

Mick's cheek tightened. "Walter told us stories, the locker room kind, but nobody believed him. When I went to tell Jade about Walter and Chloe, she... Let's just say she's a wild cat."

"Angry enough to tear the change room apart?" she asked.

"Not that kind of wild. More like the passionate kind."

"Oh, yeah." Razi nodded.

Gilda sat behind her desk when she realized what she meant, and covered her face with both hands. "Eww. I need a vat of hand sanitizer."

"Martial artists get her mojo revving," Mick said, leaning against her desk. "I don't think Xavier or Erik are her type. You won't tell anyone, will you? Especially Marion."

"What would I say that wouldn't make Jade look bad?" Gilda asked.

He stared at the floor. "If she had wild, crazy monkey sex with Walter first, she could've easily skewered him with a *katana*. The guy wouldn't be able to move."

"Way too much information," Gilda groaned, covering her ears.

Razi leaned on the desk and narrowed his eyes in thought. "What if she was here to let someone else inside?"

"An accomplice?" Her stomach ached. The man in the yellow robe. "It's possible. Maybe she has a lover."

"Unless it's a woman," Mick said. "Walter wasn't exactly being faithful. Maybe a jealous lover wanted payback."

"Then why kill Walter, not Jade?"

He sat beside her. "You heard Walter was a teacher and Jade was his student."

She shuddered. "Did you know he was a child molester?"

"Gilda, it's not like that. He fell in love with her and—"

"I can no longer listen," Razi said.

"We've been over this," Mick said. "Walter was never unsupervised."

Razi snorted. "He was always unsupervised."

"Gilda was here," Mick said.

"Oh, no. Do not put that on me," she said. "You knew about his past and let him teach. You should've been here."

Mick's nostrils flared. "Of course everything's on me. I didn't have any control over any of this either, lady. You, Walter, Yoshida, Erik, Chloe, you can all just go jump in the lake." He stormed out the front door, leaving Razi and Gilda to stare after him.

"I believe our meeting is over," Razi told her. He helped her out of her seat, locked the door, and walked her home. "I hope you will not repeat what you heard. It could be very embarrassing."

"People will cancel their memberships when they find out. But I they need to know the truth."

"They would also not like the way Yoshida behaved the other night," he said. "Particularly toward you."

"Mick doesn't seem concerned." She'd have to do some serious damage control before things got worse. Maybe it was time to learn more of the gossip. "What happened after I left that night?"

"All I can say is that things did not go as well as Sensei Mick had hoped," Razi said.

"What do you mean? What did he tell you?"

"Good night, Miss Wright." He left her at her front gate, alone in the dark in more ways than one.

With a sigh, Gilda walked up her front sidewalk in the semidarkness with a vague, uneasy feeling. She hadn't noticed Gary or his car, yet something was out of place.

Ahead on the front porch, someone flicked a lighter and a flame flared to life.

Chloe del Garda lit a cigarette, took a long drag, and blew a stream of smoke toward Gilda before extinguishing the lighter. "About time you got home. I've been sitting here half an hour. Even you can do better than Razi."

Gilda started to explain, then reconsidered. "What do you want?"

"You don't have to sound so hostile." Mick's former girlfriend shifted in the warped wicker chair as she tossed her long, dark hair over her shoulder. "Did you get this thing at a garage sale?"

"It was my grandmother's," Gilda said, climbing the steps.

Chloe took another drag. The cigarette glowed before she released a long breath. "You're a good secretary, but don't get too cozy. He's mine. I'm the one with the looks, the brains, and the money. I'm also a former bikini model. A trophy. You're nothing."

Gilda, self-esteem at a new all-time low, pulled out her keys. "I'm going to bed. I'd appreciate you leaving."

"Oh, I will, honey," Chloe said. "After I tell you to stay away from my father."

"Your father?" Her entire body tensed.

Chloe stood and teetered in her four-inch spike heels. Without the heels, she was Gilda's height. "People are talking. They've seen you and my father running around town and I want it to stop. I won't have you ruining his good name."

"His good name. Are you serious?" Gilda gagged as smoke wafted into her face. Gary del Garda had established his "good name" long before either of them were born. "I'm not having, an affair with your dad, nor would I."

"What's wrong with my dad?" Chloe asked.

He's twice my age. He's a criminal. He's stalking me. "He's not my type."

"Good. Keep it that way." She tapped her toe on the porch.

Gilda shifted her weight and longed for an ice pack. "Is there anything else, or can I go inside now?"

Chloe huffed. "Yeah. You can tell that old Japanese dude to stay away from me."

"Yoshida?"

"Every time he's in town, Mick insists we take him to dinner. Usually, I get out of it, but lately he's been hanging around more. The other day, I bumped into him in the grocery store."

Gilda frowned. "What was he doing there?"

"Probably stalking me, but I'm not sure why he had tampons. No man I've ever dated would buy them for me." Chloe took one last puff on her cigarette, then buried the butt in the planter full of marigolds. She walked down the front path and to the left. Seconds later, the Ferrari's engine roared to life and faded into the night.

"Stay away from Mick and Gary. Keep Yoshida away from Chloe," Gilda muttered as she unlocked the front door. "Sounds easy enough."

She closed the door and leaned against the cool wood. Yoshida thought women were subservient and meant to cater to him. Some woman had to have a hold on him. Through blackmail, perhaps. What had he done to give someone so much control over him?

CHAPTER 14

The next morning, with more thoughts rolling through her head than flowers in her garden, Gilda gave up on paperwork. She changed clothes to wander among the peonies and daylilies out front. Her yard had gone neglected thanks to the interruptions of the past few days. Pulling weeds would clear her mind.

The guys were right. She needed to let Thayer and Fabio do their jobs since that was why the town paid them. Hiding in her garden would keep her away from Gary and Mick. Before she could pull the first weed, a car door closed, and footsteps drew closer.

Thayer leaned on the white gate. "Do you have a few minutes?"

She dropped her attention back to the marigolds and bachelor buttons. "I'm busy."

"So am I," he said, opening the gate and walking over to sit on the third step. His face was drawn, and his hair rumpled. "But I could use your help."

"You just want me to rat out my friends." She took a stern look at him. Dark circles surrounded his eyes, and his skin seemed sallow. She couldn't help but feel an inkling of sympathy. "When's the last time you slept?"

"Which day was Walter killed?" Thayer pinched the bridge of his nose between two fingers. "What's going on at the karate place?"

Her jaw tightened. "It's a school. I'm not going to gossip."

"That's good, because I want the truth," he told her. "I was in Café Beanz earlier and heard all the gossip I can stomach, and even more that I couldn't. I need the real story."

A trickle of sweat slid down Gilda's spine like a cold finger. "What kind of gossip?"

"I thought you didn't gossip?"

She scowled. "Look, Thayer, you and I have a common goal. To sort fact from fiction and figure out who killed Walter. If you want my help, tell me what you've heard."

He rested his forearms on his knees. "Since that's not going to happen, why don't you tell me what you know about Walter?"

Some things never changed. Still a one-sided relationship. If you could call it that.

"Walter was a karate instructor who worked at the cheese factory, had a wife, three kids, several grandkids, and everyone loved him as a teacher."

Thayer rubbed his bloodshot left eye. "Do you know how he met Jade?"

She looked away.

"Stop being childish, Gilda. You just want to see how frustrated I'll get, but this isn't a game." He pulled out his handcuffs. "Let's make this clear. Tell me what you know, or I'll lock you up. Mick will have to bail you out."

"And arrest me for what exactly?"

"Interfering in an ongoing investigation. Withholding information. Being a pain in the butt. Take your pick." The handcuffs gleamed in the sunshine as they swayed.

She folded her arms across her chest. "I get the point. Walter was a high school teacher who fell in love with one of his students. He left his wife, three kids and his teaching career to marry Jade. They had three kids and moved here. Last I heard he worked full-time as a foreman at the goat cheese factory and part-time at Yoshida's."

Thayer's shoulders relaxed as he put away the cuffs. "Who taught Walter's classes when he wasn't there?"

"No one." She wished Gary would choose now to make an appearance. "Walter's never even taken a sick day. He only took a week off when his oldest daughter got married. Mick looked after his classes that week."

His jaw tightened. "Did Walter and Mick get along?"

"Mick ran the business. Walter looked after classes. Except for training, they only saw each other in passing," she told him.

The other black belts had ample opportunity though.

"What time do you start work?"

"Eleven." She frowned, hoping he didn't pester her at the school.

Thayer glanced at his watch. "You'd better get moving. If you hurry, I'll escort you."

"Escort me? Gee, thanks." Gilda turned away, climbed the steps, and closed the door behind her. If she was lucky Thayer would take the hint and leave.

Instead, he opened the door to study her locks. "You may want to change the lock on your front door. Someone could break into your house just by sneezing."

Gilda scowled. "Could you please wait outside? I don't like you invading my space."

"That's ironic." Thayer said. "Considering we once planned to share a space, and I bet it would've been nicer than this. Something with a large fireplace and a big backyard. Maybe a pool."

She balled her fists. "That was before you decided to fool around. I kicked you to the curb and moved on, so get over it."

Thayer reddened. "I'll wait outside."

"Good idea." She locked the door behind him, waiting for a couple minutes in case he did sneeze on the lock or kick the door down to make his point.

* * *

The kids' classes were full that night. Either everyone had missed training, or the parents were anxious to see the murder scene and catch up on the latest. Most stayed to watch their children, but ended up deep in conversation.

"It's great to see everyone here again," Marion said, leaning against Gilda's desk.

She nodded. "It's been a long week."

"Especially for you," a newly divorced mom told her. "It'll be different for all of us with Walter gone, but it's nice to have Sensei Mick teaching classes again. He's much easier on the eyes. Is he still seeing Chloe?"

Marion shook her head. "I heard they broke up."

The mom continued, "I also heard Walter met his wife when he was a high school teacher, and she was in one of his classes. Is that true? Oh, and is Razi still single?"

"Down, girl," Marion said.

It was hard to ignore the gossip and questions. Gilda kept her mouth shut as she typed a full page of gibberish. She'd have to delete it as soon as she could remember how.

"Yes, it is," another dads answered. "He was a teacher with a family of his own at the time. What kind of creep dumps his wife and kids for a teenage girl?"

Gilda deleted every line, then started over with more gibberish.

"I Googled him." Marion leaned closer. "Did you know he used to have his own karate school in New York? He was run out of town for molesting a couple teenage students?"

Gilda froze. Why hadn't she thought to do a search for any of the black belts? She made a note. Since the ring was a dead end, she'd need a new source of information.

A second mom gasped. "I never thought he'd do such a thing. Gilda, did you know any of this?"

Gilda shook her head. "No, I—"

"Everyone has secrets, don't they?" the woman asked. "It's not like Sensei Walter told anyone."

"Come to think of it, neither did Mick," Marion muttered when the woman walked away. "You know, honey, that man owes everyone an explanation. Do you run police checks on your instructors?"

"No clue. They were all here before me." Gilda wished she could leave before any confrontations occurred.

That wasn't meant to be. The instant Mick stepped out of the dojo, the semi-peaceful evening exploded into a barrage of accusations and finger-pointing. Questions flew like missiles as parents circled Mick. He had nowhere to hide.

When he searched for Gilda, she ducked behind the desk. Since he'd left her to deal with Walter, she dumped the angry parents on him. To his credit, he listened to everyone, then promised them discounts for the following month. Great public relations for him. A logistical nightmare for Gilda.

"Thanks a lot," she grumbled, cleaning up after the kids classes that night. "I should be able to sort it all out in a month or two."

Mick shrugged. "It'll all work out. Just remind them we have sixty students, and they have to be patient. Send them to me if they get out of hand."

"After the long weekend and two days without classes, they've had a lot of patience and little information."

He placed his hands on her shoulders. "Take the night off and go home. It's over. Besides, Thayer has a good idea who killed Walter, so it's time to move on."

She stared. "Thayer knows who killed Walter? When did you find that out?"

"We met at the deli for lunch. He's waiting for test results to prove his theory."

"Who does he think did it?"

"Erik."

"Why didn't he tell me when I saw him earlier?"

"I guess he figured you didn't need to know." Mick caught her in a hug. "Go home, Sherlock. Things will be back to normal tomorrow. The most stressful thing you'll have to worry about is deciding what to have for lunch."

Gilda hoped he was right. Deep in her gut, she doubted it. She had to find out more about Erik. As she left the school, someone fell into step beside her.

She groaned. "Twice in one day, to what do I owe the displeasure?"

Thayer chuckled. "Cute. You can tell me why you're hanging out with Gary del Garda lately."

"I haven't been." She swung her bag over her shoulder, nearly hitting him in the head and wincing at the pain she caused in her back and shoulder.

"I've seen him loitering around the school and your house. Plus, I've seen you two talking," he said. "You're either having an affair, which is disgusting, or you're not smart about the company you keep."

"Are you in that last category?" she asked.

He didn't look amused. Lowering his voice, he leaned closer. "Gary has a rap sheet longer than all the mats at your school lined up end to end."

"People make mistakes." She scowled. "Look at you and me."

"He's spent time in jail for murder, assault, and drug trafficking."

Gilda glanced around. No sign of Gary or his sedan. "He said he's going straight for his daughter's sake. I guess he's taking advantage of his second chance."

Thayer stopped and announced, "He worked for the man who killed your father."

A touchy nerve. She clenched her fists before she faced him. "Then why don't you talk to him? Maybe he's the one who killed Walter. Not Erik."

"Erik?" Thayer narrowed his eyes. "I take it you talked to Mick. What would Gary have to gain by killing Walter?"

"Ask him."

"Funny. I thought he told you his life story by now."

Gilda poked Thayer in the chest with her index finger. "You're the cop. Investigating instead of following me around. If you think Erik or Gary had anything to do with Walter's murder, then you need to find the evidence and figure out the motive. Not me."

"Are you telling me how to do my job?" Thayer asked as he glared at her. "What gives you the right to boss me around?"

She had no right to do or say anything. It just felt good. Rather than reply, she simply flashed a syrupy smile.

Thayer sputtered, then laughed. "I've missed that about you, Gilda. You and I should sit down and discuss a few things over a glass of wine or two."

"I told you I didn't kill Walter."

"Not about Walter," Thayer said, taking her hand. "About you and me. We made a great team back then. Now that we've had time to grow up, we could be even better."

"You haven't grown up. You're still a ten-year-old kid in a grown man's body."

He steered her toward her house. "I'm glad you noticed that much. At least I'm not so serious I'm no fun anymore."

She pulled away from him. "What are you trying to say?"

Thayer met her gaze. "Stop hanging out with Gary del Garda."

"Why? Because he's dangerous or you're jealous?"

"Because he's a murder suspect."

"Which he probably wasn't until you saw him talking to me." When his shoulders sagged, Gilda opened the gate, then slammed it shut between them. "You are so obvious. You're the one who cheated on me. Don't use that as an excuse to put innocent people in jail."

"They're not all innocent," he said, his voice following her up the front steps. "Someone at that school killed Walter Levy, and I'm going to find out who. Just be careful you're not next."

"Be careful?" she whispered as she unlocked the door.

Who, or what, was she supposed to be careful of?

CHAPTER 15

G ilda's Friday morning started off with stretches, then a slow, uneventful walk through the park. Uneventful meaning no signs of Thayer, Gary or Mick. After a long, hot shower and a breakfast of egg whites, turkey sausage, and whole grain toast, Gilda was both refreshed and more positive than she'd felt in days.

She popped into Café Beanz for a low-fat latte before she headed for the school and unlocked the door. As she walked toward her desk, she realized she should've turned on the lights. She set the latte on the front desk, then dropped her keys in her purse.

Something made a noise on the floor behind her.

As she turned, a blur of color flashed as before something hit her in the head.

* * *

When Gilda awoke, the school was silent. Her head ached and a kink pinched her neck. She sat up slowly trying to figure out what happened. Someone was in the school and had knocked her out. But who?

Dizzy, she kept one hand on the desk as she stood and flipped the light switch. Something lay on the mats in the dojo. At first, she squinted for a better look, then shuffled to the other light switches.

Beneath the shrine in the dojo, Erik lay face down with several small objects on his back. Ninja throwing stars. The ones they used in class were rubber. These were shiny. Someone found a real six-pointed set and honed them. Blood surrounded each point in Erik's back.

She gagged, falling to her hands and knees as she began to hyperventilate. Thayer lock her up this time and solder the door shut.

Gilda took several deep breaths as she crawled to her desk. Once the threat of vomiting passed, she dialed 9-1-1. "Marion, it's Gilda. Send Thayer to the karate school."

"Gilda? What happened?"

"Erik's... Injured." She fought back tears. "I need the police and an ambulance."

"Is he bleeding or having trouble breathing?" Marion asked, her voice calm.

"I don't know. I just came to. I haven't checked." Gilda pulled herself up onto her chair and rubbed the back of her head.

"Just came to?" Her voice raised. "Are you okay, girl? Because I'll come down there and straighten those—"

"Hurry. Please. He's bleeding and not moving."

"Is there anyone else there?"

"No, I think I'm alone. Aside from Erik."

"You think you're alone?" Marion asked. "Do you need a lawyer?"

"Not yet," she said. "If you know a good one, keep him on speed dial. Just in case."

Gilda hung up before Marion could tell her to stay on the line. Her next call was to Mick, who sounded winded.

"Please tell me there's a water leak or the printer's out of ink," he said.

"I think Erik's dead," she whispered.

"I'll be right there."

She steeled herself to peer over her desk. Where Walter's death was so violent, Erik's seemed more like a sneak attack. Like someone threw the ninja stars from behind and ambushed him.

Gilda crept into the dojo, careful not to touch anything. Erik's back was riddled with ten metal stars. Whoever threw them had deadly aim. Were the small weapons alone enough to kill him?

Thayer edged around the dojo door and called out, "Gilda? Are you in here?"

Startled, she joined him in the front lobby, the scent of greasy fries doused in cider vinegar and salt stung her nostrils. "That didn't take long."

"I was next door grabbing lunch." He set a paper bag on her desk. "You hungry?"

She glanced toward Erik. "Not really."

"Good. Keep this safe for me." He motioned toward the bag.

"That's not my job." She rolled her neck, and rubbed her head.

Thayer examined the crime scene from various angles before he borrowed a piece of paper. Gilda followed him back into the dojo to hover nearby while he used the paper to test the blades. The sheet sliced cleanly, and a thin layer of liquid soaked into it.

"Is that poison?" Gilda asked. "I didn't think the ninja stars alone would kill him. There's not enough blood."

"May I remind you that I'm the cop and you shouldn't even be near the crime scene?" He stood and put his hands on his hips. "I solve the mystery. You sit behind your desk and call your students. Classes are cancelled until further notice."

"I don't think you get a say in what I think or do. In case you've forgotten, you lost that privilege a long time ago." She wanted to say more, but another glimpse of Erik put things into perspective. Arguing was pointless and petty.

"Still clinging to that grudge, are you? Maybe I should just haul you down to the station now to do a complete background check." He waved the other investigators over and motioned to the body. "Check the whole building for clues. Different MO, but we could be looking for the same killer. I'll call Fabio. You call Mick."

"Already done," she said. "At least one of us is good at our job."

In the lobby, Mick leaned against her desk. He waved a cardboard tray full of French fries. "Thayer getting on your nerves?"

"No more than usual." She grabbed a fry and jabbed it in the glob of ketchup without thinking, then looked at it. Too much like blood. She lost her appetite. "Sorry."

Mick ate it. "You okay, Sherlock?"

"Not as good as you." She turned her focus to straightening her tidy desk, not Erik.

"My thoughts exactly. You don't seem shaken up over Erik's death." Thayer approached the desk, then frowned. "Is that my lunch?"

"Was it in the brown bag on Gilda's desk?" Mick asked.

"You know it was," Thayer replied.

"In my defense, Officer, I thought it was hers."

Thayer flared his nostrils. "That's Detective. Since when do you two share lunch?"

"We share a lot of things you don't know about," Mick told him.

Gilda's face burned as she caught a whiff of alcohol.

Thayer grabbed the cardboard tray.

Erik was dead in the next room. She had no idea how the two men could even think about eating. She sat behind her desk and sighed.

"When did you last see Erik?" Thayer asked.

Gilda turned on the computer and rubbed her face with both hands. Let the police search for clues. She was done meddling. All she wanted was to go home. Two bodies and a whack on the head was more than enough for her.

"He was at the staff meeting," Mick said.

"What did you discuss at this staff meeting?" Thayer asked.

Mick sat beside Gilda and rested his feet on the desktop. "We asked Gilda to stop playing detective before she got hurt. When I left, she and Razi were still here. Thursday we held classes as usual. Minus Walter."

"I told you that when you interrogated me in my garden yesterday." Mick frowned. "He did?"

"He even walked me to work and followed me home last night."

"That was nice of you," Mick said. "I'm amazed you didn't give her a ride in your cruiser to waste even more taxpayer money."

Fries and all, Thayer snorted and returned to the dojo.

Mick's jaw tensed. For a brief second, Gilda was sure he'd throw something. Instead, he dug out a ten-dollar bill. "Can you go pick up coffee and muffins? My treat."

"What's the catch?" She narrowed her eyes.

"I plan to yell at Thayer to get out of my dojo with his munchies," he said. "By the way, stop at the police station and file a harassment charge against him. He's also mishandling the investigation."

She shook her head, which made little stars shoot across her vision. "He'll just say the harassment is because of the murders since we're all suspects."

Mick chuckled. "Thayer already cleared you. He thinks you're a ditz."

"He does not." Gilda took the ten. "I'll get coffee and muffins, but I'm not laying false charges against anyone."

"If the guy's bothering you, you need to cut him down to size. While you're at it, tell him to lay off me too. He's had some guy in a black car tailing me all over town."

She rolled her eyes. "That's Gary del Garda, and you need to talk to him before he breaks your kneecaps."

As she left the school, Thayer yelled, "Hey, you can't leave. I have more questions."

Gilda kept walking, her head spinning. She hoped Mick would back her up. Ducking into Café Beanz, she was grateful for the air-conditioning and the aroma of freshly ground coffee. Comfort food. "Two large Jamaican Blue and two chocolate banana muffins, please."

The barista set two large paper coffee cups on the counter. "Wow. I can't believe you're having coffee so soon after your latte. Must be a tough morning."

"More than you know." She'd completely forgotten about her vanilla bean latte.

"Oh, honey, everyone loves you and Mick," the barista handed her a bag containing the two muffins. "Give me one good reason your students won't go back."

Two dead bodies and a serial killer might do it.

"You're right." Gilda took the coffees and added milk and sugars. The smell of coffee made her gag. She needed to drop off Mick's food, then go home and rest. She started to wonder if she had a concussion.

The police station stood right across the street from the coffee shop. If she stopped, their coffees would get cold. A plausible excuse. So was the nausea and the sudden yearning to sleep on a beach in Tahiti. Far, far away from the school, Thayer, and Mick.

Maybe Doc would give her a note to excuse her from work for the rest of her life. Nah, too drastic.

Thayer opened the front door and grabbed the coffee she'd fixed for Mick. "Ah, payback can be sweet."

She was about to stop him but reconsidered. Thayer drank his coffee black. Mick took enough sugar and milk to make her whole body vibrate for an hour and a half. If nothing else, Thayer's attempt at retribution was good for a laugh.

He stood in front of the desk to make sure Mick was watching before he took a huge mouthful. Then, he spit it all over the desk and floor before asking, "What's in that?"

Mick howled as he took the cup and pried off the lid. "Double milk, triple sugar. Good job, Gilda. That was even better than my idea. You're not the sharpest dart in the board, are you, Thayer?"

Thayer huffed before he disappeared down the hallway talking to the investigators who'd arrived while she was gone. "You people are sick."

Gilda handed the bag to Mick. "Chocolate chip banana. Your favorite."

"Ah, you know me well. You're the best, Sherlock," he said, then frowned. "Are you okay? You look kind of pale, and your eyes are—"

"I'm fine. It was the whack on the head." Or finding Erik's body. Or the lack of sleep. "What are the odds are of getting Thayer to clean up his mess?"

Mick snorted. "About the same as getting me to do it."

"Slim to none then." Gilda sat and tried to draft an e-mail to the students. Her eyes ached and she wanted to vomit. The more she typed, the worse she felt. "No classes until Monday. I'm starting to hate Fridays." She wiped away a tear. "By the way, I won't be here next Friday. Or any Friday after that."

He patted her hand, leaving behind a dab of chocolate. "I agree. We should close on Fridays from now on."

"I'll send an e-mail, then go home." More tears overwhelmed her before she had a chance to stop them. She buried her face in her hands.

"Sherlock?" Mick's chair squawked. "Hey, honey, are you okay?"

"No." She gasped for air as the walls seemed to close in.

He pulled her close, cradling the back of her head in his hand. "Come on, babe. You probably need a good cry. Believe me, I get it, but Thayer will see it as a sign of weakness. He'll think you have something to hide."

"But I don't."

"G splash your face with cold water. I'll keep him busy."

Gilda was back to being just one of the guys. She wiped her face with the back of one hand and staggered around the investigators to go splash her face with cold water. Mick was right Thayer would pounce on her weaknesses in front of everyone. There was no way to hide her red, puffy eyes.

She returned to see Mick at the keyboard typing a single letter at a time. He concentrated so hard that she was surprised his tongue didn't stick out of one corner of his mouth.

"What are you doing?" she asked.

"Trying to help, but it'll take me until Christmas to get this done. I don't exactly have your typing skills." He moved out of her chair.

"That's not good considering it's July."

She was almost done when Mick cleared his throat and said, "Brace yourself. Here comes the pretty boy."

She finished the e-mail and hit send. "I'm going home.."

"Tell him to take a flying leap, then leave," Mick told her, then grinned. "Better yet, let me tell him."

When Gilda stood, her vision dimmed as the room spun. "I'm leaving."

"Wait a minute. I need—" a voice said.

"Are you okay?" a louder voice asked, breaking into the conversation like a sledgehammer. Marion grabbed her by the upper arms. "Honey, you look awful."

"Somebody knocked me out."

Marion ran a hand over Gilda's scalp. "Wow, that thing's bigger than Thayer's entire brain. Did one of these clowns call you an ambulance?"

Both men stammered.

"Honey, you need a bodyguard before one of these morons gets you killed."

Mick's mouth opened before he sighed.

"You're hired," Gilda said. "I'm going home to take a nap."

"Oh no you're not. You're pale and in shock and I'm taking you to the hospital," Marion insisted.

Thayer walked out of the dojo. "Who's going to the hospital?"

"Gilda has a concussion and needs medical attention."

"She seemed fine, considering everything," Mick said. "I'll take her to the hospital."

Thayer shook his head. "She's my witness."

"You're conducting an investigation and can't leave."

"And you have to stay to lock up the school when we're done."

"Oh, pack away the testosterone." Marion snapped. "You two are pathetic. Step aside, boys, this girl needs a doctor, and you two are doing everything but pulling out your winkies to measure them."

"I'll send an officer to escort you." Thayer moved aside.

When Mick blocked their exit, Marion growled. "I'll take care of my best friend. You keep Thayer out of trouble."

"Thanks, Marion," Mick said, moving out of their way.

"I'm not doing this for you. I'm tired of seeing this girl get hurt by you—"

"Winkies?" Gilda asked.

"That fits. Let's go."

At the hospital, Gilda found herself surrounded by more doctors and nurses than necessary. Apparently, she was a local celebrity after finding two bodies in the span of a week. The lump on her head got full attention, as did the fading bruises on her face. Everyone reiterated that she needed a better hobby. She was in and out of the emergency room in record time.

Marion was leading Gilda to the front exit when they heard yelling in the waiting area.

"Where is she?" Thayer yelled.

"I'm here to take Gilda Wright home," Mick demanded, not much calmer than Thayer. "She's my employee. I need to make sure she's okay."

"What kind of boss doesn't even call for an ambulance for an injured employee?"

"You saw her before me."

"You sent her out for coffee."

Mick's next words were muffled, until Thayer yelled, "Get out of my way before I have you arrested."

Gilda groaned. "Why can't they just leave me alone?"

Marion left Gilda in the care of a nurse then stormed down the hallway and bellowed, "Both of you leave that poor girl alone. She has a serious, life-threatening concussion."

"I do?" Gilda asked.

The nurse led her into a small examination room when the voices grew louder. "Not really. It's minor, but you still need to take it easy for a while. You're better off staying here for a minute. I'll get rid of them, so Marion can take you home."

Gilda sat and closed her eyes, her hands trembling in her lap. What was wrong with those two? Two men were dead, and Mick and Thayer were arguing like kindergarten kids with a frog. Life was much better when she could walk through her day without anyone noticing her.

Marion returned ranting about what she'd love to do to either of them if she ever bumped into them in a dark alley. She closed the door and lowered her voice to a whisper, "Sorry about that, hon. No more men. No more bodies. Just peace and quiet for the rest of the day. We can watch sappy movies, eat junk food, and put our feet up."

"Sounds perfect."

Rather than take her out a back exit, Marion marched Gilda straight out the front door. "Those two aren't smart, but they are devious."

As they drove out of the hospital parking lot, Gilda spotted Mick and Thayer near the rear exit of the emergency room. "How did you know they'd be there?"

"My sister's the one who put you in that little room," she said. "She's got our backs."

Gilda smiled. "You know they'll figure out we left and bang on my door."

"And by then you'll be settled on your couch with a big mug of tea and popcorn." She pulled in front of Gilda's house. "What did you ever see in Thayer anyway? I get if have the hots for Mick, I'd get it, but Thayer?"

"He was different in high school. Sweet and athletic. After he went into the police force, he came back a total jerk."

"That's rough." Marion forced her to sit on the couch with a blanket, then went to make a pot of tea. "What's going on with Mick and Chloe? Are they together or not?"

Mick was like Peter Pan, never wanting to grow up, rarely taking responsibility, and hardly noticing anyone else. Deep inside, he had a serious side that most people rarely. Lately, she'd seen glimpses.

Gilda eased off the couch to check the doors and windows. Satisfied no one else could get inside without attracting attention, she returned to the couch and snuggled up with the blanket. "They won't last. They argue when they're in the same room. Last week, he told her not to come to the school anymore."

"I heard Erik had throwing stars in his back. Good all you got was a mild concussion." Marion handed her a steaming mug and curled up at the other end of the couch. She turned on the television and flipped channels until she found *Casablanca*. "Any idea who knocked you out?"

"I don't know. I didn't see anyone." While she inhaled the soothing scent of chamomile, Humphrey Bogart drank and played a game of chess in Rick's Café Américain. "Whoever was there was as quiet as a cat. Ninja-like."

"Poor Erik. Nobody deserves that, not even him."

"What do you mean?" Gilda asked, as she nestled into the cushions.

"That boy's been in trouble his whole life. I thought Yoshida and Mick had finally straightened him out. Last I heard, he was opening his own school."

That fit with what Gilda heard. She didn't realize the whole town already knew. "Do you know where?"

Marion sipped her tea. "He told one of the tellers at the bank that he'd rented an old store in Fort Erie. His daddy and step-mama moved there three years ago. I guess he figured he'd live in their basement until business picked up, but his step-mama nixed that. He had to find his own place."

First Walter, now Erik. Gilda set her cup aside. Someone had a serious grudge against the black belts of Yoshida Martial Arts.

How long would it be before the next one fell?

* * *

After Marion left the next morning to get some sleep, Gilda paced the living room, then rechecked every door and window. Her head hurt and she was exhausted, but she was tired of feeling caged. She checked the time, then headed for Happy Harvey's Hangover Hut in search of a friend.

Happy threw his arms open wide when he saw her. "Gilda! *Senti tanto a sua falta*. You hardly ever come in since you broke up with that cop, yet suddenly you here twice in week. I am blessed. You look pale and tired, *amiga*."

When he pulled her close, the scents of stale coffee and Doritos surrounded her. She allowed herself to relax as she took comfort from her friend. Thayer was the least of her concerns.

"I've missed you," Gilda told him. "I thought I'd pick up a bottle of wine for later."

Happy raised his eyebrows. "Big trouble in Little Japan school? Mick getting out of hand. You get job somewhere else. Here, maybe."

She swallowed hard, relieved the store was still empty. "It's been trying, but it's nothing to do with Mick." Well, not entirely, anyway.

"Ah. Walter." He hugged her hard again. "I am sorry, *amiga*. His death was bad. Did students come back after funeral?"

"They started to." Her chin quivered.

He dragged her behind the counter and forced her onto a stool. "*Mi amiga*, sit. What happened?"

"Erik." She burst into tears.

"I never liked that one. What that two-faced *parasita* do?"

She sobbed as she reached for a tissue. "Someone killed him."

"*Santa Maria mãe de Deus!*" Happy pulled her off the stool, sat down, and wiped his brow. "That poor *parasita*. He was killed at the school, like Walter?"

"When I went into work, someone hit me from behind. When I woke up, Erik was dead." She blinked away tears. "Happy, I swear that place is cursed."

Happy crossed himself, then scurried around the counter and returned with a cardboard carton that held four small bottles. "Any more than this, you get out of control and do stupid things, *amiga*. You take, have bubble bath and next week, come to me for work. I treat you right. No murders or crazy stuff. Better money."

"Thanks, Happy. I'll think about it." Gilda reached for her wallet.

He waved a hand before sticking it in a paper bag. "You take. A *presente*. Get a new life before that place ruins you."

Gilda should've gone for coffee and breakfast. Instead, she wandered down the beach to the large driftwood tree and sat down to crack open a mini-bar sized bottle. "Here's to you, Walter. Hope things are much better where you are."

"Honor," she whispered before drinking the small bottle.

Why couldn't she shake the thought of the kanji and the missing scroll? If the killer followed the pattern of the four possessions, Erik's death would be over "Integrity." Walter had dishonored his first wife and kids. What had Erik done?

No time for silly, sappy thoughts. She cracked the second bottle of pinot grigio open. "Erik, I have a feeling you're in a much warmer place than Sandstone Cove. I hope you're happier there."

Once she'd guzzled the second bottle, she sat back, nearly falling right off the log as the alcohol quickly numbed her. "Honor." "Integrity". HI.

"Hi." She giggled as the alcohol kicked in, then glanced into the bag. Two bottles. Two kanji. Three black belts. Only one receptionist.

Gilda slid onto the sand and sat against the log to think. She'd already discovered two bodies. This time, the killer could've included her in his spree this time. He had an opportunity to strangle her or worse while she was unconscious, but hadn't. Were the deaths about the black belts and the kanji, or had Gilda missed the motive altogether?

As tourists began to flood the beach, Gilda wandered home along the trail that followed Lake Erie's coast. Once home, she put on the stereo, cranked the volume, and tucked the remaining two wine bottles in the fridge. A distraction was in order. After locking the front door, she checked the windows again before she sauntered into the bathroom.

Immersed in warm water and bubbles, her mind traveled worlds away from Sandstone Cove. As she sank beneath the bubbles, she daydreamed of a tropical beach with a cabana and a scantily clad man. For the first time all week, the school and black belts took a back seat.

A doorbell rang somewhere in the distance.

"Go away," she mouthed.

A few seconds later, the doorbell rang again.

Just as Gilda relaxed again, a loud bang rattled the house. The bathroom door rattled. She floundered in the water as heavy footsteps stomped across the hardwood.

"Where are you?" a man bellowed.

How on earth did he get inside? Her heart knocked at her ribs. She'd locked all the doors save one. The bathroom.

When the bathroom door flew open, she sank as much of her naked body beneath the bubbles as possible. Pulling the curtain closed, Gilda peered around the pink fabric as Mick wavered in the doorway.

"What are you doing here?" she shouted.

"Oh, geez. You're okay. When you didn't answer your phone, or the door, I got scared."

"I needed some peace and quiet."

He turned slightly but didn't leave when he said, "I called a dozen times and rang your doorbell. What were you doing?"

Gilda raised a handful of bubbles. "Taking a bath. Now get out of my house!"

"I can't. Not with you in the tub." He hesitated, then added, "Especially since I broke down your front door."

"You what?" she gasped.

His gazed returned to the tub—to her—and he flashed a sheepish grin. "I got worried when you didn't answer. I knocked first, then I got scared you were dead, so I kicked down the door."

Dread filled her stomach as Gilda closed her eyes. "You mean you kicked it in."

"Nope," Mick said. "It's lying on the floor."

. "Have you been drinking?" she asked.

"A little. We all have lately."

Guilty. Gilda hid behind the curtain. "Why don't you go home and sober up? We'll talk later."

He sat on the toilet lid, dropping his face into his hands. "I don't have a home."

"Sure, you do. You have a condo on Balsam Avenue."

"Sort of," Mick said. "Chloe move in, changed the locks, and forgot to give me a key. I've been sleeping at the school for the past few days." He looked dejected enough for her to believe him. "I guess I should've known better."

"I don't know what to say," Gilda told him.

She reached for the towel on the rod and missed by inches. On her second attempt, she leaned over the edge of the tub onto the shower curtain and pulled down the rod and all. The fabric draped over her, covering her backside, while the rod clunked her on top of her lump from Erik's killer. Her vision sparkled with tiny stars and the sharp pain made her cry out.

Mick lunged to pull the rod away. "Geez, Gilda, are you okay? Keep it up and you're going to take yourself out."

When he started to lay the curtain and rod on the floor next to the tub, she grabbed the fabric for cover. Her face grew hot, and a rush of pain pulsed through her head.

"I'm fine. Can you please get out of my bathroom? I need to get dressed.""

"You know, I thought it was a fluke when Walter got killed," he said, staring at her over the fallen curtain but didn't seem to see her. "Now Erik's dead too and I could be next. I need your help, Sherlock."

She shifted the wet curtain to cover her nakedness as she sat up. "Why don't you go make a pot of tea while I get dressed? Then we'll talk."

"Okay." Mick stood, then groaned. "I should try to stand your door back up. I seriously knocked it to the floor. I'll get someone to fix it tomorrow."

Except for the throbbing pain in her head, she was it was all a bad dream. Was it possible she was still unconscious and never found Erik? Wishful thinking.

Gilda sighed. Fixing her door couldn't wait. "Can you at least pass me a towel?"

That was when he suddenly realized she was naked. He paused to take in the sight of her beneath the flimsy shower curtain. The surge of energy coming off his body could've reheated the water in the bathtub as he grinned and said, "You look good wrapped in plastic. Kind of like a microwave dinner."

He tossed her a towel, then closed the door behind him when he left.

"Jerk." Gilda got out of the tub, wrapped the towel around her, and locked the door. For all the good it would do. Twice in one week, Mick had arrived at her house inebriated.

She peered out the bathroom door and was met by silence. When she crept down the hall and peered around the corner, she realized Mick had passed out on the couch. The front door lay on the floor, just as he said. She picked up her phone and called for reinforcements.

The safest person to call was Razi, who appeared on the front step ten minutes later and asked, "Shall I take Sensei Mick home?"

Gilda almost said yes, then shook her head. "Let him to sleep it off here. Apparently, he has nowhere to go. He's relatively safe here. Could you help fix my door?"

"Do you have a hammer and a screwdriver? I can do a temporary fix, enough to keep the skunks out. I recommend calling a professional."

"Thanks. I'm sure Mick's snoring will keep the bad guys away for tonight."

Razi's eyebrows squished together. "Which bad guys? The killer or the other ones who are after him?"

She dropped into the lumpy wicker chair. "What other ones?"

"My mistake," he said, his face darkening.

"No mistake. What other guys? Who's after him?"

"Sensei Mick likes to make money, but he also likes to..." He paused. "What are the words he used? Bet on the ponies. He introduced me to Gary at the sports bar."

Her stomach churned. Gary again. "Mick gambles?"

Razi shifted his weight and leaned on the wooden porch railing. "Only occasionally. He lost a horse race and now owes fifty thousand dollars."

"Fifty thousand?" She stared. No wonder Gary was stalking him.

"Now he is worried they will break his legs." He fidgeted with a set of keys. "What is worse is that he is Chloe's father, and I believe Sensei Mick called him a grandfather."

"Chloe's pregnant?" she gasped.

"No." He shook his head. "Gary is a gangster."

"Oh, you mean a godfather." The weight of the words struck her, and she buried her face in her hands. "Oh, crap. Mick, what have you gotten us all into?"

"Please, do not tell him I told you. He already has enough problems with the school."

Gilda frowned. "Erik was murdered."

"I am aware." Razi nodded. "Sensei Mick called when you left. When I told him I saw you leave Happy Harvey's Hangover Hut, he was not happy."

"When did he have time to get so drunk?" she asked.

"He started to keep a bottle of scotch in his desk after Chloe came back. He must have opened it."

Scotch in his desk? "Why?"

"Walter. Erik. I do not think he was very happy about your life being in peril for a second time. He considered firing you."

"Firing me? I didn't do anything.?"

Razi turned away. "He does not want you to be harmed. I should fix your door, so you can lock it."

She led him to the kitchen, then rifled through a drawer. "Does Mick think the murders have something to do with his gambling?"

"Mostly, he believes it is some demented psychopath."

"That sounds right." Gilda handed him the tools, then followed him past Mick snoring on the couch. "Razi, did you notice anything missing after Walter's death?"

"Of course. The photograph of Shihan Yoshida and Sensei Mick that used to hang in the front hall."

She hadn't even noticed that. "Huh. Anything else?"

As he lifted the door into place, he told her, "Yes. The scroll of the Four Possessions of the Samurai that was in the change room. We all have one just like it. They were gifts from Sensei Mick when we received our black belts, just as he received his from Shihan Yoshida."

So much for narrowing down her suspect list. At least she knew where the Four Possessions came in. But why?

CHAPTER 16

As the morning sun peeked through the windows, Gilda glared at Mick, who slept peacefully on her couch. How dare he snore, blissfully unaware of her restless night, despite her exhaustion, or of her damaged front door?

She stomped past him and grasped the doorknob. As soon as she pulled, the top hinge popped off, so the door hung off kilter by only the bottom hinge. She leaned the sagging door against the wall before sitting on the front step to sip her coffee and simmer.

How could Mick bring such unsavory characters into her life? Into all their lives. It was like he had no idea his vices would put his students in danger.

Did Gary del Garda have anything to do with the deaths of the instructors? She supposed it was possible. He had told her he only wanted to talk to Mick but...

After a deep sigh, she finished the last of her coffee. There was a full pot in the kitchen, but getting more required walking past Mick. After all the horrific thoughts she'd subjected herself to all night, she didn't trust herself near him. Not when she had an urge to hold a pillow over his face.

Inside the house, a door closed. Mick was no longer on the couch. A few minutes later he strolled into the kitchen, then stepped out onto the porch with two cups of coffee and a frown.

"I think I owe you an explanation," he said.

"You owe me a lot more than that, pal," she told him. "A new door, for one."

He sat next to her. "Thanks for not smothering me with a pillow."

"The thought was there." She took the fresh cup, setting her empty one aside.

"By the way, I'm sorry about the door. Who fixed it?"

Gilda wrapped her hands around her mug. "Razi. He wanted to make sure it kept out the rest of the skunks. One of the hinges came off when I opened it."

"I know a guy who can fix that." Mick pulled out his phone.

"From what I hear, you know a lot of guys," she snapped. "Unfortunately, some of them kill people."

He yawned and rubbed his jaw before asking, "Where'd you hear that?"

"Razi told me you bet on the horses and lost."

He snorted. "For being the strong, silent type, he can be a real blabbermouth. Look, Gilda, I can explain."

She shook her head. "Of course you can. Don't bother. You know, I took the job at Yoshida's because it seemed like a safe place to work. I like learning how to defend myself, but two instructors are dead, you got drunk and kicked down my front door, and I got conked over the head walking into work. I don't want to know what you're involved in, but it needs to stop before…"

"Are you trying to tell me you quit?"

"Yeah."

He ran a hand through his hair. "Look, I know it seems like I don't appreciate you sometimes, but I don't know what I'd do without you."

"Sometimes? When Walter died, you left me to deal with the police. When Erik died, you sent me to get coffee, even though I had a concussion."

"You make it sound way worse than it was."

"Really? Here I thought I was sugar-coating things." Gilda took a deep breath and fought hard not to yell at him. "You need to leave."

"We should talk about this."

"I don't want to talk anymore." She stood, her hands shaking. "I need someone to fix my door. Don't be here when I come back out."

Mick followed her into the kitchen. When she reached for her phone, he placed his hand on hers. "Give me a chance to explain."

"You've had a week to explain, and to help deal with the aftermath," she reminded him. "Instead, you blew fifty grand gambling and got kicked out of your condo by some psycho chick you let move in. Now we're both being stalked by her father."

"Are you done? I've got something I want to say."

She tried to pull her hand away, but he tightened his grip. Finally, she sighed. "Say your piece then get out of my house."

"What do you mean Gary's stalking both of us?" he asked.

A couple weeks ago, she would've savored his nearness. "He's been following you, yet I'm the one he talks to. You need to deal with him before I have a nervous breakdown, or he does something stupid to you."

"You're worried about me?"

"No, I'm mad at you for knocking down my front door. Now get out."

He grasped her by the upper arms and gazed into her eyes. Warmth spread up her arms and left her breathless. "Gilda, I love you."

"No!" She recoiled, then kneed him in the groin.

That was the one reaction Mick wasn't prepared for. He gasped and collapsed against the cupboard. "What was that for?"

"Get out." Her voice crackled. Tears spilled down her cheeks as she grabbed her phone and walked around him.

"We're not done with this," Mick told her as he stood as upright as possible. "Once we know who killed Walter and Erik, all bets are off."

"For all I know, you killed them and I'm next," he retorted.

"And for all I know, you killed them and I'm next."

Checkmate. Her heart seemed to sink into her stomach. Once he'd gone, Gilda let the tears fall in a torrent. She couldn't even slam the door behind him. How dare he play on her emotions like that?

By the time the repairman showed up, she was drained. The man took one look at she and her door and assured her he'd call the police. She managed to convince him everything was a misunderstanding, then she sat to make a list of the Four Possessions.

Someone had tucked "Honor" in Walter's breast pocket at his funeral. In the week since, she'd discovered he was far from honorable. As a schoolteacher, he'd had an affair with a much younger student that he eventually married, then cheated on regularly. As Happy always said, "A leopard doesn't change its stripes."

"Integrity." Erik, now dead and awaiting burial, had none. Planning to start his own karate school without his sensei's back—plus paying a healthy residual—was a definite no-no. Mick should have kicked him out long ago and probably would've if Erik hadn't turned up riddled with honed and poisoned ninja stars.

When she came to "Loyalty," she paused.

She'd assumed the killer was after the four instructors but what if Mick was right. Was he also a target? He was positive both Xavier and Chloe tried to poison him. If there was one thing Mick had issues with, it was loyalty. Not only with his girlfriends, but with his students in general.

Xavier's loyalties were also questionable after bringing poisoned coffee to her and Mick. Other than that, she didn't know much about him.

Nauseous, Gilda pushed her pad of paper away when she realized her stomach was growling. The clock read one, and the air grew thick with humidity. The deli was four blocks away. She could get there and back before the rain fell. Since Mick was currently living at the school, it was off-limits. She shoved the notepad into a drawer, paid the repairman, and locked door behind her.

The streets were quiet save a loud crack of a bat and the roar of a crowd. Most people were either already at home, the beach, or the baseball diamond a couple blocks over. Gilda ordered a thick ham and cheese sandwich with a side of sour pickles and a diet cola, then sauntered home and opened the front gate.

When she reached back to close it, a hand grabbed hers. She sucked in a sharp breath, spinning around and stepping away, ready to use her self-defense techniques. Razi probably wouldn't even notice if she did hit him.

"What do you want?" she asked.

"We need to talk, Miss Wright." The tone of his voice made her knees threaten to buckle. He was the one member of the school she knew little about and had talked to even less until recently. "I would like a few moments of your time."

"What's going on?"

He glanced around them. "Could we step inside? I wish to discuss Walter and Erik."

She closed the gate, feeling the need to put distance and a solid object between them. "We can talk right here."

"After all I have done, you do not trust me?"

She closed her eyes and sighed. "I'm sorry. Razi, for all I know, you're a serial killer and I'm next."

"In my own defense, you could also be the killer. Could we sit in a public place? You can enjoy your lunch while I talk."

"We can sit on the front porch."

He followed her up the steps and sat on the bench that doubled as her table. "I am sorry you are afraid of me."

She set her food down and offered him a pickle. "None of us knows who to trust anymore. I'd never even seen a body before last Friday."

"It is not an experience I wish to repeat either," he said. "I am trained to kill, Miss Wright. I could snap your neck and make it look like you fell asleep."

"Thanks for the heads-up." She had a dozen questions, but held her tongue.

"I have no reason to harm you. I want to help. Walter knew about something about my past I would rather keep private. He asked for money to not tell Sensei Mick."

"Walter blackmailed you because you were a soldier?" she asked.

"He tried to blackmail me, but not because I was a soldier. Because of something I did that forced me to leave everything important behind." Razi gazed toward the street. "I did not play his game. I have kept no secrets from Sensei Mick."

Curious, Gilda offered him a cup of tea. "I have cookies in the freezer."

"Thank you, but I must go," Razi said as he stood. "Would you like to know what I told Sensei Mick?"

She wiped her hands as she thought, then asked, "Did you kill Walter or Erik?"

"No, Miss Wright," he said without flinching. "I swear on my life."

"Then I guess it doesn't matter, does it?"

"It does not. Thank you." He smiled, then left her in peace.

Relief washed over Gilda, but the question remained: Who killed Walter and Erik?

She did yoga, then curled up with a novel, hoping to take her mind off things, even for a short time. In the back of her mind, she replayed the events and relived the fear of learning she wasn't alone in the school.

What had she missed?

Absorbed in her novel, she'd read nearly half before Mick called late that afternoon. "Why aren't you at work? When I got here, you were gone."

She stared at her candle and fought to keep her breath even. "I was never there."

"When Walter died, you were always here. What changed?"

"You're a jerk." Gilda hung up, then set her book aside and stormed into the kitchen. After tearing apart an entire head of lettuce with her fingers, she was almost calm by the time Mick phoned back.

"What do you want?" she asked.

He sighed. "I'm sorry. You're right. Yesterday was rough for all of us."

"I told everyone not to come back until after Erik's funeral."

His tension was palpable even over the phone. Having no classes was financial suicide. Finally, he told her, "I'll check the messages and e-mails then we can get things back on track."

"How? In case you missed the newsflash, we've lost two instructors in the past week. They were murdered, Mick. Someone killed them in the school."

"I get it, Gilda."

"No, I don't think you do." She hacked a tomato in half. "None of this is random. Someone's targeting our school. Our staff. Either one of us could be next."

"Not you," he said softly.

"Why not me? Aren't I important enough to kill?"

Mick chuckled. "All I'm saying is there seems to be a pattern. Remember that HILT thing? The four possessions?"

"How could I forget it? It's all I've thought about since Walter's funeral." Well, that and Mick kissing her in her kitchen. She attacked a miniature cucumber as though chopping it into fine pieces would make her feel better.

"Five black belts. Four kanji. Three black belts left. Two kanji. The odds are not in my favor, honey."

Her breath stuck in her chest. "Could Razi or Xavier be the killer?"

"I dunno. Gary's been nosing around. With his background, it's hard to say what he'd do." After a prolonged silence, he told her, "Watch your back and be careful who you talk to, Sherlock."

When he hung up, she stared at the fragments of lettuce and other assorted vegetables on the counter. Her appetite gone, she put them away for later, laced up her shoes, and headed out for a light run. Despite the afternoon heat, she was too restless to sit and fret.

How were they supposed to catch a killer and how was she supposed to know who to watch out for? Short of setting up surveillance cameras in the school.

When a dark sedan slowed beside her, Gilda gasped. She should've run through the park where no one would see her.

Gary leaned out the window. "You're one popular lady."

"What do you mean?" she asked.

"You've had several gentlemen callers lately."

She eyed the upcoming path to Ponderer's Point. The point was a dead end. On her side of the street, a dirt trail led to the riverside park. "What do you want?"

"I won't tell your mom. I just hope you're charging enough."

Outraged, Gilda stopped. "Are you calling me a prostitute?"

Gary chuckled. "You're creating a scene. Get in. We need to talk."

"Absolutely not," she told him, putting her hands on her hips. "Unless you know who killed Walter and Erik and have a mountain of evidence, I have nothing to say to you."

"You sound like your dad." Gary pulled his car into the lot at Ponderer's Point.

She closed her eyes and groaned. When he turned off the engine, her heart pounded. Did he know something or was she his next target?

She could run in the opposite direction and disappear into the maze of trails that crisscrossed Sandstone Cove. If she went home, she could barricade the doors and windows from the inside. She banished both thoughts before crossing the street, her curiosity more overwhelming than her fear.

Gary leaned against his car. "You're a lot like your dad, you know. More nosy than cautious. You even walk the same."

"I'm not here for a stroll down memory lane. What do you want?"

"What do you want to know?" He nodded toward the wooden boardwalk. "My legs are stiff. Walk with me."

Gilda stood her ground. "To the end of the Point? You're not planning to kill me and dump me in the surf, are you?"

Gary gave a deep laugh. "Honey, you're young, fit, and know karate. If we got into a fight, you'd have the upper hand."

"Unless you have a gun."

He held his hands out. "You want to search me?"

"No, thanks."

"That's probably for the best. From what I hear, people are already talking. No point giving them more fodder."

People like Thayer and Chloe. She blew out a breath. "What do you know about Mick and the karate school?"

As they walked toward the wooden boardwalk, Gary stuck his hands in his pockets and asked, "How long have you known Mick?"

"I thought this was your story, not mine."

"You're the boss," he said. "I've known Mick since he moved to town five years ago. He wanted to invest in Yoshida's school, but his money was in other investments."

"But he had the money?"

"Oh, yeah, he was good for it." Gary paused, then added, "Up until his wife left. He's not the kind of guy who'd blow a lot of cash on just anything."

"Except gambling on horses."

He chuckled. "That wasn't his doing, but I love making him sweat."

"What do you mean?"

"Five years ago, Mick asked to borrow money. Yoshida had set a deadline and refused to cut the kid slack. He came to me for a short-term loan."

"How short term?" She glanced around, dismayed there was no one else in sight. Gary could throw her in the lake, and no one would ever find her.

"Thirty days," he said. "Mick repaid the full amount plus interest in ten. I liked him from the start. He was smart, honest, and hated owing money."

"That's it? He borrowed money and repaid it. The end?"

"Hardly." Gary stopped to meet her gaze. "Yoshida never wanted a school in Sandstone Cove. Mick pushed to open the school near the beach. Once he had the money and found a building, Yoshida upped the ante. When he realized Mick's crazy idea would work, he wanted a bigger cut."

"And Mick went back to you for more money."

"Nope. He was smart enough to liquidate more than enough assets, so he could renovate and buy merchandise. The next time we met, it was by chance in a local bar. He joked about hiring a hit man to make Yoshida disappear."

Her breath stuck in her throat. Could Yoshida be the next victim? "Are you sure it was a joke?"

"When I made him an offer, he refused," Gary said. "That was four years ago."

"What if he changed his mind since? He and Yoshida have had some ugly run-ins lately."

"So, I've heard. Were there any attempts on Yoshida's life?"

"Not that I know of," Gilda told him. "How would I find out?"

He scratched the white stubble on his chin. "Maybe he filed a police report."

"Yoshida doesn't seem like the type to run to the police. He'd probably stew about it, then get revenge." Gilda sucked in a sharp breath.

"Seriously?" Gary took her arm as if he sensed the sudden weakness in her legs. They resumed their walk toward the Point. "Do you think he'd seek revenge on whoever wronged him? He'd have a lot to lose."

"It's more likely than him going to the police." Her head throbbed. "How well do you know Yoshida?"

He grimaced. "Well enough he strikes me as cold-blooded and greedy."

It was an accurate assessment as far as she was concerned. Yoshida frightened her, especially after her last class with him. Suddenly, he was putting in appearances at funerals. Mick had hosted dozens of events over the past two years, yet Yoshida remained distant. Now it was like he wanted to be seen. What had changed?

"Yoshida's been in town more lately, hasn't he?" Gary seemed to read her thoughts.

She raised her eyebrows. "Yeah. It's a bit unnerving."

"And you're wondering what he's up to."

Gilda shrugged him off. "The thought hadn't crossed my mind until now."

"He has a girlfriend."

"Jade Levy. So, I heard."

He chuckled. "Mick was right. You're shrewd."

"It was a guess. I've heard different rumors." She turned to let the wind blow the hair off her face. Billowing black storm clouds rolled across Lake Erie toward them. "When did you and Mick talk about me?"

"We bumped into each other at the café the other day and spent more time talking about you than anything else," he said. "We both have an interest in your personal well-being."

Gilda flinched. "I thought you would've talked about Chloe and Mick's debt."

"We did." Gary laughed. "Don't get me wrong, honey, business first. Mick heard rumors people have seen you and I together lately. I had to promise not to hurt you."

"He threatened you? Is he crazy?"

"Oh, he's something, but I'm not sure crazy's the right word," he said. "He cares a great deal about you."

"He's got a funny way of showing it," she told him. "The only person Mick Williams cares about is himself. As far as he's concerned, the whole world revolves around him and whatever he wants."

Gary picked up a stone and tossed it into the waves. "Maybe losing both Walter and Erik made him realize what's important."

"He told you that?" She pulled wisps of her hair out of her face again.

"That and much more, honey."

"How did you know about Yoshida and Jade?" She wasn't ready to hear about what Mick wanted. Not yet.

"You and I have a mutual friend," he said, scooping up another stone and clenching it in his fist as though he could make a diamond from it. "I hear Chloe stopped by to see you. What did she want?"

Gilda hesitated. "She warned me to stay away from you and Mick."

"Me?" He laughed. "Is she afraid you'll become her new stepmother? Let the girl worry. It'll do her good. She's all bark and no bite. She might carry my last name and my DNA, but that's all she's got."

"Good to know." Gilda picked up a flat, white stone and tossed the stone into the waves. "What else does your friend know about Yoshida?"

"The less I tell you, the safer you are," Gary said.

"Why's that?"

He handed her a business card that was blank except for a phone number. "Word is that you're under my protection. Anyone who lays a hand on you will be dealt with accordingly. That's my number. Put it in your phone and call me if you need anything."

Gilda's stomach sank as he strolled back to his car.

What would her father think to hear she was being protected by a bookie? Even worse, her mother would lose her mind when she found out.

Despite having her nerves rattled, Gilda did a slow jog across town and through the park to think then back to the beach. Slipping off her running shoes, she waded through the water to cool her feet before she padded home barefoot.

She wanted to call Marion and find out if she'd heard more about either murder. Odd how Marion was scarce since their trip to the hospital. They hadn't even talked about their weekly brunch at The Cove. Was she afraid Gilda was the killer?

"You don't listen very well, do you?" Thayer asked as he caught up to her on her way home. "I told you to stay away from Gary del Garda."

"If you're stalking me, you need a better hobby."

He opened her front gate, then followed her to the front steps. "I'm investigating two murders, and you happened to find both bodies. I'm not out of line to think you're involved."

Gilda shook her head. "I told you before. I never killed anyone."

"I know you didn't," Thayer said. "You couldn't hurt a bug."

She tossed her shoes near the front door and sat on the top step. No way was he getting into her house without a warrant. Not that she had anything to hide. It was more about making it clear where he stood.

"Then what do you want?" she asked.

He straightened his pale blue shirt. "Gary's a bookie and a convicted murderer, not to mention he's at least twice your age."

"I'm aware of that. "What's age got to do with anything?"

Thayer sat next to her and said, "You should date someone younger. Someone who would do anything for you."

"Like Mick or Razi?" she asked innocently.

His face reddened. "You and I had a great thing going. Maybe we should give it a second chance."

"You're a liar and a cheater who never thinks of anyone but himself," she told him, picking a giant rhododendron next to her.

"That's hurtful."

Gilda sniffed the blossom. "Hey, I've had to deal with the mess you left me for two years. I don't plan to make that mistake again. Go find someone who's happy to swallow your lies."

"There is no one else, sweetie," Thayer said as he reached for her hand. "You're the only girl I want in my life. You're sweet and honest."

"And a sucker. No, thanks. You can't have me, so suddenly I'm far more interesting than before." She tapped his face with the flower. "The answer's still no."

He lunged toward and planted a firm kiss on her lips. When he sat back with a grin, she shoved him into the rosebush behind him.

He thrashed amid thorns and a shower of red rose petals. "Get me out of here. This thing's trying to eat me."

"It's a rosebush. The worst it can do is prick you and draw blood," she told him. "You both have that in common."

Thayer crawled onto the walkway, leaving a trail of foliage. "You're a witch."

Gilda prepared to defend herself if he tried anything else. "Because I'm over you? At least you'll smell nice at the office."

"Funny." Thayer brushed petals and leaves off his clothes. The whole time, he cursed her and her garden.

"I'll tell Fabio to get you some rose dust, I don't want you getting bugs."

With one last curse, and a rude hand gesture that made her laugh, Thayer stormed away picking thorns out of his clothing.

Her gaze locked on Gary's sedan across the street. Gary howled, wiping tears from his eyes. At least she'd made his day.

After a quick shower, she made a protein shake before the doorbell rang. She scowled, not wanting to talk to anyone let alone get arrested for shoving Thayer earlier. Six rings later, curiosity got the best of her.

Xavier stood on the front step holding a bouquet of burgundy sunflowers, their faces drooped to the wooden floor. "I'm sorry. I never meant to kill you."

Gilda curled her fingers into a fist and prayed for the strength not to punch him "I could've died, you know."

"I never intended for anyone to die, which is why I used a small amount over a long time," he said.

She stared. "How long?"

"A couple weeks. I was mad at Mick and took it out on you. Not a smart move, considering you're Thayer's girlfriend."

"I'm not Thayer's anything," she told him.

Xavier frowned. "Weird. He's telling everyone in town you're back together and getting married on Ponderer's Point next summer."

She wanted to ask if he had any cyanide left. "I'm sure he got the point after I shoved him into a rosebush. Just how many times did you poison me?"

"Five." He stepped out of her reach. "I'm sorry. It was wrong and I feel like dog doo. If it helps, I turned myself in to the police."

Not sure how to react, she accepted the sunflowers and stammered, "Thanks, just... I just... Don't do it again."

"I won't. I promise." Xavier held up a pinky, then asked, "Did Thayer cheat on you?"

"Repeatedly." She sat on the top step.

"I should've poisoned him instead." Xavier sat next to her and nudged her with his elbow. "You deserve better."

Gilda was both flattered and repulsed at the same time.

"Doc lectured me until my ears burst into flames. Considering the minute dose, he said he'd tell Thayer to give me a misdemeanor assault charge or something."

"Did he?"

Xavier fidgeted with a red petal that lay on the step beside him. "So far Thayer hasn't mentioned it. Does that seem odd to you? I mean, I know he's focused on finding a murderer, but after what I did, I thought he'd lock me in a dungeon."

Gilda kicked away a broken twig. "Unless Thayer blew you and Doc off because nothing happened. I mean, technically, no one got sick or died, right?"

With two recent murders, the lack of police action did seem odd. Were Doc, Thayer, and Fabio focused on another suspect or did they consider the poisonings more evidence and were biding their time?

"I should go talk to Doc. I need to settle this before it festers."

Gilda patted his arm. "I'll talk to Doc. It was my coffee cup, after all. If you do it, he might think you actually want to go to jail."

"Jail's probably safer than the karate school right now," Xavier said. His face softened. "You'd do that for me? Even after what I did?"

"Yeah." Mostly to help figure out who murdered Walter and Erik. She hoped Xavier's attempted poisoning was a small piece of the problem.

He hugged her, then left.

Gilda remained on the front step absorbed in thought. Just like with Walter's murder, the front door of the school was locked. She'd used her key when she found Erik.

Logically, the killer must've locked the door to conduct the murder, then escaped after knocking her out. If someone did see the killer leave, it had to be a person witnesses were used to seeing coming and going. Unfortunately, only she and the instructors fell into that category.

CHAPTER 17

G ilda's work life invaded her dreams, and the black belts made special guest appearances. All of the wrongs. All of the secrets. A mountain of the lies that swirled into a suffocating fog. Walter. Erik. Xavier. Razi. Mick.

She sat and opened her eyes with her heart beating like she ran a marathon.

Mick said he loved her.

Her reaction was to knee him in the crotch and quit her job. She pulled her pillow over her face and groaned. Not her finest moment. He'd hold her to her word.

That meant she needed a new job, a new place to train, and new friends. Maybe even leave Sandstone Cove. Her other possibility was moving in with her mom.

Did Gary have a contact who could help her create a new identity and disappear?

The world didn't seem any brighter after a shower and breakfast. She slid on her sunglasses to take a walk before she began her job search and apartment hunt in Fort Erie. There was no way she wanted to live with her mom.

When she opened the front door, she froze. "What happened to you?"

Mick sat on the top step wearing the same clothes as the day before. He handed her a paper cup and averted his gaze. "You."

"You still think it's a bad idea for me to look for Walter and Erik's killer." She took the cup, hoping he needed her too much to add poison.

"I think it's a bad idea for you to team up with Thayer, for one."

Gilda sat next to him. "And for two?"

"I was serious," Mick told her. "I think I love you."

"You think you do?" Her heart seemed to hover in her chest, waiting breathlessly for a punch line. "Were you drinking again?"

"No. Once I sobered up, I threw out the rest of the scotch."

When the lid on Gilda's cup popped off and coffee splashed her hand, she relaxed her grip and refastened the lid. "What about you and Chloe?"

"Chloe placed a large bet with Gary on my behalf," he said. "She lost a ridiculous amount of money, then locked me out of my condo. She also posed as my wife to change my phone number."

"How could she do that?" Gilda resealed the cup lid. "Isn't that fraud?"

Mick smirked. "I'm cancelling the phone and selling the condo."

She raised her eyebrows. "Ooh, devious."

"Glad I could make you smile." His face softened as he took her hand. "Forget about her. Can we get back to the problem at hand?"

"Which one?"

"That I'm in love with you."

Her heart fluttered. How could she forget? She remembered from head to toe. "You're on the rebound, and it was the scotch talking."

"Maybe, except now it's morning and I'm sober." He entwined his fingers with hers. "You're the only one who's watched my back when I made a mistake, and have to pick up the pieces to start over."

"What is it you want?" she asked.

He met her gaze. "To be with you."

As much as she'd daydreamed about what that would be like, Gilda wasn't convinced. There were too many other things going on. "What if it doesn't work out? What if we can't stand each other? I'm not sure if I can work for you if—"

"I know." He picked a rose Thayer hadn't destroyed off the bush. "I'd be upset, too."

"Maybe for a minute."

"Show's what you know. I'd give up on women and become a monk."

Gilda laughed. "That I can't see."

"To be honest, me neither." Mick tucked the rose into her hair, then dropped his head onto her shoulder. "You're the only person I can count on, Sherlock."

"Even if you're still at the top of my suspect list?"

"Especially," he said. "You have no illusions about me, which is a good place to start considering."

"It's a lot to think about," she told him.

He gave her hand a squeeze. "I just wanted you to know I was serious. If you want to talk, you know where to find me."

Gilda frowned. "Where?"

"At the school. My clothes are in my car."

"The Ferrari?"

"Yup. It's still my car until Chloe gets her hands on the keys again, which she won't." He rocked his head from side to side like he had a stiff neck. "Do you get nervous when you go to the school? If I were you, I'd be a basket case."

"Why do you think I haven't been there since Erik died? I'll come in once classes restart to pick up my things."

"Rather than quit, why don't you take time off? I'll deal with things at the school. You deserve that much."

"I deserve a lot more," she muttered.

"Yes, you do." He gave her a hug. "Don't worry, babe. I'll make sure you get what you deserve."

What did he mean by that? Her stomach turned a somersault with a double twist.

While Gilda worked in the yard later, elbow deep in a blue hydrangea, one sentence coiled around her brain. She washed her hands, changed her shoes, then ran to the karate school. This time, front door was unlocked, and voices filled the lobby.

"I do not think you understand how serious this situation is," Yoshida shouted. "Someone stole thousands of dollars in merchandise. It could ruin my school."

Missing merchandise? Why hadn't anyone told her? She peered around the corner. The men were in Mick's office with the door ajar. She ducked behind her desk.

"It's my business, too. You said not to go to the police about the thefts, so I'm looking into it. What more do you want me to do?" Mick's anger was palpable.

"Get rid of that woman. There is no way one man did this alone."

"There's no proof anyone stole anything," Mick replied. "Besides, what would she have to gain?"

Yoshida snorted and his voice raised a full octave. "A job at his school. She is the only one here all the time who had access and I want her gone."

The she in question was Gilda. Her hands shook.

"She wasn't the only one with access. You and I have keys. All the black belts have keys." Mick's office door closed like he knew she was there.

If only she'd stopped to grab a coffee, Gilda would've missed hearing how much Yoshida doubted her. Hated her. No wonder he'd attacked her. There was no way Mick would let her go without a fight. Would he?

Not unless he was dead.

The odds of that had risen significantly in the past week. There were still two kanji left and three black belts.

The reverberation of muffled, raised voices came from Mick's office. Gilda leaned forward and strained to get the gist of what they said. No such luck.

Suddenly, the door opened. Yoshida stomped around the corner and stopped with his dark eyes wide. "Miss Wright."

She refused to look away from him. Her arms tensed, ready to block if he threw a punch. Instead, he left the building. She stared after him, not quite sure what to do.

"For the record," Mick said, leaning on the desk and blocking her view of the door, "you didn't hear anything we said."

"Actually, I just got here."

"Good answer. Here I thought you quit. Oh, and I told you to take a couple days off. Do I have to tell you the opposite of what I want you to do?"

"You also told me where you'd be if I wanted to talk to you," she reminded him as she studied the faint lines etched into his face. He seemed to have aged five years over the past week. "You never mentioned we were missing merchandise."

"You didn't need to know. You've had enough to deal with lately."

"Is that why Yoshida's here?" she asked. "Do deal with missing merchandise?"

"He thinks you and Erik stole things to pawn, so Erik could start a new school. "Now that he's dead, Yoshida wants me to fire you and close the school. I stopped listening after he started screaming like a teenage girl at a concert."

Gilda struggled to catch her breath. Yoshida despised her more than she thought. "I would never steal anything let alone jeopardize the school. What's missing?"

"I have a list."

"You already did an inventory?"

Concern flickered across Mick's face. "Yoshida noticed we didn't have as many sparring gloves as usual. He thought our stock was low for the summer."

"It is," she said. "I always keep minimal stock until late August, then refill the shelves. Yoshida was the one who drilled that idea into my head for the past year."

"That's interesting. You keep a running inventory on the computer, right? Can you print me a copy?"

"Do you think Yoshida fudged the list?" she asked.

Mick sighed. "I don't think anything. So far, I've gone on his word. With you on my side, I can get."

"I'll print two copies and do a physical count," she said.

"Just print one copy. I'll worry about the count. You grab coffee." He met her gaze and handed her a twenty. "Please. This could take us a while."

She was reluctant to leave since she wanted to know what was going on just as badly as he did. After printing the list, she ran up the street for two coffees and cinnamon buns, hoping to bribe him to let her stay.

When she returned, he set his cup and bag on the counter, then steered her toward the door. "Go home. You're already nosy enough and I don't want you getting hurt or..."

"Killed" hung unspoken in the air.

She sat on the floor, blocking the doorway. "If you want me out, you'll have to pick me up and throw me out."

Mick rolled his eyes and sighed again. "You're a stubborn little thing, aren't you? Fine. You count. I'll dig out Yoshida's list."

Considering she'd done inventory in June and no stock had come or gone since, a recount would be easy. She already knew what should be in stock. Armed with her coffee and her list, she walked into the backroom.

The minute she opened the stockroom door, she saw the problem. There were twenty belts where there should've been forty. Six gis sat in the drawer, all in different sizes where there'd been twelve last month and only sold two. All of the T-shirts were accounted for, but five pairs of sparring gloves and ten mouth guards were gone.

She leaned in Mick's doorway with her revised list. "Yoshida's right."

He swore, crumpling a page on his desk. "What's going on around here, Gilda? You've warned us not to touch any stock without letting you know. Where did it go?"

Organization was her biggest strength—or weakness, depending on how you looked at it. Mick and Erik knew she kept meticulous records. Yoshida wasn't as aware.

She slumped onto the thin plastic chair, flimsy to ensure his private meetings were short and sweet. "Why steal from the school?"

"Erik wasn't the brightest bulb in the socket," Mick said. "Either someone either put him up to it, or set him up."

"Someone like Yoshida?"

Mick frowned. "Do you really think he'd steal from his own school? It would have to be someone with no idea how good you are at tracking inventory."

Until lately.

"All Yoshida had to do was walk in and take things. No one would stop him."

He waved to the wall behind her where a pyramid of five yellow meditation candles stood on a narrow shelf by her head. "Do you know how long it took Yoshida to arrange my candles? Ten minutes. He used that ruler to space them exactly an inch and a half apart like it was its own meditation. When we opened this place, everything had to be placed just so. Pictures hung certain distances apart. Objects clustered in fives. If they were moved when someone cleaned, he'd notice."

Gilda leaped from her chair and strode to her computer to figure out the significance of the number five. The four possessions she understood. The number five was a mystery.

"What did I say this time?" Mick followed her to her desk. "Was it about the stacks of five? Maybe he's Obsessive-Compulsive."

"That would explain things, wouldn't it? I thought it was because of his training," she said. "Is there something significant about the number five in karate?"

Mick moved around her desk. "No idea."

Before he crouched beside her, she'd pulled up a website. "OCD. A personality disorder. Control. Perfectionism at the expense of .

Preoccupied with details and rules. Stubborn, self-righteous, unco-operative. Unable to complete tasks due to their desire for perfection."

"That's Yoshida in a nutshell," he said. "Do you think he's capable of setting someone up to go to jail just to take a few things that already belong to him?"

"Capable? Yes. But why bother? He could just take what he wanted."

Mick moved around to the chair beside her. "As long as he told you first."

"As if I'd yell at him. He's scary."

"You yell at me. Aren't I scary?" He coiled a strand of her hair around his finger.

Gilda bit her lower lip. Mick scared her on so many levels she didn't know where to start. "You know what I mean."

"Yeah. You like me."

"You're my boss. It helps." Her face grew so hot she could've pressed linen with her cheeks. "What are you going to do about Yoshida?"

"Ignore him." Mick leaned so close his cheek brushed hers. "I think that's my best option. He's too stubborn to compromise, so I'll wait until he brings it up again."

"What if he doesn't?" Gilda asked.

"Then I'll assume he has a split personality and run for the hills." He pulled up the calendar icon in the corner of the screen.

"Sounds reasonable enough. You surf. I'm going home."

"I have a thought," he said. "Isn't Friday the fifth day of the week?"

A chill ran down Gilda's back. "If you consider Monday the beginning of the week, then yes. That means the murders happening on Fridays isn't a coincidence."

"Which also means if he's following the list of the four possessions we have an idea when someone else might die and why. Sort of."

"Told you I hated Fridays." She stared at the next Friday on the calendar. "Does this mean we have new evidence for Fabio? Maybe we should tell him about the missing merchandise."

Mick shook his head. "I'll talk to Razi and Xavier first. Maybe they know something. I'll call Fabio later."

"When do we do that?"

"We don't. I'll arrange a meeting. You're taking time off."

Gilda wanted to hug him, but had a feeling the fear wouldn't end until the killer was caught. "What should I do in the meantime?"

"Keep your eyes and ears open." He took her hand as he turned to face her. "And if you see Yoshida, run and hide."

CHAPTER 18

G ilda never even found out about half the instructor meetings until after the fact. This one Mick not only invited her to, but he personally walked her down the street that evening. They passed the karate school and Ponderer's Point, heading toward the far end of town, where magnificent brick homes overlooked the lake.

"Where are we going?" she asked, padding beside him in her rattan flip-flops with a beach towel draped around her neck.

"Black belt meeting." Brusque and vague, just as he was when he called an hour ago. He'd spoken to Fabio and Thayer about the missing merchandise but hadn't said more than that.

"Wearing bathing suits?" She laughed. "I'm not even a black belt."

"Call it a staff meeting then."

She stopped, sweaty, and hurting from matching his brisk pace. "Hey, you called me, so stop being snippy. Are we late or can we slow down before I lose my flip-flops?"

"Sorry," he said. "I'm a bit distracted."

"I'll bet you are. Meetings with Thayer peeve me too, but I can't walk any faster. Where are we going for this staff meeting?"

"Razi's. We need to sort out some things." He lowered his voice. "Like who to trust and what we should do next."

Gilda frowned. "You still don't trust me, do you?"

He draped one arm across her shoulders. "Honey, you're the only one I can trust. That's why you're with me."

"Like a sidekick?"

"If that makes you happy."

"I can live with it," she told him.

Razi's plain white bungalow with dark green shutters stood back from the cliff along the shoreline. Mick led her to a side gate through a jungle of lush hydrangeas, rhododendrons, and ferns. They emerged into a backyard lined with flagstones that surrounded a stone barbecue and hot tub. Flat stones dotted a line to the far end of the yard where there must've been stairs that led to the lake.

"This place is amazing," Gilda whispered.

Colored solar lights around the yard twinkled like delicate fairies. She never knew Razi was such a devoted gardener. It was a relaxing spot perfect for meetings or parties.

"Welcome to my humble abode," Razi said with a bow. "I am glad you could join us, Miss Wright."

Xavier stood next to a lounge chair with a towel hung around his neck. He clutched a beer bottle in one hand. "This is a black belt meeting. What's she doing here?"

"Under the circumstances," Mick said, "it seemed like a good idea."

"No one's hunting nosy receptionists that I've heard." Xavier told them.

Gilda hung back in the shadows, her arms crossed over her belly. If any of the men made a move toward her, she'd run for the iron garden gate. They might be stronger and faster, but she was smaller and could duck beneath the foliage. The men had to fight through the leaves.

"This affects her as much as us. We need to stick together to protect each other." Mick slid his arm across her back, then told her, "He's always a jerk after a couple drinks. Give him one more and he'll morph into a pussycat."

"What happens after four?" she asked.

Mick grinned. "He'll either do anything you want, or pass out."

"This is a bad idea." She stepped back behind the gate. "There are three of you and one of me. Throw in a hot tub and alcohol and those aren't great odds. Xavier's right. I should leave."

He followed her into the shadows and wrapped his arms around her. "None of us would ever hurt you. If you want to leave, I'll take you home. If you stay, I'll make sure these guys behave."

"And you?" When she met his gaze, a surge of heat shot through her body.

Mick ran a finger along her jaw. "Don't you trust me?"

"Yes." Gilda let him pull her back into the yard toward the hot tub. Currently, she had a problem trusting anyone. She felt like a fly soaring toward a web.

"Well, the gang's all here." Xavier cracked open bottle number three. "You gonna tell us why?"

Razi opened a pink bottle and handed it to Gilda. "Yes, why are we here?"

"I figured we needed to relax and give each other some moral support." Mick climbed into the hot tub.

The others exchanged glances before they joined him. Gilda was grateful for the warmth on her aching body as she sank into the bubbles. The cooler Razi gave her smelled like fresh strawberries.

"That's it?" Xavier asked, looking skeptical.

"That's it," Mick said. "No ulterior motives."

Xavier narrowed his eyes. "Do the cops have any idea who's targeting black belts?"

"None they're sharing." Mick reached for a bottle of beer in the cooler packed with ice that sat on a table next to the tub and raised it high. "To our fallen brothers. May justice be swift and sure."

"Cheers." Xavier clinked his bottle against Mick's.

"To Walter and Erik." Gilda joined them.

"*Le'chayim*. To life." Razi clinked his bottle against each of theirs, then asked, "What is going on? I have heard rumors at Happy Harvey's Hangover Hut and Café Beanz that someone has stolen merchandise as well."

When Mick looked her way, Gilda shook her head.

Xavier sat back in the swirling water before his gaze fell on Gilda. "Well, it wasn't me. And nobody better say it was."

"Nobody did," Mick told him. "This last week's been tough. We need to stick together, not fight among ourselves."

Xavier sucked back half his beer before he belched. "Kinda feels like someone's out to get us, doesn't it? With no real pattern, how do we know who's next?"

Gilda shrugged. "Hopefully, nobody's next. Maybe someone had problems with Walter and Erik and that's the end of it."

She wanted to mention the missing scroll and her theories about the kanji. Instead, she sat back to listened, hoping to hear something she didn't know.

"The scroll containing the Four Possessions of the Samurai is missing," Razi said.

Mick paused with his bottle midway to his mouth. "Did Gilda point that out?"

Razi frowned. "No. When I replaced the mats. When did you notice it missing?"

She bowed her head. "The day Walter died."

"And you didn't say anything?" Xavier's face hardened.

"I told her not to. Then she found something else." Mick was about to throw her to the wolves. Was this a test of her loyalty or was he trying to draw out more information?

"What was it?" Xavier asked, narrowing his eyes.

"A goju ring," she said.

He frowned. "As far as I know, I'm the only one in the school with one. It went missing weeks ago. Do you still have it?"

"I gave it to Fabio."

"Figures." Xavier chugged more beer.

"Was it missing for weeks? Or just since Walter died?" Mick asked.

Xavier stood and leaned on the edge of the hot tub. "I don't have to take this. All of you can just go to—"

Razi stuck out an arm to stop him. "Xavier is not the only one with such a ring. Shihan Yoshida has one."

"There are two rings?" Gilda asked.

"Mine was a gift from my ex-wife." Xavier polished off his drink. "She ran off with a mechanic from Louie's Garage. The ungrateful cow had no idea about the great opportunities coming my way."

"What opportunities?" Gilda asked, hoping the pussycat side would peek out soon.

Razi rolled his eyes. "You have had enough to drink, Xavier. Perhaps water would be a better—"

"No way. I wanna 'nother beer, then we can get down to some serious relaxing." Xavier stepped out of the hot tub and fell out of sight. He landed on the stones below with a sickening crunch.

Razi jumped out and hoisted Xavier off the rocks like he was little more than a watermelon. Xavier's face was bloody as Razi carried him toward the white bungalow.

When Mick stood to help, Razi shook his head. Mick sat next to Gilda. "I forgot Yoshida had a ring. I haven't seen him wear it for a while."

"I've never seen him wear it to the school." She sipped her cooler.

"Mostly at banquets and tournaments," he said. "I wanted to get one, but he'd never tell me where he got his."

The strawberry drink made her giddy. "Maybe he got it from the Secret Order of the Goju Water Buffaloes."

He chuckled. "Great. One cooler and you start making bad *Flintstone* jokes. Have you always been such a cheap date?"

"Correction," she said, holding up her bottle. "Half a cooler."

"Even better." He winked. "I should check on Xavier. I hope he's okay. We're already shorthanded."

Gilda didn't relish the idea of sitting in Razi's hot tub alone. The murderer could be hiding in the bushes waiting for the right moment to ambush whoever was there.

Mick touched her chin with his knuckle. "You okay?"

"I guess I'm more spooked than I thought," she admitted. "What if the killer's lurking in the shadows?"

When the patio door opened, she jumped.

Xavier limped out of the house with a large white bandage around his right leg and slumped onto a lounge chair. "Somebody grab me a beer."

"No ambulance required." Razi climbed back into the water. "He tore some skin and has a bruise."

"I'm fine. Thank you. Don't worry about me. I'll survive." Xavier hobbled over to grab another beer, then droned on about how no one cared about him and how he'd be better off dead.

Gilda wished Mick had let her leave earlier. When she shot him a nervous glance, he shook his head then reclined against the edge of the tub.

"Beer number five," he muttered. "Let's hope he passes out soon."

"This is why we usually meet for coffee," Razi told Gilda.

"Xavier's an alcoholic? Was he drinking when he tried to poison us? That's why you never pressed charges."

Mick lowered his gaze. "He's had problems lately. We arranged this meeting to make sure he didn't do anything else stupid."

"So, you not only lied to me, you tricked me," she said.

"Technically."

Gilda stood, then stepped out onto the textured stone deck. She turned to glare at both Razi and Mick. "I'm going home. You're both despicable."

"Sherlock, wait." Mick followed her across the yard and grabbed her by the shoulders. "I'll walk you home."

"Why?" She pulled away. "I've lived here my whole life. Besides, I'm not in danger. You said so yourself. Why should I worry, aside from the fact Xavier poisoned me, and Yoshida wants to maim me?"

Razi opened his mouth, then closed it. He kept a watchful eye from the hot tub.

She wrapped her towel around her hips. "Like Xavier said, no one's hunting receptionists. Just black belts."

"You work for me That makes you a target," Mick reminded her.

"Oh yeah? What happened to me being too nice and naive to be a target?"

Mick grabbed his T-shirt and towel. "I'm taking Gilda home. I'll be back."

Razi raised his bottle. "Take your time."

"Don't bother. I don't need a bodyguard." Gilda stomped through the foliage, intentionally letting branches go to hit Mick.

Mick chased her through the shrubs and grabbed her hand. "At least leave your drink here. Thayer doesn't need a legitimate reason to throw us both in jail."

She turned on him. "Seriously? With everything going on, you're worried Thayer will throw me in jail over alcohol?"

He pulled her back through the greenery, then set both their bottles in the grass. Putting one arm across Gilda's shoulders, he said, "You, my dear, are enough to make a man drink some days. Most days, actually. Days that end in a y."

"Don't blame your drinking on me." She shoved through the rhododendrons before asking, "How long have you known Xavier's an alcoholic?"

"About a year. I tried to get him help, but he keeps sliding back," he said. "He's never come to the school drunk—"

"That you know of."

"That I know of. I should have kicked him out a long time ago."

"You think?" She snorted, then turned to face him. "Between Walter dating teens and Xavier's booze... What were you thinking?"

"That I need people who are good at karate, even though they've made bad decisions." Mick rubbed his jaw. "Don't you think I want our karate school to have the best instructors possible?"

Gilda closed her eyes as the world spun around her. It had to be the alcohol. There was no way anyone drugged her. Razi had opened the bottle in front of her. "Yoshida overruled you, didn't he?"

"If I didn't go along with his demands, I'd lose the school." He cradled her chin between his finger and thumb, pressing his forehead to hers. "Razi and Xavier are good men. I'd trust them with my life."

She met his gaze. "I still want to go home."

"I know." When he kissed her, he tasted like beer with a hint of mint gum. Just when her knees threatened to buckle, he backed away but still close enough to feel the burst of heat surge through her body when he whispered, "Let's get you home."

Temporarily disoriented, she let him steer her to the sidewalk. His kiss had altered her senses and wiped her mind blank. What was she so worried about?

Mick gave her hand a squeeze as they approached the beach. "You got quiet. Did I miss something?"

She waited for the tingling in her fingers and toes to subside. "No."

"I wouldn't have brought you if I'd known that was going to happen."

"The kiss?" She was breathless.

"I meant Xavier," he said, then stopped. "Is that what's bothering you? Our kiss?"

"No. I'm good."

"Liar." Mick nudged her toward the lake.

Panic washed over her. "What are you doing? I want to go home."

"In a bit." He led her to where the waves rolled in and crested with caps of foam.

Her flip-flops filled with grit. She kicked them off and picked them up with two fingers. The sky darkened beyond its usual velvety black. They'd have another half hour before the rain hit. Her garden would perk up and be full of snails by morning.

"What are you doing?" she asked.

Mick tossed his towel onto the sand then took off his shoes. "Going for a swim."

"Gilda glanced back up at the looming clouds and clung to her flip-flops. "I don't want to go for a swim. I want to go home."

He locked her in the circle of his arms with clasped hands. "Look, I know you think I'm insincere, I'm unreliable, and I drive you crazy."

She was too nervous to look him in the eye. "Most times."

"I've wanted to pour my heart out to you for the past year. Until I managed to the other night."

Yet Gilda mistook his flirtations for teasing until he'd kissed her. After Thayer, she'd given up on men and focused on what she wanted. Yet, aside from work and training, all she had was her garden.

"You mean when I kicked you?"

He chuckled. "That was a great knee kick, by the way. Do that in class one night, just not to my groin."

Her face burned. "What does this have to do with going for swim?"

"Dive in, Sherlock." Mick moved her hands to his shoulders and pulled her closer until every curve of their bodies seemed to touch. "Take a chance."

Gilda shuddered. She didn't want to get her hopes up. "How am I supposed to trust you? You have an ex-wife. Girlfriends. You gamble. Then there's Yoshida."

"I'm not the greatest catch, am I?" he asked.

"And I'm the crazy woman who beat up Thayer and aggravated Yoshida." She laid her head on his chest.

"Which makes you worth the frustration in my book." He raised her chin to kiss her again. "You ready for that swim?"

Heat surged from her lips to every part of her body leaving her breathless as he held her. Touched her. As much as she wanted more, alarm bells rang in the back of her head.

Breaking his grasp, she tossed her flip-flops onto the sand, then tugged her towel off her hips and left him standing alone on the beach as she waded into the surf. The storm was blew in faster than they'd anticipated..

Mick walked her home in the pouring rain and helped towel dry her hair.

He didn't stop there...

CHAPTER 19

Mick left around dawn. His musky scent, a reminder of the long, lingering kisses and passionate caresses stayed with her. It was well after the sun rose when she finally slept for a few hours.

Still smiling, she pressed her black dress and hung it in the bathroom before sitting on the front step with her coffee. The mourning doves cooed from a roof across the street.

What did she think she was doing? Mick Williams was the worst man to get involved with. Even worse than Jason Thayer. Why didn't her hormones know that? Sure, he was handsome and built like a marble statue, but still...

"You look like a cat that drank a whole bottle of cream," Thayer commented as he strode through her front gate. He scowled as he sat next to her. "What's going on?"

"Nothing." Heat burned her cheeks and radiated to the roots of her hair.

"That's an awfully bright color for nothing." Fabio joined them carrying a tray with three cups of coffee. He handed her the cup with a black G on top. "Vanilla latte. I had the girl froth the milk, then add cinnamon and chocolate curls."

"Are you here to arrest me or something? If you want answers, we can go downtown after Erik's funeral."

"That sounds like something out of a gangster movie. I'm surprised you still watch those old movies," Thayer said, grabbing his coffee, which sloshed onto his hand and shirt cuff. He frowned the cup to his left while he wiped his wet hand on his pants.

"Where were you last night?" Fabio asked. "We stopped by, but you were gone."

"Staff meeting. Mick wanted to sit down and make sure we were all on the same page." She sipped the coffee and got a mouthful of foam and cinnamon.

"We checked the school, but no one was there. Is Mick trying to close ranks against us?" Thayer asked.

Fabio indicated the porch swing. "Do you mind if we sit up there? My sciatica's acting up. That storm kept me awake half the night."

"No problem." Gilda and Fabio took the swing, leaving Thayer the wicker chair with the lumpy cushion.

When Fabio took the lid off his cup, froth clung to the inside. "The deaths of two instructors is a major inconvenience. It can't be easy going to work."

"It's not." She blinked back tears.

"Do the rest of you have any suspects in mind?" Fabio asked. At least he tried to befriend her, not like Thayer who seemed intent on offending everyone. Mostly her.

"Not really."

Thayer snorted. "She probably has a ton of evidence against Mick, but won't turn it over. She's in love with him and doesn't want to lose her job."

Gilda refused to let him goad her. Her next sip of coffee and scalded her tongue, but she refused to let Thayer see her pain.

"Do me a favor?" Fabio said. "Go down to the beach and see if anyone there saw anything strange Thursday or Friday?"

Thayer grumbled. "I know you're trying to get rid of me. Next time, just tell me to get lost."

"That's funny." Gilda smirked. "He's clueless when I try to get rid of him."

Fabio waited until Thayer was several houses away before he turned his full attention on her. "Some days he's smarter than he looks. You're lucky you got away before you were stuck with him. I have to work with him until he gets shipped off to Nunavut or Saskatchewan."

"I'd work on that if I were you," she muttered.

He sipped his coffee. "Mick and I trained together for years, both in karate and at the gym. When I got shot, he made sure I had whatever I needed. There's no way he'd murder anyone."

Tears blurred her vision. Finally, something positive about Mick she didn't know. "Who's on your suspect list?"

"Aside from everyone in town? Razi and Xavier are at the top, but I hoped you could tell me about Yoshida. I stopped training with him a long time ago."

"Was he always so strange?"

"Strange how?"

She thought a moment. "Angry."

"From what I hear, he's got a few more screws loose than he did back then," Fabio told her. "I know he's been hanging around Sandstone Cove more than usual since his wife left him six months ago. Any idea why?"

"His wife left him. Chloe told me she ran into him in the store." She hesitated. "He bought tampons."

"That explains things. Who is he seeing?"

"I have no idea." Was that who was at Jade's house the day Gilda dropped by?

"Relax, Gilda. I don't suspect you of anything. Well, unless you're dating Yoshida. I don't think you're seeing anyone right now, are you?"

"Thayer would've told you if I was."

Her thoughts drifted to swimming with Mick at the beach, then running home in the rain and drying each other off. Her face warmed.

"The right guy will come along soon enough." He patted her knee.

"Are you planning to set me up?" she asked.

"Just giving unwanted advice."

"Oh, is that why you're here?" She savored her latte, enjoying the tastes of cinnamon and chocolate.

"Two of your coworkers are dead. I assume you have a few ideas about who'd want to kill them."

Gilda's stomach churned. "I thought I did. Now I'm not sure of anything. I don't even know if I'll go back to the school."

"No one would hold that against you." He turned her face toward him to study her. "Who gave you the shiner and fat lip?"

"Yoshida," she admitted. "We did kumite in our workshop Tuesday."

"I take it he also tagged Mick's face."

The memory sent shivers up her arms. "Yoshida started to spar me, then went completely nuts. I should've been able to fight back, but the look in his eyes scared me. It was like he was possessed or something. That was when Mick stepped in."

"Possessed or stoned?"

She froze. "I don't think he does drugs. Does he?"

"Just a story I heard. Something Marion Yearly told Happy." He paused. "How well do you know Marion?"

"She's one of my best friends. She took me to the hospital when I got hit on the head. I haven't seen her in a few days though." Gilda hesitated. "Chances are, if it was something serious, she'd know. Of course, if it was gossip, she'd know that, too."

"That's good to know. Would you do me a favor? If you hear anything, please let me know. Don't worry about Thayer. I'll deal with him."

"Sure." She stared at the card.

"If you're keeping things from us, we may have to arrest you for your own protection. Make sure whoever you're protecting is worth it."

"What makes you think I'm protecting anyone?"

"I'm a cop. Call it a hunch." He pushed to his feet. "I hope you know what you're doing, honey. Tell Mick to work on his back stroke the next time you two go for a late-night swim."

Gilda stared after him as he limped away. She was positive she'd closed the drapes last night before they went to Razi's house. She glanced at the window, she noticed they were open. Hopefully, no one took photos of she and Mick, especially after they got back to her house.

Were the police following her or Mick?

CHAPTER 20

E rik's funeral was far different from Walter's. Where the crowd at Walter's service was older, more refined. Most of the people who came to say good-bye to Erik were young, beautiful, and spent more time texting than talking. Across the room, his stepmom held his younger sister, a teenager with heavy black makeup streaked across her face, while his dad greeted people with a frozen smile.

Erik looked more like an elegant tailor shop mannequin than a corpse. He was the best-looking dead guy she'd ever seen. The makeup artist at the funeral home must've had a crush on him.

Gilda sat on a pew in the chapel with a heavy heart. This wasn't how things were supposed to go. Her friends and coworkers were supposed to pass on after long lives of hard training and making her life miserable. Even Erik.

"I thought he was moving to his mom's place." said a tall, blonde woman in a black dress, which barely concealed her considerable assets. She stood with two men and a woman. All four wore pouts more appropriate for magazine covers than a funeral.

A dark-skinned man wearing a dark shirt and thick gold chain shifted his weight as his gaze darted toward the casket. "He was. He quit his job at the moving company and couldn't wait to tell his sensei to kiss his lily-white butt."

A thin, raven-haired woman laughed and told them, "Oh, please. Mick's a pussycat. Did you see that creepy old dude? He's the one I'd worry about. He beat Erik up after we had that party at the school. The dude was livid."

Yoshida.

They all exaggerated shivers, then chuckled.

"Anyone know how Erik's meeting with the karate guys went?" the man asked.

"No," the blonde said with a sigh. "We were supposed to go for dinner afterward. He never showed up."

He snorted. "It wouldn't surprise me if one of them lured him to the school and killed him. To ambush him with ninja stars is just cold."

Why hadn't Mick told her they'd met with Erik? If all the black belts were present, her suspect list hadn't whittled down any. If not, she was down to Yoshida and Mick, which gave her little comfort after their intimacy last night.

Across the room, Mick pushed away from Erik's father, a lanky, balding man. Erik had definitely inherited his swarthy looks from his dad. "Get out of my face."

"I want to know the truth." Erik's father shouted, following Mick toward Gilda.

Mick turned and replied, "This is neither the time nor the place. You want to talk to me, call me after the funeral."

A tiny, dark-haired woman grabbed the man's arm and reprimanded him in a hushed voice as she led him back to the rest of the family.

Mick slid onto the pew beside Gilda, cursing beneath his breath. He hadn't walked her to the funeral home this time, nor had he called since leaving her house. It seemed he'd gotten what he wanted from her, then ran for cover. Was he afraid of his reaction or hers?

"What's going on?" she asked.

"Erik's dad thinks I killed his son," he whispered. "Do you think anyone would have enough brass to go to the funeral of someone they murdered?"

"Guilty people do weird things," she said. When he scowled, she leaned toward him. "I have to know something."

Mick patted her thigh. "Yeah, I know. I left and didn't call. I was trying to get Chloe out of my condo. Then the police dropped by to chat some more. During the interrogation, my phone died."

Although that thought weighed on her mind, she told him about overhearing Erik's friends discussing a meeting he had with Erik the day he was killed.

"What does that have to do with anything?" he asked.

"Rumor has it one of you lured Erik to the school and killed him."

He paled. "Can we talk later?"

"Why didn't you tell me about the meeting?" she asked.

Mick glanced behind them and did a double take. "Yoshida's here. At least his appearance takes the heat off me."

Gilda's gaze followed Yoshida through the crowd. There was a man who could probably kill someone, then attend the funeral later. Cold as frozen lemonade.

Yoshida spoke briefly with Erik's parents. He seemed to linger near the open casket longer than most people had.

"What's he up to?" Gilda murmured.

Mick leaned closer. "What do you mean?"

She inched away. Mick's cologne was distracting. Disorienting. "Before Walter died, Yoshida rarely came to the school. He's shown up at both funerals and done training at the school."

"We need some good publicity," he said. "It would look worse if people found out we were robbed on top of everything else."

Gilda raised her eyebrows. He had a point

Mick held a finger to his lips, then grasped her hand and pulled her toward the casket. "Yoshida's gone. Let's make sure no one left a gift for Erik. If the murderer's following the sequence and leaves it in the casket, 'Integrity' will be next."

"What's the hurry? He's not going anywhere." She stumbled into him when he stopped.

"See anything unusual?" Mick asked, draping his arm around her waist. "Anything in his pocket?"

"Aside from the fact he looks like he should be on a date with Barbie, just the usual."

"Focus, Gilda."

"What do you want me to do? Search him?" she asked through gritted teeth.

"Do we have time?"

"You're a sick puppy." Her gaze fell on a piece of material sticking out of his left hand before she whispered, "Left hand."

"So, grab it."

"I'm not touching him."

Mick reached into the casket, pulled the cloth from Erik's pale fingers, then tucked it into his suit jacket. "Looks like someone left a gift. He won't need it as much as we do."

Gilda put her hand to her mouth and moved away from him. She hoped he'd go sit with Razi, Xavier, and Yoshida and nowhere near her. Since the three men sat close to Erik's family, she had no such luck.

Mick touched the small of her back and led her to an empty pew. "We can go to Café Beanz later to take a look."

"What is wrong with you?" Erik's dad stormed toward them. "Isn't it bad enough you killed my son? Now you're desecrating his body?"

"We were just saying good-bye to our friend," Mick explained.

His face grew red as he folded his arms across his barrel chest. "Maybe you and your girlfriend should leave. In fact, you can take the whole karate gang with you. Go home and leave my family alone."

Mick's body tensed against Gilda's. "If that's what you wish, then out of respect for you and your family, we'll leave.."

"Okay. That's good." Erik's dad seemed ill prepared for Mick to back down so easily. "The rest of you, too. Get out."

"Just one more thing." When Mick held up a hand, the room went still.

"Oh no," Gilda whispered. "Please, don't make a scene."

"Erik was a good kid. I'm proud of all he accomplished at our school, and he would've made a great sensei. I'm sorry for your loss." With that, he draped an arm around Gilda's waist and led her out of the chapel.

"Where did that come from?" She asked, not looking back to see if the other black belts followed them. "That was actually really nice of you."

"I'm not always a jerk."

"I wouldn't work for you if you were."

"Good to know." He gave her a squeeze. "You want to go for a swim?"

Her step faltered. "I'm not really dressed for it."

Mick grinned. "If we go late enough, you won't have to be dressed at all."

"Skinny-dipping?" Heat surged through her and radiated out the ends of her hair. "I'm not sure that's a good idea. Won't we get caught?"

"Not where I go," he said.

Gilda's imagination worked overtime as they walked toward the coffee shop. Had he kept his distance from her earlier to give her time to think. She hoped their tryst last night wasn't an attempt to throw her off his trail. Either way, it was a huge mistake.

Mick nudged her over by the window and slipped onto the bench beside her. He unrolled the scrap of cloth he'd taken from the casket. "The second kanji"

"We were right."

"A lot of people paid their respects. How do we narrow it down to one person?"

"We both know who—" Interrupted by the server, he scrunched the fabric in his hand. "Large coffee, cream, and sugar."

Gilda ordered a low-fat latte with cinnamon and chocolate curls.

When the server left, Mick skirted around to her side of the table and lowered his head. "Well, aren't they cozy?"

"Who?" She frowned.

He pointed over his shoulder with his thumb. Chloe sat at a table across the room head-to-head with Thayer.

"Do you think he's asking questions about you?" Gilda asked.

"I think she's cheating on me."

Considering what they'd done the night before, her palms sweated. Cripes, that made Gilda the other woman. Gilda bit her lower lip before she said, "I thought you two broke up." Gilda bit her lower lip.

"We did." Mick narrowed his eyes. "We can talk about the kanji later. I've gotta go."

When he stood, Gilda grabbed his sleeve. "You're not planning to do anything stupid, are you?"

"Would that bother you? You hate Thayer as much as I do." Mick winked. "I've got work to do."

"I could come to the school to finish some paperwork. It would be less stressful if I wasn't alone."

"Go home and play in your garden. I'll take it from here."

He walked away leaving Gilda alone like nothing had happened between them. When the barista handed him a cup of coffee, he left like he never saw Chloe, Thayer, or Gilda. Like he had things on his mind that didn't include any of them. After all he'd done to get so close to her, why put so much distance between them now?

Gilda strolled past Thayer and Chloe to get her coffee to go. She overheard Chloe mention something about abuse right before meeting Gilda's gaze.

As Gilda walked away, Chloe gave a slow smile. What was she up to and was Thayer only another pawn in her game?

* * *

"Hello, Gilda." Gary leaned against the hood of his car. Today he'd parked in front of her house facing downtown and enjoying the afternoon sunshine. "Sorry about your friend. I knew him through Chloe. Good kid. A bit messed up, though. The funeral home made him look good."

She folded her arms across her stomach. "I didn't see you or Chloe."

"You and Mick were leaving when we arrived," he said. "Something about a disagreement with Erik's father. There's something to be said for appearing fashionably late. Is there something I should know about? The two of you seem chummy lately."

"Me and Erik?"

"You and Mick."

She walked over to sit on the porch swing. "What do you want from me?"

He followed her up the steps then leaned on the railing. "To make sure you don't get hurt. Bad things are going on around here lately and you're too nice a girl to get pushed into a bad position."

"What position is that?"

"Hanging out with a murderer."

"Why would you care?" Gilda asked.

He picked a marigold out of the planter Chloe had butted her cigarette and tucked it in his buttonhole. "Despite our differences, I had nothing but respect for your father. I also know Mick and the boys you work with. Your friend Yoshida is a shady character, even from my perspective."

"Funny. That's what everyone else says about you, including Mick." Or that's probably what he'd say if she asked.

Gary sighed. "I chose a bumpy road through life, Gilda."

"To say the least."

"So, you know, I was in jail when they killed your father. I thought the man who shot him was a good friend until the day I got arrested." He paused. "While your father put the cuffs on me, he asked me one thing that made me think hard about what I was doing with my life."

Gilda shivered despite the heat. "What did he ask you?"

"When the last time was that I saw my daughter." Gary's voice cracked. "I spent ten years in jail and missed seeing her grow up. Her mother refused to bring her to see me. I know I can't make up that time no matter how hard I try."

Her eyes stung. "At least you get to try."

Gary handed her a small packet of tissues. "I'm aware of that, which is why I'm here now. Those men are trouble. I'm trying to keep you safe without being obvious."

A jolt of fear pulsed through her body. "You didn't kill them, did you?"

"I had no reason to hurt any of them," he said, "but if you asked me to, I'd be glad to make anyone disappear. Free of charge."

"No thanks." She shook her head. "There's been enough blood."

"You're sweet on Mick, aren't you?" Gary asked. "Chloe suspected something was up. She only dated him because everyone else wanted him. That, and she thinks I don't like him. Apparently, she inherited my people skills."

"Trust me, yours are far better than hers."

"A lovely compliment, considering I've done nothing but make you nervous. You know you can call me. Day or night. Think of me as your godfather, so to speak."

His offer didn't exactly give her warm fuzzies. Gary scared her, especially since the only side he was on was his. If she ever crossed him, she'd be on the naughty list, along with Mick and Yoshida, in a heartbeat.

"So, to speak." She laughed, then covered her mouth.

"Go ahead and laugh," he said. "You look good when you smile, even bruised."

"Thanks." She cleared the emotion from her throat. "I mean that. My dad would've appreciated you looking out for me."

"Yeah. I doubt that, but thanks." Gary winked then sauntered toward his car.

CHAPTER 21

The next morning, Gilda rolled over and opened her eyes, hoping for a glimpse of the clock. Instead, Mick lay inches away—practically nose-to-nose with her. Was she dreaming?

When he opened his mouth and exhaled, the scent of stale scotch assaulted her.

She shrieked, pulling the blankets to her chest. "What are you doing?"

Clad only in blue plaid boxer shorts, Mick seemed as surprised as she was. He tugged on a blanket. "I was sleeping until you screamed."

"What are you doing in my bed?" she asked. "How did you get into my house without me knowing?"

"Your spare key," he mumbled. "Don't worry. I put it back. This was the safest place to hide."

A safe place to hide. Was that all she meant to him? "Hide from who?"

He nestled beneath the blankets. "Chloe. The killer. The guy I owe money to. You have a comfy bed, you know. I've been sleeping in my office since Chloe locked me out. Anything's more comfortable than that."

Gilda sat up. "I get that you owe Gary money, but why did Chloe kick you out? Did you drink milk straight from the carton or something?"

"Daily." Mick leaned on his elbow. "Since I owe Gary fifty grand, he took my condo as collateral. That's how Chloe got the keys. She and I never lived together, nor do I want to. I've been trying to shake her off for weeks."

"Fifty grand?" She struggled to breathe. "Who owes fifty grand to a bookie?"

"One that trusts his former girlfriend to place a bet for him. Instead of betting fifty bucks, she bet five thousand to get even for me dumping her."

"Oh, brother." Gilda fell back onto her pillow. "I never thought I'd say this, but get out of my bedroom. You're an idiot."

"You never thought you'd tell me to get out of your bedroom?" he asked.

She hit him with her pillow.

"Seriously, babe, I'm in danger here," he said. "Someone killed two black belts in my school and a gangster wants my head. Your bedroom's the safest place in town."

"That's not exactly flattering. Why didn't you tell Gary you'd never make bets you couldn't pay?"

"Because I can pay my debts. I did explain, but since Chloe made the bet in my name, I'm doing the right thing. It's just taking longer than expected."

Gilda hugged her pillow. "Then why not kick Chloe out and take back your condo?"

"I needed time to cash in some investments. She's not willing to wait until I free up the cash and convinced him to kick me out."

"I doubt Gary would rather break your legs than wait for his money."

"Speaking of Gary," he said, "I ran into Happy the other day. He's seen you and Gary hanging out lately."

Gilda hesitated. If she expected Mick to be honest, she should be in return. "Gary feels some weird sense of responsibility for me, especially since I work for you, and he knew my dad."

"Does your dad owe him money?" Mick asked.

"My dad was a cop."

Mick covered his face with both hands. "That explains why you're so nosy. You have the cop gene. We could use his help about now."

Tears sprang to her eyes. "He was shot by one of Gary's crew during a robbery."

His eyes grew wide, and he reached for her hand. "Oh, man. I'm sorry, babe. That's why Gary's keeping watch. He doesn't trust any of us near you."

"Why are you really here?"

"In Sandstone Cove or in your bed?" he asked. a sheepish grin covering his face. When she scowled, he moved closer. "I'm kidding. Honey, you're the only person in town who still talks to me, besides Razi and Xavier."

"You're a bad liar."

"Okay, you're right. There are the girls at Café Beanz and Happy, who makes me nervous. I don't think he likes me."

"He doesn't."

Mick brushed the stray strand off her face. "How can someone like you be so sweet? Life throws you curveballs and you deflect them every time."

"What do you mean?" She ached to melt against the warmth of his body.

"Thayer, for one," he said. "Finding Walter and Erik. You're either in denial or—"

She winced. "I'm not a killer."

He met her gaze. "I never thought you were."

"After what I did to Thayer, people must think I'm..." She grasped for the right word.

Mick nuzzled her ear. "Nope. Still sweet and innocent."

She moved back before he could distract her. "No, I'm not. I'm mean and evil."

"Sure, you are."

"Thayer called me a witch after I shoved him into a rosebush."

Mick burst into laughter. "I'm sure he deserved it. You probably tell us off in your head all the time."

"Now you're a mind reader?"

"Body language reader." Mick placed a hand on the curve of her waist, then gave her a lingering kiss that made her stomach flutter and her toes curl. "Good to know I have a friend who will let me hide out when I'm in trouble."

A friend. After the other night, they were back to being friends.

When he rolled out of bed and padded down the hall to the bathroom, her self-esteem took a fast rollercoaster ride. She was finally getting to know Mick better than she'd ever dreamed. Too bad all he wanted was a friend.

How dare he strike where she was most vulnerable? She groaned and pulled the blankets over her head. The thought was disheartening. When the bathroom door opened, she lunged to slam the bedroom door and yelled, "You're a louse!"

"What did I sat?" He rattled the doorknob.

She threw the blankets into a heap on the bed to wash later. "I am so tired of people using me. Doesn't anybody care what I want?"

"Have you lost your mind? Come on, Gilda. Let me in, so we can talk."

Gilda pulled on shorts and a tank top. "No way. I'm getting dressed."

He thumped on the door. "All I want are my clothes."

"You should've thought of that before you left them in here." She pulled off the tank top and yanked on a sports bra. What was he doing to her?

Her mind was no longer in the bedroom but on Mick Williams standing out in the hallway in his underwear. Ironically enough, that led her thoughts back into the bedroom. She growled. What was wrong with her?

Desperation.

She hadn't dated since she broke up with Thayer. She'd poured her heart and soul into her work, her garden, and training. With Mick.

"Are you losing your mind? Let me in." There was a pause before he said, "What are you doing here? This isn't what you think."

She pressed her ear to the door. "Who are you talking to?"

"Me," Thayer's voice reverberated through the wood. "Why are Mick's clothes in your bedroom?"

She pulled on her tank top for the second time, then picked up Mick's clothes. They still smelled like musk and spearmint gum. Her heart skipped a beat. "I don't need to explain anything, especially to you. How did you get in my house?"

"Gilda, can you hurry?" Mick asked. "I don't like the way he's looking at me."

"Why are your clothes in her bedroom?" Thayer asked.

Mick snorted. "Take a guess."

"None of your business." She opened the door and threw the jeans and T-shirt at Mick, then pointed at Thayer. "What are you doing in my house?"

"I knocked, but considering everything—"

Gilda clenched her hands on her hips. "Did it ever occur to you I could be in the shower or asleep?"

When Thayer's face reddened, she guessed they had entered his head. He'd broken into her house to catch her with her guard down. "Not after two murders."

"Good point." Mick, still shirtless, zipped his jeans. "I would've done the same."

"You did, and I should press charges. Neither of you has a good reason to be here."

Mick shook his head. "That's not true. I came in because you didn't answer the door. For all I knew, the killer found out where you lived."

"Is this true?" Thayer asked.

She pushed between both men toward the kitchen. "No. He broke in to hide in my bedroom to save his own bacon, just like when he broke down my front door. Which you still owe me money for."

Thayer's eyebrows shot upward. "You broke her door?"

"Only once. This time I used the key," Mick said.

Hands shaking, she poured water into the coffeemaker.

Thayer sat at the table. "I have some questions for you."

"Then come back in a couple hours. Maybe I'll be in a better mood."

"I'm not leaving until he does," Thayer said, folding his arms across his chest.

"Oh, grow up." Mick and leaned so close to Gilda that his breath warmed her cheek. "I'll get rid of him, then we'll talk."

"Mick. Get out."

He seemed genuinely surprised as he held out his hands. "And go where?"

She folded her arms over her stomach. "Don't make me give you directions."

Mick's lips brushed her ear, resurrecting thoughts of him wearing nothing but boxer shorts. "I'll be back." Then he turned to Thayer. "Let's get breakfast and give the lady some peace. I'll buy."

Thayer start to object, but Mick slapped a firm hand on his shoulder to steer him out of her house. When Thayer tried to turn back, Mick yanked him out the door.

Gilda brought the spare key inside and tossed it in a drawer, then she locked the front door, the back door, and every window until she was convinced no one could enter. She even stuck duct tape over the mail slot. Agitated, she took a long, cold shower, polished off half a pot of coffee, and made a protein shake.

The phone rang while she blended the shake. S ignored it, in no mood to speak to anyone. The ringing stopped when she pressed the blender's off button. The caller hadn't bothered to leave a message.

She poured the mango and pineapple concoction into a travel mug and sipped. If she headed for the beach and tried hard enough, she could imagine herself alone in the tropics. She grabbed a steamy Katarina von Herrington romance Marion had loaned her weeks ago. Murder mysteries were no longer welcome in her house. Ever.

She hoped no one would find her until she had time to think. Thayer was all talk and no action. He claimed to want her back, but hadn't made a real attempt.

Not until he broke into her house while she was locked in her bedroom with Mick pounding on the door.

A surge of heat pulsed through her from head to toe and all points between. Mick had professed his love for her, crawled to her when he was drunk, and let her cry on his shoulder repeatedly. Waking up next to him, was exactly what she'd longed for since the day they met. Now that he needed a friend and came to her, she'd rejected him.

Why did her attraction to him feel so wrong when he was all she'd desired for two years? Her best guess was that she didn't want to become involved when he could be a killer, or a likely victim.

"Hey, slow down." Fabio called out. When he fell into step beside her on the way to the beach, she noticed two cups of coffee and a paper bag. "You haven't seen Thayer this morning, have you?"

"I kicked he and Mick out of my house a while ago," she said. "Last I heard, they were going for breakfast."

"They were there at the same time?" Fabio's asked. "Why were they at your house?"

She sighed. "You don't want to know."

"Try me." He followed her onto the beach.

Gilda kicked off her flip-flops to carry them. "Mick used my spare key to come into my bedroom last night to hide. Thayer used it this morning when I didn't answer the door. He caught Mick pounding on my bedroom door trying to get his clothes back. What was Thayer doing there anyway?"

Fabio chuckled. "Oh, Gilda, I have so many questions. Thayer was supposed to watch your house while I got coffee."

Glad to see her favorite log unoccupied, she sat on the names, dates, and initials etched in the weathered surface to sip her shake. "Why are you being nice to me?"

He eased onto the log before reaching into the bag. "Because I think you're stuck in the middle of a storm and could use a friend."

She eyed the muffin he pulled out. Chocolate chunk. A dose of chocolate would go a long way.

Fabio held out the muffin. "Want one? Thayer can get his own."

"No, thanks. Walter and Erik are dead," she said. "I found them. Doesn't that make me look guilty?"

He handed her the muffin anyway. "No. None of the guys you work with suspected you, so we haven't either."

"Never?" She raised her eyebrows. "Seriously?"

"You sound oddly disappointed, which scares me." Fabio sipped his coffee. "Finding two bodies does look suspicious, but you have no motive."

Waves lapped the shore as tourists slowly invaded the beach. She admired the confidence of anyone who wore skimpy bathing suits, since she didn't have that kind of intestinal fortitude. She still needed more confidence.

"Mick never doubted you," Fabio said, breaking the silence.

She fumbled what was left of the muffin. "Mick? Why would you say that?"

"It was no coincidence I ended up in Sandstone Cove, you know. He and I trained together before Mick got his black belt. When I called the other day, he told me to never to show up at his school again."

"That was you?" Gilda asked. "The call that came from Mick's condo the day Walter died. I thought it was Chloe."

Fabio shook his head. "No, I made that call. Chloe called because someone broke in. She thought it was Mick. Now he's convinced I'm her latest fling."

"She's no good for either of you anyway." The breeze blew hair across her face. "Why would he break into his own condo?"

"Because she'd changed the locks and told him to take a hike." Fabio frowned. "Mick insisted it wasn't him. When I looked around, it looked like someone wanted to plant evidence, which probably would've netted us a killer if Chloe hadn't contaminated it first."

"Contaminated what?"

"A fabric scroll with pieces cut out. Mick had one just like it. Chloe threw it in the trash."

"A scroll?" She sat up straighter. "Rust colored with Japanese writing?"

"Yeah."

Gilda grew lightheaded. "The Four Possessions of the Samurai. It went missing from the school the day Walter died. Mick and I..." She trailed off when she realized she and Mick had compromised the pieces they'd found.

"HILT. Honor, integrity, loyalty... I don't remember the last one. Why didn't anyone mention the missing scroll earlier?"

"The last one's Time," she reminded him. "The scroll didn't seem important until Walter's funeral. Then Mick and I started to find them at the funerals. 'Honor' was in Walter's breast pocket. 'Integrity' in Erik's hands. We guessed the killer is using them as reasons to kill people. There are three black belts left and two kanji."

"Which means time's running out." Fabio crumpled his muffin wrapper and dropped it into the paper bag. "We'd better keep an eye on all three of them. I can't believe you took evidence out of their caskets. There are better ways to—"

"How many suspects do you have?" she asked, cutting off his lecture.

He looked away. "A couple."

"If it helps, I didn't notice the scroll was missing until after the police were gone. It used to hang in the change room."

Fabio nodded. "That's where I'd seen it. Thayer and I have checked out alibis and backgrounds, but until we get lab results, we have no proof." He paused. "Do you have suspects?"

Gilda finished the last of her protein shake and hoped her surprise wasn't obvious. "The killer keeps whittling down my list. Do you think Xavier, Mick, or Razi did it?"

"You forgot one," Fabio told her. "Yoshida. Do you think someone would want to kill him?"

"There's a long line."

"I'm going to the office to do some research. Yoshida has access to the school, Mick, and the others. To you, too, Sherlock. Watch your back."

Sherlock. Fabio had spoken to Mick. Apparently, he and Mick either made up since he made the call from Mick's condo, or called a truce until the murders were solved.

Maybe Gilda needed to take a page from Fabio's book and do some more digging.

CHAPTER 22

G ilda's head pounded with a dull ache. Neither breakfast, meditation, nor a morning run under threatening skies eased the
pain. She arrived at the school that afternoon in time to see the first
splatters of rain slap the front door behind her.

"Is that you, Gilda?" Mick called out. His voice sounded scratchy
and tired.

She flinched, turning the lights on before she sat behind her desk.
"Why are you in the dark?"

When her question was met by silence, she shrugged. He hadn't
called out for help, nor asked for an ambulance. What if he only had
enough strength to shout once?

"Mick?" With her heart beating faster, she pushed back her chair
and peered into his office. "Are you okay?"

No reply.

She reached around the corner to the light switch, expecting to find
Mick dead in his chair. No body, just fast-food containers, half empty

coffee cups, and rotting fruit. Where was the police cleanup crew now? She doubted even they'd touch those biohazards.

"Hey, what's up?" Mick asked behind her.

Gilda spun around and shoved him away. "Where were you?"

"The dojo." He wiped a trace of blood off his lip. Fresh cuts crossed his face, and he wore the first blush of a black eye.

"What happened to you?" she whispered.

"Chloe got mad at me. Why are you here?"

"We have classes today, remember?" She folded her arms across her stomach. "Why is Chloe mad now?"

"She demanded I sign over the deed to my condo." He skirted around her to sit. "When I refused, she tried to claw my eyes out. That' chick's crazy."

That explained the papers Chloe gave him several days ago. Gilda frowned and leaned in the doorway. "I thought once you repaid Gary you'd get your condo back. You still haven't paid him, have you?"

He stared at the floor. "It hadn't seemed like a priority until now. I'll get things settled before Chloe comes back with some muscle."

"She must really like your condo."

"No, she just really hates me," he said. "She's doing everything she can to get me out of her life and out of town."

Chloe hadn't even come close to her suspect list until right then. "Including killing people?"

Mick stared, then shook his head. "She's not the hands-on type. Well, aside from mangling my face. She'd never be able to pull off a murder without bragging. I guess we'd better do some serious cleaning in here. Hopefully, a couple students will show up."

"Yeah. Hopefully." Gilda turned away to return to her desk, a thousand things on her mind. As she passed the dojo, she thought she saw light from the doorway. It was there and gone so fast she decided it was a side effect of her headache.

Mick bolted from his office, opened the back door, and peered outside before turning back to ask, "Did you hear that?"

"Hear what?"

He flipped on every light in the building, before looking into the back room. "I thought I heard the back door close."

"That's weird. I thought I saw a light but figured it was from my headache."

"A flashlight or daylight?" he asked.

Lightheaded, Gilda stumbled to her desk to sit. "Daylight."

"The killer must've been in the school." Mick sat next to her, beads of sweat glittered on his forehead. "I was a sitting duck. He could've taken me out before you got here."

She shuddered as she reached for the phone. "I'm calling Fabio."

"I don't want him here."

"He and Thayer need to know someone broke in here again. They can keep an eye on things while you focus on classes. I'll feel safer."

"They won't make me feel safe." He scrubbed his face with both hands. After a long minute, he nodded. "Fine. We have students to protect."

Gilda's hands shook. "I'll ask Razi to come in early."

"You're the best. Thanks." He smiled, but fear haunted his eyes.

She called the police station, not surprised when Fabio and Thayer arrived five minutes later. They searched the school, then directed a two-man forensics team to dust for fingerprints near the vent and back door. Thayer disappeared out the back door with the forensics team.

"Are you sure you didn't see anything?" Fabio asked.

"Just a flash of light," she said. "Mick was in his office and heard the door."

"Why didn't you hear the door?"

Gilda frowned. "I have a pounding headache and a thousand things to worry about before classes resume this afternoon. I wasn't paying attention."

"Has there been anyone else sneaking around before?" Fabio asked.

She hesitated long enough that he raised both eyebrows. "The day after Walter died. When I came in to send e-mails, a man with bare feet ran out the back door. By the time I got there, he was gone."

Fabio shook his head. "You didn't think that was important enough to mention?"

"Mick knew," Gilda said.

"Mick's not a cop."

"I thought he'd tell you." She focused her energy on cleaning toilets and floors to keep busy.

Before long, the door opened. Marion strolled in with two cups of tea. "Gilda, honey, you look dreadful. I brought you chamomile tea. Did something else happen? Why didn't you call me?"

"Thanks."

Fabio smiled. "We're just making sure things don't get out of hand today."

Marion looked doubtful, even more so when Gilda folded her arms across her stomach. Mick's office door was closed. She hoped he'd found an ice pack and wouldn't scare the kids. Before she could move away, the door opened, and Mick strolled out and forced a weak grin.

"Whoa." Marion stepped back. "You look ready for Halloween. That's quite the shiner. The kids will be well behaved tonight."

"You should see the other guy," Mick said.

Gilda returned to her desk without comment. No point trying to talk to him with everyone else eavesdropping.

"Miss me, honey?" Thayer strolled through the door with a cardboard tray. "I got you to calm your nerves. You sounded a little stressed."

"Marion brought me herbal tea. No caffeine." She refused to give him brownie points, no matter what he did.

"You're here to observe and keep the peace, not bother my receptionist." Mick scowled. "Maybe Fabio should investigate you. You've wanted me run out of town since Gilda started working here. I wouldn't put it past you to hire someone to put me out of business permanently."

Thayer snorted. "If I wanted to kill you, I wouldn't hire someone else."

When everyone fell silent, he bowed his head, then skulked to the seating area.

"Let me know if he bothers you again," Mick said. "I'll convince him to come into adult class, so you can spar him. That'll teach him."

Unconvinced, Gilda logged onto the computer and wrote down a list of tasks. The phone rang before she could tackle the first one on her list. She hesitated for three rings, afraid to get another caller asking about the murders. "Yoshida Martial Arts."

"It's Gary. Meet me out front."

She shook her head. "It's raining."

"I never took you for a wimp," he said.

"What do you want?" Her question prompted Thayer to approach the counter. She waved him off, then asked, "What's going on?"

"Chloe stopped by to see Mick earlier," Gary said. "I heard he tried to beat her up, then threw her out."

Gilda chuckled. "I wasn't here, but he looks like he tangled with a wild cat."

"Sounds right. Did my spoiled little princess provoke him?"

"That was my impression," she replied.

"Thanks for your honesty. Let Mick know I'll come by tomorrow to settle things."

When he hung up, Gilda frowned. Getting back into a regular routine wouldn't be easy. Not with people breaking into the school and the local bookie's daughter making threats on Mick's life. She missed the good old days when all she had to worry about were broken toes and bloody noses.

CHAPTER 23

G ilda longed to sleep in Thursday morning, but her head pounded. Wednesday night had drained every ounce of energy she'd managed to retain from dealing with curious parents, both in person and on the phone. "Why are the police here?" "Who gave Sensei Mick a black eye?" "Who's the guy in the dark car parked out front?" "Do you think there'll be another murder?"

By the last class, she was ready to snap.

Things only got worse when Mick invited—no, lured—Thayer into class.

She pulled the blankets over her head to block out the memory, but the thumps persisted. The pounding was at her front door. Someone wasn't about to let her sleep in.

"Coming." Gilda's throat ached. Her voice rasped like she'd screamed all night, which was close. She swung her legs out of bed with a groan. Clad in her long T-shirt and pajama shorts, she opened the front door.

Marion held two extra-large cups. The scent of coffee was hypnotic. "I figured you could use this after class last night. I'm so glad I stayed to watch you put Thayer in his place. Honey, I am seriously thinking about signing up after watching you in action. You're my new hero."

Gilda groaned. "Don't remind me."

"Why not?" Marion asked, handing her one of the cups. "You're one scary chick. I'll bet Thayer had nightmares after that fight. He'll never cross you again."

Which was why Mick paired them up in the first place. Payback.

"Probably. He deserved every shot I gave him." Gilda motioned her inside and flopped onto the far end of the couch.

"Especially that last one," Marion said. "When you left, he was still lying on the mat counting stars. No man in that school will ever tell anyone they hit like a girl again. Honey, I know you and Thayer have a history, but what was all that about?"

She huffed. "He shouldn't have called me a wimp. Do you know he and Fabio have never taken me seriously as a murder suspect?"

"And that bothers you?" Marion asked, then rolled her eyes. "Be glad you're not under surveillance twenty-four seven and getting dragged to the station to answer questions about everything from birth to now."

"I just hate that Thayer never takes me seriously."

Marion chuckled. "He will now. Good thing Fabio gave you a ride home. You looked exhausted. That wasn't the reason I came over. When I was in Café Beanz last night, I overheard Chloe tell some guy she needed some muscle to convince 'a guy' to sign his condo over to her."

Gilda gagged on her coffee. "Why didn't you say anything? Do you know who was she talking to?"

"You were busy. I've never seen him before," Marion said. "I assume he's one of Gary's goons. The guy's got people everywhere."

Possibly, but Gary wouldn't let anything happen to Mick if he owed money. Chloe, on the other hand, would use whatever means it took to get Mick's condo. Maybe even his businesses.

"Are you okay?" Marion waved a hand in front of her face.

She rubbed her eyes. "I should warn Mick and Gary she's up to something."

"Let's go. I'm off today. I'll tag along for support." Marion headed for the door.

"I'll text them."

Marion peered out the window. "You could, but Gary's out front. I can wave him in."

"I just got out of bed. I'm not even dressed yet, let alone had a shower."

"Then get a move on."

"Do you want to go for a walk?" Gilda asked. "I need to clear my head."

"What about Gary and Mick?"

"Texts sent."

Marion took a long drink of coffee. "Okay. Keep in mind I'm not in great shape. If you make me walk too far, I could have a heart attack. I need to start a diet tomorrow."

Gilda chuckled. "No torture. Just an easy walk to clear my head, move my body, and avoid every man in my life. Maybe we should start going for walks instead of brunch."

"Did you get hit in the head last night?" Marion asked. "I need my weekly dose of bacon. Besides, if I lose too much weight, I'll have to buy a whole new wardrobe. I don't know about you, but I don't have the money for that. I'd rather eat bacon."

Laughing, Gilda glanced out the front window. Smoke curled out the driver's window of Gary's car as he sat back against the leather upholstery. Good thing there was more than one way out of her house.

She got dressed, then led Marion out the back door. They snuck through the dew-covered garden and through the gate before heading toward the beach. Breaths of wind swirled off the lake and dried the fear from her forehead.

"You're one sneaky girl." Marion said. "I'd hate to be on your bad side, especially after last night."

Gilda glanced over her shoulder, keeping watch for Mick, Thayer, Gary, or Fabio. "Thayer always makes me feel so incompetent. Mick seems to know I can do things before I know I can."

"Like beat up police officers, hold together the karate school, and solve crimes?" She raised her eyebrows. "Thayer's gonna think twice about bothering you now. Plus, you've got the local bookie on your side and Mick's head over heels for you. You should've seen him last night. It was like he wanted to stop you and Thayer, but—"

"How on earth did he find us?" Gilda asked, when she spotted Gary up the beach.

"Just pretend we're out for a normal walk on the beach."

"We are out for a normal walk on the beach."

She raised her eyebrows. "Then why did we have to sneak out the back door?"

"Because I feel like a fugitive lately. I might as well act the part."

Marion let out a loud laugh. "And that's why we're friends. Don't worry, I'll run interference. But if he gets out of control, you take him down."

"How'd you sneak past me?" Gary, still wearing his dress shoes and socks, walked toward them. "I was waiting for you."

"We ducked out the back door. How'd you find us so fast?"

"I know people," he said. "People who tell me I need to talk to you because you're one tough little cookie who can kick my butt if I step out of line."

"Yes, she can." Marion grinned. "I watched her throw Thayer to the ground after she knocked him around in class last night. I'm signing up to take classes with her."

Gary studied both women, then shook his head. "Is Mick still living at the school?"

"As far as I know," Gilda said. "Why?"

He grasped her arm and steered her toward the street. "You and I are going to get him to settle up his debt with me."

She wrenched her elbow out of his grasp. "Why do you need me? I have nothing to do with any of this. It's all on Mick."

"Yeah. Leave her out of this," Marion said. "She's not involved."

Gary grabbed Gilda's arm again. "She works for Mick and can get me through the front door. We're going to get this cleared up before I get tough."

When Gilda stopped on the sidewalk, she pulled out of his grip. "Are you going to use the same muscle-head Chloe hired?"

His gaze darted from Gilda to Marion. "What are you talking about?"

"I overheard Chloe talking to some goon in the café last night. She wants him to get Mick to hand over the deed to his condo," Marion told him.

"You'll probably foot the bill for him whether you know it or not," Gilda said.

He raised his eyebrows. "What did he look like?"

After Marion gave him a brief description until he nodded and said, "Let's go."

"I'm serious." She clenched her teeth. "I'll help you, but you have to tell Chloe to get out of Mick's condo and leave town."

Marion nudged Gilda. "Either that, or you need to spar Gilda in class. Trust me, you don't want to do that."

Gary stuck his hands in his pockets. "Consider it done. I'll ship my princess off to New York. My brother can set her up with a job or something. Anything else?"

Gilda shook her head. "Nope. I'm good. Marion?"

"All good. Let's track down Mick."

They discovered him in front of the school, unlocking the front door. He wiped the sweat off his forehead, taking one look at the trio before he groaned. "I'm hot, I'm sweaty, and I'm not in a good mood. Can we save the intervention for later?"

"No intervention," Marion said, holding the open door. "Just problem solving."

He led the way into the lobby then met Gilda's gaze. "Gary, I didn't know you hired female bodyguards. That's a progressive concept, even for you."

"Stop playing dumb. You know why I'm here. Where's my money?" Gary asked.

Mick stood in the middle of the lobby. "I'll give you the money. But first, you need to get Chloe out of my condo, away from my Ferrari, and out of town. Agreed?"

Gilda shook her head. "I don't think you're in a position to bargain."

Gary winked at Gilda. "I understand the problems you're having with my daughter, and I wholeheartedly agree. I thought I'd like having her around, but she's turned into her mother. I'll send her to New York and set her up with some rich plastic surgeon."

"So far, so good," Marion said. "Gilda, let's get out of here."

"Don't go anywhere, you two. I want witnesses." Mick led the way to his office and handed Gary a small canvas bag. "I trust cash will be fine."

"How much cash are we talking?" Marion asked.

"Fifty grand." Gary took an envelope out of his pocket. "I'll trust all the money is here since your life's on the line. Gilda assures me I can count on you."

Mick met her gaze. "Good to know."

The men shook hands, then Gary left.

Once the door closed, Mick slumped into one of the plastic chairs lined up for parents to watch their kids in classes and let out a deep sigh.

"That's it?" Marion asked, shaking her head. "Geez, for fifty gees, I expected a shootout. At least a fist fight or a little more mayhem. All you two did was exchange packages. I had more fun watching Gilda clobber Thayer last night. Call me if you need anything, Gilda. I'll see you later."

Once her wannabe bodyguard left, Gilda sat beside Mick on a flimsy chair and frowned. "I agree. That was too easy, and that bag looked too light for cash."

"Newspaper," Mick admitted.

She groaned. "And what did he give you?"

"A plane ticket." He opened the envelope and let her see. "Chloe's coming by later. I'll give her the ticket to New York and convince her to leave town before the trouble between me and her dad escalates and gets caught in the middle."

"What do you get in return?" she asked.

"He moves her out of my condo and changes the locks." Mick tapped the corner of the envelope on his leg. "He came by after Fabio took you home last night. We had a couple drinks, while Thayer came to his senses. I settled my debt, and we both decided it was best if Chloe left town."

Gilda narrowed her eyes. "Then what was the whole duffle bag thing about? Gary grabbed me and Marion off the beach and freaked us out for nothing."

He shrugged. "In his line of business, it serves him not to trust people. There are people around you right now who bother him."

"You and Thayer mostly," she replied.

Mick chuckled. "Fabio and Razi among others."

"In short, he doesn't trust anyone."

"He trusts you, which is why he wanted to put your mind at ease."

Weird to think she got all warm and fuzzy thinking a known bookie thought of her as a step up from his daughter. "I need a shower. You people make me feel dirty."

Mick winked. "If I wasn't expecting company, I'd go with you."

As flattered as she was by his offer, she cringed. "Chloe."

"Relax." He pulled her close to kiss her. As he moved away, his lips brushed hers when he spoke. "Chloe should be here soon, then Xavier's coming to train. After that, we'll go grab lunch. What could go wrong?"

* * *

While she burned off her nervous energy ripping out weeds, Gilda replayed her discussion with Mick so many times since she was no longer sure what was fact and what was fiction. Something felt wrong. Mick and Xavier trained alone at the school where two other men died. Was one of them the killer, or did the killer know they were there?

Wine would be the best antidote to calm her irrational thoughts, but she settled for hot tea with honey. Frustration bubbled beneath her skin until tears burned her eyes. She didn't want to run to the school to check on them and look like a fool, yet she couldn't sit and do nothing. Her landline phone rang as she poured boiling water into her cup. Her hands shook as she set the kettle aside and let her parents' old answering machine pick up the call.

"Gilda. It's Marion." The panic in her friend's voice was palpable. "Whatever you're doing, drop it and get to the school."

She bobbed the bag in hot water and struggled to ignore the pressure rising in her chest. Afraid of what she'd hear if she answered the phone, she shook her head. "No way. Mick can take care of things without me."

When the phone rang again, Marion shrieked into the answering machine. "I know you're there. Pick up the bloody phone. Now."

Alarmed, she ran to answer it. "What's going on?"

"I'm at work and don't have time to explain. Get to the school. It's an emergency."

Lately, the only emergencies at the school involved bodies. She set her cup near the sink. Had Mick discovered one of the other black belts dead? Worse. What if Mick had been murdered?

"Oh, crap." Her throat tightened. She'd never forgive herself for leaving him alone with Xavier. She bolted out the door, then returned for her purse in case she needed her keys to lock up. She brushed off the morbid thoughts and raced out the front door.

Gilda spotted the flashing lights of the police cruisers from two blocks away. She broke into a sprint. This was no prank. People milled around outside the front door, trying to get a glimpse inside.

"Get out of my way. I work here." She shoved through the crowd and flew past the officer guarding the door. "What's going on? Where's Mick?"

Fabio and Thayer stood over a figure seated behind the front desk. Her desk. Drops of blood dotted the floor. Her heart hammered as she tried to get a better.

"Who let you in here?" Thayer asked, lunging to stand between her and Fabio. "You need to go home. We'll talk to you later."

"Let her stay," Mick said.

At the sound of his voice, relief washed through her. "Mick, what's going on?"

Fabio and Thayer moved aside.

Mick sat in her chair covered in blood. When his gaze met hers, he frowned. Combined with the black eye and contusions from Chloe, at first glance he looked like he'd murdered someone.

Gilda swallowed the fear her first impression was right. "Please tell me you didn't do anything stupid."

"Don't know yet. Neither of them are talking," Thayer said.

"Neither of them?" she asked, her eyes widening and her stomach sinking.

She caught a glimpse of Xavier on his back beneath the shrine. His arms and legs sprawled as the handle of a dagger stuck out of his chest. The ornate Japanese dagger Mick kept in a box in his office. A cherished gift from Yoshida when they opened the Sandstone Cove school.

Footprints had thinned patches in the pools of congealed blood nearby. She refused to believe Mick killed Xavier. He must've arrived after the murderer left and checked Xavier for a pulse.

Thayer towered over Mick and put on his tough guy act. Apparently, he'd forgotten Mick could knock him to the floor with a flick of his finger. "If you don't tell me what happened, I'll lock you up for the rest of your miserable life."

"Maybe you should let Detective Wright take a bash at him," Fabio suggested. "I'll bet she'd got her own ways to make him talk."

"More than you know," Thayer growled.

Gilda wasn't so sure she wanted to hear the truth, especially not after Xavier tried to poison them.

"Sit," Mick said.

"No." Her hands shook, and her knees weakened. "I can't do this. First Walter, then Erik, now Xavier. I'm going home and locking my door. I quit, Mick. For real this time. Deal with this yourself this time, I'm done."

"Sit," he repeated, motioning to the chair beside him.

"Not a chance. You were right. I give up. I don't need to play detective. Thayer and Fabio can handle everything. I'm going home." She turned to walk away.

Thayer steered her to the desk. "Your boss told you to sit."

She folded her arms across her chest. "He's not my boss. I've already quit twice this week. As far as I'm concerned, I don't work here, and I'm not coming back."

"It's okay, Gilda," Fabio said. "You're scared and in shock. We all understand." He looked past her and frowned. "Mick, I need your clothes for evidence."

"Sure." When Mick stripped off his shirt to reveal rippling muscles, a female officer tried to hide her stare. "Gilda, can you do me one last favor? Grab me a change of clothes from the desk in my office."

"No," she snapped.

"I'll get them," Thayer said.

"Gilda knows where my things are," Mick insisted.

She scowled, curious why he wouldn't trust anyone else. "Fine, but after that I'm leaving."

"Thanks," Mick said. "After you get my clothes, you can leave. I'll mail your last paycheck."

Gilda wove through the maze of people and paused in the doorway of Mick's office. Pristine was the first word that sprang to mind. Too pristine, considering the current state of the rest of the building, and how messy the school was just a short while ago, especially with Mick living in it lately. He wasn't normally so tidy.

"You will wait in my office. I will deal with you later." Yoshida's words had bothered her the night of the workshop, but now they swirled in her head as if on a loop.

Mick's clothes were folded on the desk, not slung over the back of a chair. His sandals, the only thing out of place, sat under the desk, not on the shelf out front as usual. Beneath his clothes, lay a stack of papers. Rental agreements for a building in Toronto. Yoshida's signature was on them. He'd stuck bright yellow arrows where Mick was to initial and sign.

Gilda grabbed his clothes, sticking the papers beneath her shirt with a sudden yearning to hear what he had to say. She clutched the papers against her stomach with one arm before she rejoined the men at her desk.

When she handed Thayer the clothes, she asked, "Do you want to search them? You'd better make sure I didn't smuggle him a weapon"

When Mick blanched, she shook her head a fraction of an inch.

Thayer shook out each item of clothing before handing them to Mick. "He can change, but I want one of my officers to keep an eye on him."

"Fine by me." Mick unzipped his jeans and dropped them to the floor. He stood behind the desk, wearing nothing except a pair of Snoopy boxer shorts, then stuck his thumbs in the waistband. "Did you want these too?"

"No!" Both Thayer and Gilda hollered.

The female officer's eyes grew wide.

"Put your pants on." Fabio chuckled.

Gilda turned her back. She was used to seeing Mick with no shirt, but not in his skivvies. Aside from when he carried her to her bed, then she woke up next to him. First he'd professed his love to her, now he was practically naked in front of her and most of the local police force. How much more could she stand without long, cold shower?

"Come and sit." Mick patted the chair beside him. When both officers moved closer, he held up a hand. "Just Gilda. The rest of you take a hike."

"Keep in mind she's not a lawyer," Thayer told him. "There are no confidentiality rights between an employer and employee."

Fabio yanked his partner away from the front desk. "Give them two minutes before you walk Mick to the gallows. You can interrogate them separately."

Gilda had barely sat down before Mick pulled her so close their noses bumped as he whispered, "Did you find the papers?"

When she lifted the bottom of her shirt and showed him, he kissed her then grinned. "Anything else under there?"

"Where these for Erik's school?" she asked.

"I know whose ring you found."

Gilda stared. "Whose?"

"Xavier was looking for it the other day. His father-in-law's a goldsmith. The same goldsmith who made a copy of Xavier's one-of-a-kind ring for Yoshida a couple years ago after Xavier and his wife split."

"When I asked him about it, he never said a word," she said. "Not even when you mentioned it at Razi's."

"Shh!" He pulled her by the front of her T-shirt until their noses touched again. "He hid it from one of his ex-wives and didn't say anything or he would've been a suspect."

"He already was," Gilda reminded him. "Then who killed Walter and Erik?"

Mick glanced toward the dojo where Fabio leaned in the doorway, doing a bad job of pretending not to watch them. "I don't even know who killed Xavier. Someone knocked me out and left long before I woke up, just like they did to you."

"I guessed that by your footprints in the blood."

"Huh?"

"The blood was already congealed when you stepped in it. If it was still wet and runny, I don't think your print wouldn't be so clear." She hesitated, sure his eyes glazed over. "This doesn't matter, does it?"

Mick grinned. "You amaze me. All I know is that Xavier and I planned to train for a couple hours. I went to my office to make a phone call and change into my gi. When I came out, I heard a noise, then someone hit me from behind. When I came to, I saw Xavier and tried to give him CPR. Then I heard another noise."

"The killer was still here?" Gilda tensed.

"A cat."

"How did it get in here?"

Mick motioned his head toward the wall. "The vent is loose. It leads to the roof and would be a handy way for someone to sneak in and out without being seen."

But only for someone a great deal smaller than either Razi or Mick. She shivered. So much for her theory. Yoshida was a black belt. He was smaller than both men, but could walk in and out of the school without anyone paying much attention. Why bother to hide?

"When did you call the police?" she asked.

He reached for the hand sanitizer on her desk. The bottle sputtered when he squeezed it. "After I checked his pulse and before I checked out the vent. Marion took the call."

"Yeah, she phoned me."

"And you came running thinking I was dead."

Gilda frowned. "She said there was an emergency and told me to get over here."

He gave her a hand a squeeze. "I thought maybe she told you I was the murderer and to stay away from me if you valued your life."

"Why would she tell me that?" She tilted her head.

"Because I was a blubbering idiot when I called, and probably said I was covered in blood." He studied his hands as though they belonged to someone else. "I need a hot shower and something to scrub with."

"And I need a word with your boyfriend." Thayer announced. He shooed Gilda away. After fifteen minutes of interrogation, he let Mick go. "Don't leave town or else."

Mick stared at the computer. "Thanks, but I live at the school and have nowhere to go until Chloe leaves town. She was supposed to pick up her plane ticket earlier." He hesitated, then asked, "Gilda, do we have more hand sanitizer?"

"Yeah, in the back. I'll get you some." She bit back an offer that Mick could go home with her. Not only would Thayer take it the wrong way. So would Mick. She opened the utility room door and frowned.

Bleach wasn't something they used in the school, yet there were five, extra-large jugs that would've taken her both hands to move. When she reached inside for a bottle of hand sanitizer, the smell from the jugs made her gag. Whatever was in them didn't smell like bleach—more like gasoline.

"Mick," she called out. "Did you put these here?"

He came around the corner, with Fabio and Thayer close behind. "Bleach? "You know I never use the stuff. What're they doing here?"

"They weren't here the other day," she said, "and they don't smell like bleach."

Thayer shoved her aside, grabbed a jug, and sniffed the contents. He set it down carefully, then told everyone to clear the building. At first, no one moved. They all seemed to hold their breaths.

Fabio peered around him. "What's going on?"

"The room's full of jugs of gasoline," Thayer said. "Enough to burn the school, and half of Main Street to the ground. I think we all need to go to the police station."

"This wasn't my doing," Mick insisted. "Dust them for finger-prints. This place is all I have, so why would I want to torch it?"

"If you don't come peacefully, I'll have to cuff you," Thayer said.

Mick met Gilda's gaze. "I'm probably safer there anyway."

She agreed until something caught her attention. The jugs were stacked neatly, not set inside in a line. Three bottles on the bottom with a board wide enough to balance the remaining two jugs on top of the lower three. Someone with an obsessive-compulsive disorder had cleaned and reorganized the utility room.

Yoshida.

She shot a concerned look at Mick, who said nothing.

Fabio turned to Gilda. "I'll need your keys to lock up."

When Mick peered into the closet again, the fear on his face spoke volumes. "She's not safe either."

Thayer narrowed his eyes. "What did you see?"

"That either of us could be next."

Gilda craned her head for a better view. Five thick rolls of paper towel were stacked in the same pattern behind the bleach jugs. All it would take was for someone to toss a match on the paper towels. The school and the consignment shop next door would explode. She struggled to catch her breath.

"Can Gilda grab one last thing from my office before we go?" Mick asked.

"Quickly," Thayer said.

"My wallet's on the shelf with the candles." Mick leaned closer and lowered his voice. "Call Razi. I'll text you later. We'll meet at Café Beanz."

She half-ran to Mick's office. On the shelf above his desk, stood the tower of candles Yoshida had built. Three on the bottom with a ruler supporting the remaining two. Everything stacked so there was an object between the two layers. Just like the bleach and the paper towels. Was Mick trying to let her know he'd figured it out?

She returned with his wallet, her hands shaking and whispered, "Are you okay?"

"I will be when this is over." He gave her a one-armed hug, hard enough for the papers in her shirt to crackle between them. "Give Fabio your key, then go home. I'll call you when they release me."

Gilda grabbed her purse and scurried out the door, armed with the lease documents. Now all she needed was to put it all together.

CHAPTER 24

Despite having quit her job twice and no longer wanting any involvement with the school, the murders, or Mick, Gilda called Razi when she got home. "Sensei Mick is at the police station. Can you make sure he gets home okay?"

"That is not what Sensei Mick asked."

So much for quitting and not getting involved. She should've ~~walked~~ run when she had the chance. What was wrong with her?

"He will meet us at Café Beanz once Thayer releases him," Razi said.

"Which could be hours from now."

"That is true," he said. "He also wanted me to ask if you are upset with him."

"Upset?" Anger burst through her carefully constructed dam. "How could I not be upset with him? He never mentioned the missing merchandise. Didn't tell me about Walter's past or the whole mess with Chloe and Gary until I was in the middle of it. I could've been killed being anywhere near him." She sucked in a sorely needed breath. "How in heaven's name could I not be upset?"

Razi spoke slowly, "I will meet you at Café Beanz at four o'clock. We will sit in a booth near the window. Then you can try to convince me you do not care what happens to Sensei Mick. Okay?"

"Huh?"

"I will see you at four o'clock," he said. "Please try to think of a way to help stop the murderer."

Razi was right. Even after everything that had happened, the murders, the whack to her head, and her misguided night with Mick, the three of them had to stick together. The men needed her to set her anger aside to help them catch a killer.

Unable to relax, she cleaned the house. Her hands did the work, while her mind sifted through evidence and events. Had she missed something? Was there a suspect she hadn't even considered, someone who had grievances with the instructors and the school?

All her thoughts returned to Yoshida and Mick, who could've set up the crime scene around Xavier. He would've had the time and ability.

The phone jolted Gilda away from her mental checklist. Her stomach slithered in and out of knots as she let it ring until the answering machine picked up. She really needed to get rid of that thing.

"Gilda, don't you ever answer either one of your phones?" Marion groaned over the speaker. "You're not at the school. You're not at home. Where are you?"

She grabbed the phone. "I didn't hear the phone over the vacuum cleaner."

"You're a bad liar, honey. I'm standing at your front door. I haven't heard a vacuum cleaner since I got here five minutes ago."

Gilda really needed to give up trying to lie. She was bad at it. Opening the door, she said, "I should've called you when I got home, but I was too wound up. Coffee or tea?"

"Water's fine. I walked over after work. You're right, I need to work out more. Walking six blocks knock nearly killed me." Marion followed her to the kitchen. "I saw Mick at the police station. Do the police think he killed Xavier?"

Gilda poured two glasses of water. "He's the closest thing to a witness they have. They'll interrogate him then let him go."

She hoped.

"You don't think he killed anyone, do you?"

She leaned against the cupboard. The only viable suspects she'd come up with, aside from Mick, were Razi and Yoshida. They each had keys to enter the school. Yoshida had motives and the ability to sneak in undetected. Razi had no motive that she knew of, and there was no way he could sneak in without being seen. He did, however, have a military background and was a trained killer.

"Are you okay, honey?" Marion asked. "You look pale."

She glanced at the clock. Almost time to meet Mick and the trained killer. Her phone chimed. A text from Razi saying Mick was on his way. "Sorry, I have to go."

"I'll walk with you."

"Are you sure? That's not necessary."

Marion set her glass in the sink. "I might not be a karate master, but I am intimidating. Besides, I'm worried you could be next."

The thought had crossed Gilda's mind since Walter's death, but Mick managed to convince her otherwise. Until now. Her hand shook when she reached for her purse. "I'm not worried."

"You're a bad liar," Marion said, giving her a hug. "You're scared to death and don't know who to trust or what to do next. I'm the only real friend you've got right now."

Gilda swallowed back tears. "I don't want you to get hurt."

"Me, neither, but I'd never forgive myself if I handed you off to a killer." Marion stood her ground. "Stalemate. What now?"

She took a deep breath. "We face Razi and Mick together and hope for the best."

Seated in a corner booth in Café Beanz, Razi flinched when Gilda and Marion walked in. He scowled before flashing a weak smile. "Miss Yearly, you were not on the guest list."

Marion glowered, letting Gilda sit near the window. "Look, buddy, I've taken all the calls about the guys at the school. Gilda's my best friend and I don't trust you or Mick."

Razi turned to Gilda. "Why have you brought this woman?"

"I'm her bodyguard," Marion said.

"You are?" Gilda asked.

"You do know Miss Wright is a green belt in karate and perfectly capable of taking care of her own body," he said.

"Look, tough guy, she's my friend, and I'm here to look out for her, so get over it."

Gilda's jaw tightened. "We want answers."

"As do we," Razi said.

She handed him the papers from Mick's desk. "Mick had these. You need to look them over before he gets here."

"Do I get to read them?" Marion asked. "I didn't kill anyone, but I have a vested interest here. My bestie's life's in danger."

Razi's cheek twitched. "I will read them then decide if that is appropriate."

"Muscle head," Marion growled. "You think you're all that just because you have a black belt in karate. Boy, do I have news for you."

When the server brought their coffees, Gilda reached for her cup. "I wouldn't mouth off to him if I were you. He's trained in Krav Maga, Jiu jitsu, and karate."

Marion raised her eyebrows, keeping her gaze on Razi. "I could use a bodyguard."

His face reddened as he rifled through the papers and frowned. "I would understand if Shihan Yoshida wanted to open a school in Toronto, but why destroy the school here? We are doing well, are we not?"

"I would have thought so," Marion said. "The school's busy and you have half the town on your roster. Unless he wanted to get the insurance money."

Gilda filled them in on the bottles of gasoline and the kanji she and Mick found on each victim. "If the murderer's following the pattern, Xavier will have 'Loyalty' in his casket, but what made him disloyal to Yoshida?"

"I do not think things are so simple." Razi stirred his tea like a form of meditation.

Marion huffed. "Well, what do you think? Stop leaving us in suspense."

"Keep your voice down and listen, woman," Razi snapped, then cleared his throat. "The Four Possessions of the Samurai are not mere suggestions. They are requirements every samurai lived by, or they would bring dishonor to their fellow samurai and shame their families."

"What happened if they did dishonor their families?" Gilda asked.

"They would commit seppuku." Razi stabbed at his stomach with his teaspoon, then trailed it across his torso.

Marion's eyes grew wide. "They'd gut themselves? That's nasty."

Gilda sat back to think. "If Yoshida thought the black belts had dishonored him, it makes sense, on some warped level, that he'd take matters into his own hands. Why not reprimand them, though? He could expand the business and give everyone what they wanted. Instead, he planned to torch the place."

"Like Miss Yearly said, money," Razi told them. "Insurance money, to be precise."

"But the school was doing well. Although, we've lost students recently. It's creepy to train in a school where people died."

"Greed?" Marion asked.

Gilda shook her head. "Yoshida gets a cut of all earnings, plus he gets paid to teach seminars."

"Lust?" Razi asked.

"How do you figure that one?"

"What's she doing here?" Mick slid into the booth next to Razi.

Marion scowled. "I'm protecting Gilda. Start talking."

Mick glanced to Gilda and Razi, whose face turned strawberry red. Finally, Mick said, "It all comes back to Jade Levy. She's the one who started this mess."

Marion gasped. "Walter's wife?"

"Are you sure? How?" Gilda asked.

"Jade likes having guys fawn over her, which drove Walter crazy. For her, Yoshida was a challenge. He wouldn't even look at her the first few times she flirted with him."

"What changed?" Razi asked.

Mick hesitated then pointed a finger at Marion. "Don't you dare tell anyone what I'm about to say or I'll drag you into class by your bottom lip and spar you myself."

"Are you kidding? You could kill me with your pinky." She pretended to zip her lips shut. "Not another word."

"I'll hold you to it," Mick said, before ordering coffee and pie. "Yoshida's wife went back to Japan for six months last year. He thought it was the best time to invite us to train at his school in Fort Erie. When we went to dinner after, he and Jade spent most of the evening talking and pouring Walter sake."

"They did more than that, as I recall," Razi told them. "I had to drive Walter to the hotel. Jade stayed behind with you and Shihan Yoshida."

When Marion opened her mouth, Mick shot her a glare. She clapped a hand over her mouth before she met Gilda's gaze.

"Jade spent the rest of the evening alone with Yoshida. I assume it wasn't a one-time thing. Mick said. "They saw each other in hotel rooms after that."

Gilda dropped her head back against the bench. "Hotel rooms with king-sized beds and Jacuzzi tubs. The same thing he asked for when he was here for the workshop. You covered for them, didn't you?"

"What?" Marion forgot her vow of silence. "How could you do that? I thought Walter was your friend."

"Keep it down." Mick scowled.

When the server set a coffee cup in front of him, he added cream and sugar. "Walter knew how much we relied on him. He wanted more money, more classes, and either a share of the school or his own school. Yoshida wouldn't budge as long as Jade did everything he wanted."

"That's why he got rid of Walter," Gilda said.

Mick frowned. "When Yoshida's wife returned, Walter told her about Jade. She divorced Yoshida, took his money, and went back to Japan. That's when Yoshida wanted Walter gone and Jade for his wife. Without another messy divorce."

"But why kill the other black belts?" Gilda asked. "They had nothing to do with it."

"For a quiet lady, you have many questions," Razi said.

Marion nudged her arm. "You're good at this interrogation thing. Forget being a receptionist, you should be a cop."

Mick cleared his throat and shot Marion a scowl. Then he lowered his voice, so Gilda and Marion had to lean forward. "Greed's a great motivator. The government came after Yoshida for back taxes. If he filed for bankruptcy, it would follow him for years. If the school burned down, there'd be an insurance payout, and he'd get everyone off his back. Since he owns part of the school, there are as many legitimate reasons for his prints to be there as the rest of us."

"Did the police check the bleach jugs for fingerprints?" Gilda asked.

"They will, but somehow he'll be able to prove he was in Fort Erie," Mick said.. My guess is he's hiding out with Jade."

Gilda thought about the man she saw at the Levy home. "How do we prove it?"

Mick sipped his coffee. "We set him up and make him confess."

"I'm in," Marion told them.

"If he kills me, Mick is the only one left," Razi said. "If he kills Mick, the school closes. I will not be happy to be the only black belt."

"What do we have to do?" Gilda asked.

Mick met her gaze. "Talk to the police and set a trap."

"No way. I quit working there twice. I don't even know why I'm here."

Marion stood, then glanced at Razi and Mick. "Come on, Gilda. Let's go back to your place and figure out career options. Maybe you can drive fuel trucks or teach kindergarten. Something nice and safe."

Gilda agreed. No matter how charming Mick was it was time for her to move on. "I'll bring Happy my resume. Maybe he'll let me start next week."

"Please stay." Mick got up, pulled Gilda close, and wrapped his arms around her. "I need you."

When he kissed her, Marion let out a whoop and Razi chuckled. Breathless, Gilda pulled out of his grasp. "You need therapy."

"You're so easy to fluster," he said with a grin.

"It's about time." Marion nudged Gilda. "Definitely call me later, unless he's still at your house, in which case, I'll talk to you tomorrow for details."

Gilda turned, ready to call Marion back until she noticed Chloe at the counter. Chloe's gaze bored right through her to Mick.

"Wait. I'll come with you." Gilda followed Marion to the door, keeping her gaze averted from Chloe.

This day could only get worse if Mick and Razi expected her to be part of an elaborate trap they set for the killer.

She glanced back over her shoulder. Did Chloe have anything to do with the murder? Chances were, she knew people who could pull the whole thing off without a flaw.

CHAPTER 25

"Are we going to your house first?" Marion asked as they left the café. "I can't imagine you carry around an extra resume just for times like this."

"Yes. Just you, me, and a big bottle of wine," Gilda told her. "Maybe Happy has some application forms handy."

Marion chuckled. "As if you'd need to fill one out."

Mick grabbed Gilda's hand. "First, we go to the police. We need help."

"No, you need help," Gilda said.

Razi shook his head. "Do not worry. I will not make you go alone."

"I'm not about to miss a second of this." Marion grinned.

Gilda would've preferred they rip her away from Mick and walk her home to lock herself and Marion away from the world with junk food and wine. Instead, Mick gripped her hand so tight her fingers turned white as he marched her across the street to the police station.

Fabio glanced up. "Well, it if isn't Nancy Drew, Bess, and the Hardy Boys."

"Now what?" Thayer slammed his coffee cup onto his desk. Splatters of brown liquid dotted the paperwork scattered around the surface. "I thought we agreed you'd let us solve the murders and you guys would look after the karate school. Gilda, do you really think you can catch the bad guys?"

"No, I—"

"Bad guy," Marion corrected. "Gilda thinks there's only one killer."

"Oh, good. Now I can take a vacation and sleep at night. Hallelujah!"

Mick sat in the chair across from Thayer and stared him down. "And we think she's right. One killer, who might have an accomplice."

Gilda kept her mouth shut. She'd been inside the police station too many times this week alone. They all had.

"I see." Thayer didn't appear convinced. "That's assuming I believe whatever you have to say. I have evidence against Mick and Razi. Either one could be the killer. In fact, you each have lots to gain with the others gone."

"I have more to lose than I have to gain," Mick pointed out.

Thayer shook his head. "All you have to do is knock off Yoshida and you own it all."

Gilda frowned. "Is that true?"

Mick folded his arms across his chest. "If that were the case, his would've been the only body and I would've disappeared weeks ago."

Even if the school closed, Mick could make a living flipping houses. He and Razi could train elsewhere. Gilda had the most to lose. Her job, her house, and her pride. She'd end up working for Happy, or moving in with her mother.

"Gilda? You have something to say?" Fabio asked.

"I'm good."

Marion put her hands on her hips. "Seriously? You don't think Gilda killed them, do you? She'd never hurt anyone. Well, except Thayer, and that was fun to watch."

"Not that I want to be pegged as a murderer," Gilda said, "but I'm not as sweet and innocent as everyone around here seems to think."

Thayer chuckled. "Yeah, I know. I'm the one who caught Mick in your house wearing nothing but underwear."

"Why didn't I hear about that?" Marion's eyes grew wide. "Gilda, honey, we need to chat over that bottle of wine later."

"This sounds like a story I'd like to hear." Fabio grinned.

"No, you don't," Mick said. "Either of you."

"Perhaps the ladies should leave," Razi said. "Sensei Mick and I have all the information and evidence we need."

Gilda scowled. "Works for me. Come on, Marion. Let's go get that wine and I'll tell you everything."

Mick lunged at her so fast he knocked over both chairs in front of Thayer's desk before he wrapped his fingers around her bicep and growled, "Don't you dare."

"Let me go or I'll scream." She lowered her voice.

"What do you want, Gilda?" Mick asked. "A bribe? I can't give you a raise if we go out of business, you know."

"I don't want a raise. I want out." Tears rolled down her cheek. "I'm tired of finding bodies and of having nightmares about finding you and Razi dead."

"You're exhausted," he whispered, trying to hug her.

She nudged him away. "I'm exhausted, I'm scared, and I've quit so many times this week I've lost count."

"Go home, babe. I'll call you later."

"No." Gilda pried his fingers from her arm. "Don't call me. Don't text me. Don't include me in your drunken meetings. Don't show up at my house. I'm done. You can deal with everything on your own. I quit."

"Razi, give Fabio the papers," Mick said. "I'll be right back."

"She needs time to cool down," Marion told him.

"Alone with you? I'm sure that'll help." He followed them into the sunshine, leaving Razi with Thayer. "I just need to talk to her."

Gilda wiped her face. "Marion, go pick out wine at Happy's. I'll be right there."

"But what if Mick—?"

"He won't try anything." Gilda blinked away more tears. "He could've killed me more times than you know, and didn't."

Marion backed away, keeping a wary eye on Mick as she headed to Happy Harvey's Hangover Hut. "If you don't show up in five minutes, I'm coming after his sorry hide."

"Ten minutes," Mick said.

Marion tapped the face of her watch. "Five. Starting now. Talk fast."

When she walked away, Gilda folded her arms over her stomach. "You heard the lady. Talk fast."

"There aren't many people who scare me, but she's definitely one of them," Mick admitted. "Why the need for a bodyguard when you're a green belt?"

Gilda avoided his gaze, afraid her resolve to quit her job and stay away from him would crumble. "Because she's my best friend and she wants to help."

Mick ran a hand through his hair. "Look, Sherlock, she's right. You should go home, have a glass of wine, and lie low. Razi and I can manage things."

She winced. "By things, you mean the cops and Yoshida. Why did you want me to meet you at the café, then drag me to the police station if you don't want me involved?"

"Because I'm selfish. You were right. You quit and I need to respect that. You're safer staying far away from me."

Was he trying his hand at reverse psychology or being honest? She searched his face for signs he was toying with her but found none.

"Then I'm going home." She didn't bother to add "if you need me." The last thing she wanted was for him to need her.

He hugged her hard before murmuring, "Stay safe, Sherlock. I'll be at the school if you want to train or talk, or whatever."

When Marion emerged from Happy's with a paper bag, Gilda followed her to the nearby Chinese restaurant for the takeout Marion ordered while she and Mick talked. Fifteen minutes later, they carried containers of Sesame Chicken, fried rice, egg rolls, and Beef and Broccoli back to Gilda's house.

After a large gulp of wine, Marion blurted out, "Okay, now I want details. You kissed Mick before and never told me."

Gilda didn't bother playing dumb. "We did more than that."

Marion drank half her glass. "What were you thinking? Never mind. I know what you were thinking. Just tell me details."

"We went for a swim late one night."

"How romantic." Marion wiggled into a comfortable position.

"Not really. He was walking me home after..." She hesitated. "After a staff meeting, we took a walk along the beach."

"Anything that involves wet and naked sounds romantic. You were naked, right?"

Gilda squirmed. "The staff meeting was in Razi's hot tub."

"Ah. Mick planned ahead." She burst out laughing. "Why didn't you call me? I like a hot man with a hot tub as much as the next girl."

Gilda tried to focus on the sweet, crunchy chicken rather than her discomfort. "I didn't know where we were going until we got there. For all I knew, Mick and the others were setting me up."

"Others?" Marion asked. "Was this before the murders?"

"After Erik died."

"Is this the night Mick was running around your house in his underwear?"

"No. It was the night we... We slept together."

Marion whooped and fanned her face. "Oh my. And you never told me?"

"He acted like it was no big deal. Then I woke up the other morning and he was in my bed to hide from Chloe. That's the day Thayer caught him."

"I can't believe Thayer caught Mick running around your house wearing his skivvies. That man's so jealous he can't focus on the case. I can't believe that poor sap still hasn't taken the hint."

Gilda chuckled, warm from the wine and the spices in the food. "I wish you could've seen his face when he saw Mick half-naked in my hallway."

"Wait. Mick wasn't in your bedroom?" Marion asked.

She set her food aside. "The other morning, I woke up with Mick lying beside me in my bed. He was hiding from Chloe, who kicked him out of his condo and changed the locks. And from Gary, because he owes a lot of money after Chloe made a bogus bet in his name. And from the killer who wants the black belts dead."

Marion's mouth dropped open. "You woke up with Mick Williams in your bed and you didn't tell me anything about it?"

"I kicked him out."

"Honey, that man is hot." Both her eyebrows shot upward. "Are you nuts?"

Gilda sipped her wine. Apparently, she was.

"I thought I was seeing things at first, but I saw the way he looked at you in the café today," Marion said. "He's crazy about you. He doesn't want you around to get hurt, but he doesn't want to let you go either. That's why he won't let you quit. You're more than just some boring old receptionist."

Gilda's phone buzzed. Mick. *You ok?* Less than a minute later, another text. *Call me when she leaves. We need to talk.*

"Is that Mick?" Marion asked. "You need to tell me if it's juicy."

Five more texts in the next two minutes to say he wanted her to join him at the school to either train or just hang out. She guessed he either wanted a distraction or ideas of what they could do about Yoshida. Mostly, it seemed he wanted to spend time with her.

She punched him up on speed dial on the way to the kitchen, her fingers too clumsy from the wine to text back. When he answered, she told him, "I'm drinking copious amounts of wine and I'm not going anywhere. As a matter of fact, I'm never setting foot in the school again. Ever."

"You don't mean that," Mick said. "You're still just mad."

"Darn right I'm mad. You and Razi treat me like a kid even though I'm the one who put all the clues together."

"Either you're in or you're out, Sherlock. Are you quitting, or do you want to help?" he asked.

He had a good point. She quit her job, then showed up anyway. She kneed Mick in the groin then sent him mixed signals. While she was determined to avoid Mick, Razi and the police, they'd all encircled her like beefy, egotistical, testosterone-fueled planets.

"We need to pull together to stop Yoshida. Help me catch him and I'll make sure you and your job are safe."

"Is that a threat?"

"No."

Gilda leaned against the cupboard. "You'd keep the school going despite everything?"

"I can't do it without you and Razi," he said.

"How many times do I need to quit?" she asked. "You're as dense as Thayer."

He chuckled. "At least thirty more before I believe you. I have to make some calls tomorrow morning. Come to the school for training at ten."

She bowed her head to hide her tears.

"Are you okay?" Marion paused in the doorway with both wine-glasses. "I was right, wasn't I? Did he profess his undying love?"

"Worse," Gilda said. "He wants me to meet him at the school tomorrow. How am I supposed to do that with a nasty hangover? He's such a jerk."

Marion topped off their glasses singing, "Mick loves Gilda. Mick loves Gilda."

"You say that like it's a good thing."

"Oh, give the guy a chance. Go train with him tomorrow."

Gilda reached for the wine bottle. "What if I do and he's the next to die?"

Marion shrugged. "At least Thayer won't suspect you."

CHAPTER 26

G ilda awoke that morning with her phone clutched in one hand. She frowned. When had she picked it up? Once she realized she'd received four texts from Mick in the past ten minutes, she buried her head beneath the pillow. The phone chimed three more times.

When she still didn't reply, he called and said, "Meet me at the school."

"Go away."

"Forget it. We both need to vent and if you don't show up, I'll keep calling."

Gilda groaned. "I vented last night."

"I meant physically." The way he said it sent a pleasant chill over her body. Within seconds, her entire torso tingled.

"No." She hung up and burrowed beneath all the blankets.

This time when the phone rang, Mick shouted, "What is wrong with you?"

"I don't want to talk to you."

"Come to the school. We don't have to talk if you don't want to."

More shivers. What was he trying to do to her?

"You're not helping." She hung up again.

When he called a third time, he didn't give her a chance to speak. "Get your sorry butt over to the school or I'll kick in your door, throw you over my shoulder, and haul you out down here like a caveman."

When he hung up, Gilda swore, then shouted, "That man is such a jerk."

All the way to the school, Gilda's head pounded, and her eyes throbbed behind her sunglasses. Her feeble attempt to keep up with Marion drink for drink last night hadn't paid off. A vat of coffee held more appeal than a run or anything else Mick had to offer.

She tugged on the front door of the school, dismayed when it opened. After their earlier conversation, she hoped he'd invited other students. From the lack of voices, she guessed she was the first to arrive. Either that or she'd find another body.

Her stomach lurched and bile rose in her throat. "Mick? Are you here?"

"Yeah." Already dressed in his gi, he sat behind her desk resting his head in both hands. His hair was disheveled, and his eyes were bloodshot like he hadn't slept all night.

"You look like crap." she said.

"No one else is coming," he said. "I should've told you not to come."

She set down her duffle bag. "Who else did you call?"

"Everyone. They think this place is cursed. Even Razi. Too much bad karma. You should go home."

"Okay." That suited Gilda. She desperately needed a pot of coffee and more sleep. Picking up her bag, she turned to leave.

Mick leaped to his feet and sent the chair flying backward. "You'd leave because no one else is here?"

"You told me to."

He pulled her toward the dojo. All the missing tatami mats were replaced by thin puzzle mats. "Don't go. Please."

Gilda removed her sunglasses. "Usually, when people tell you to go home, that means you don't have to stay."

"You look like hell." Mick gave her a hug.

She didn't resist. "Too much wine. What's your excuse?"

"I got jumped by a bottle of scotch."

"Looks like the scotch won." She backed away. The others were right about the cursed feeling hanging in the school.

He ran a hand through his hair. "Just because no one else is here, doesn't mean we can't train. Right?"

"I suppose."

"Give me one hour, then we can get breakfast. I won't push you so hard you puke."

"Okay, but only if you're buying."

"That's my girl." Mick winked. "You're a trooper."

"I'm an idiot, and I'm not your girl."

"You're also not Thayer's girl." He winked. "That's good enough for me."

She headed for the change room, thinking Mick could be right. Maybe training would clear her head. Although, she'd prefer not to train where three men were murdered. It was downright creepy. She had no idea how he could live there and stay sane. Is that what the scotch was for?

"We should go train on the beach," she said. "Being in here isn't healthy."

Mick knelt in the dojo facing the birch shrine. "If I leave, the killer wins."

"And if you stay, he'll kill you," Gilda told him as she bowed in. "No one will judge you if you get out of here now and then. You didn't kill anyone. Did you?"

"No." His eyes were closed. "Did you?"

"You know I didn't."

Mick opened his eyes. "Then let's do katas. If you work hard enough, I'll feed you."

"Sounds good."

He nudged her arm. "Does this mean we're friends again?"

"As long as you don't make me throw up."

Mick grinned. "I can't make any promises."

She got to her feet and jogged slow circles around the dojo, which was enough to make her nauseous. Mick dispensed with formalities. After half an hour of kata work Gilda became conscious of someone else in the school.

Thayer stood in the doorway, his gaze on Mick as he corrected Gilda's stance. For the first time in weeks, Thayer wore his full uniform, rather than a suit and tie.

"Are you signing up for classes or snooping?" Mick asked.

Thayer's jaw hardened like cinder blocks. "I'm here for Gilda."

She broke the horse stance—shiko dachi—she'd held so long that her thighs quivered. "I didn't do anything."

"I'm not here to arrest you."

"She's busy." Mick shielded her from Thayer's gaze. "We're training."

"Is that what you call it?" Thayer asked. "How convenient. You teach karate classes and women flock straight to you, hoping they can spend a night with you."

Mick's back stiffened. "At least I don't have to handcuff my dates."

"You'd better watch your mouth," Thayer said. "You're nothing more than a muscle head who couldn't make a go of it in the big city because of your reputation for messing around with students."

"You should leave before you say something you'll regret," Gilda warned.

"Let him say his piece," Mick said. "I'd kind of like to hear what he thinks he knows. I'm up for a fight today."

Thayer's eye twitched. "You might not want Gilda to hear what I have to say. She's not into guys who play the field. From what I hear, you play the bad boy role to the hilt."

"Like you?" she asked.

Mick chuckled. "Sounds like the playing field's pretty level then. There's nothing I haven't done that you haven't equaled."

"Maybe we should step outside," Thayer said.

Gilda groaned. "Oh, that's mature."

Mick placed his hand on her shoulder. "Why not settle things right here and now? This isn't public, Thayer. This is personal."

"On your turf? Do you think I'm stupid enough to take you on with all your weapons within reach?"

"I have all the weapons I need right here," Mick said, holding out his hands. "What are you so afraid of? You have a gun and a baton."

"And handcuffs." Gilda hoped they weren't serious. She had half a mind to lock them in the building to beat each other senseless. Fabio would probably handcuff the two of them together and tell them to work things out.

Thayer took off his shoes, then set his utility belt in the dojo against the wall.

Mick cleared his throat. "Out of respect, I'd rather you leave the gun outside."

"Seriously? With my luck, Gilda will shoot me in the back."

"Oh no, don't drag me into this," she told them. "I'm leaving."

Mick untied his black belt and folded it neatly. "You're already involved. He's beating his chest because he doesn't want you near me. This is about Thayer's pride."

"I don't see you backing down," she said.

"Then I'd look like a wimp." He set his obi on the floor near the shrine, then took off his gi top.

Gilda threw her hands in the air, then headed for the change room.

"Where do you think you're going?" Thayer asked.

"Home. There's too much testosterone in the air." She turned to bow at the door.

"He's the one trying to impress you," Mick said.

"And you're not?" Gilda closed the dojo door behind her. Why should she care if they killed each other?

Bad choice of words. She should call Fabio to come settle things, but he'd probably referee the fight before he'd mediate.

Mick and Thayer barked insults and accusations for several minutes. Suddenly, the school grew quiet. Their voices faded, then the lights in the dojo went out.

"Oh, no. What now?" She changed before rushing down the hall.

Mick's office door was closed. She knocked, then stepped back. Thayer opened the door with a wry smile. No bruises. No blood.

"What's going on?" Gilda asked, looking from one to the other.

Mick chuckled. "You mean why aren't we beating each other senseless?"

Thayer hitched up his utility belt. "I'm a cop. I'd have to arrest him for assault."

"Hey, buddy," Mick said, holding up a finger in warning. "I told you the other night, once you sign the waiver and put on sparring gear, anything that happens in the dojo is perfectly legal."

Including Yoshida trying to beat her senseless. Gilda heaved her bag over one shoulder and shook her head. "You're both nuts."

She got halfway to her desk before Mick called out, "Don't you want to know what we've decided?"

"Nope."

"We're teaming up." Thayer said. "The more I've thought about your suspicions, the more I think you're right. Yoshida's got the most to lose if this place fails and the most to gain if it goes up in flames. We're going to set a trap for him with Mick as bait."

Gilda hesitated. "Do you think he can be tricked? He's a smart man."

Mick joined them in the lobby. "A smart man who's desperate to get rid of this school and out of Sandstone Cove. He'll bite."

"Unless it's Razi he's after, not you," she told him.

"Not a chance. Yoshida and I have butted heads for years. Razi never steps out of line. He's a bigger asset than I am."

Thayer frowned. "But what if Razi's the murderer?"

"He wouldn't be dumb enough to kill me in front of a school full of cops," Mick said.

Gilda sat on a plastic chair and closed her eyes. "Either way, it won't turn out well."

Thayer frowned. "What do you mean?"

"The killer has nothing left to lose. Mick's the last black belt, aside from Razi, and since Yoshida and Razi were trained to fight to the death."

Mick sat and placed a hand on her leg. "You should go home and update your resume. You don't have to be part of this."

"Um, I'll be right back." Thayer headed down the hall to the washrooms.

Gilda blinked back tears. "Did the police get the results back from the lab? Did they search the vent?"

"Those tests take time, which is what we're out of. I don't want anyone else to die."

"Isn't there another way we can catch him?"

"If you have a better idea, I'd love to hear it."

"Not really."

He kissed her. "Razi and I don't have a Plan B. This is it. Are you with us?"

* * *

As Gilda left the school, she realized she still hadn't had coffee or breakfast. So much for Mick's promise. Her hands shook and her knees were weak. The shaking was partially from the workout and mostly from the mere thought of Mick and Thayer teaming up to catch a killer. She hoped Fabio would keep them focused, because if their ideas didn't work...

Lost behind a veil of tears, she wasn't even aware of the car next to her until Gary called out, "Gilda, wait up. We need to talk."

Startled out of her reverie, she shook her head. "I'm done talking. I'm going home to eat, pack, and move in with my mother."

"You don't mean that."

"Way more now than I did a minute ago." She swiped one arm across her face. "I'd rather live where people aren't dropping dead around me."

He got out of the car to give her a hug. "I'm sorry you feel that way. I have something that might help."

"An extra-large coffee and breakfast?"

"A motive for the murders."

"Yeah, me too. Yoshida's greed."

"Mine's better," Gary said. "Let's go for a drive. This will make your day."

Reluctantly, she got into the passenger seat. "Where are we going?"

"Walter's house."

"Walter's dead," she sniffled.

"Yeah, but his widow isn't, and she has a secret." He refused to say more until they parked across the street from the Levy house with its three-car garage. "A friend tells me our prim and proper widow is expecting a package in about six months."

Gilda groaned. "Why do I care what Walter's widow is expecting? I need food and coffee. Just take me..." She stares at Gary. "Jade's pregnant? Who told you that?"

He lit a cigarette, drew in a lungful of smoke, then held the cigarette outside the window. "We have a mutual friend in the medical profession who wants justice done."

"Doc? Doesn't that violate doctor-patient confidentiality?"

"Jade isn't his patient. He saw her buy a pregnancy test in the hospital pharmacy. Considering he was waiting for her to identify the body, that seemed surreal."

Gilda shrugged. "So, she and Walter were expecting. They were married."

"Except that Walter had a vasectomy seven years ago," he said. "Doc confirmed it. The lovely widow was sleeping around."

Yoshida walked out of Jade's house into the sunshine, then got in his car.

"That's old news. Aside from the pregnancy, you're not telling me anything I didn't already know."

"Oh, Yoshida's not why we're here."

"Then what are we—"

Gary held up a hand to silence her, then said, "We're here because of that one."

When a familiar figure walked through the hedge and up the sidewalk, Gilda gasped. "Razi? What's he doing here?"

With a quick glance over one shoulder, Razi tapped on the front door. Jade peered out and spoke to him, her face pinched with anger. She handed him a paper bag.

Razi opened it and peered inside before he pushed past her into the house.

"What's going on with Razi and Jade?"

"That's where my connections came up with dead ends." Gary butted his cigarette. "I assume, it has something to do with his stint in the army, and the fact he and the merry widow have a history."

CHAPTER 27

A fter Gary brought her breakfast and an extra-large coffee, he dropped her off at her house with more questions than answers. Sipping her coffee, she paced the garden and tried to piece together what was going on.

Why would Razi walk straight into Jade's house like he owned the place? If Razi and Jade had a one-time fling, there was no way he'd be so comfortable.

She started to text Mick about Jade's pregnancy, then stopped. Half the men in town could be the father—including Mick. How was she supposed to sort out the truth when Jade probably had no idea who the father was?

Texting Razi would be a bigger mistake. He'd gone straight back to the top of her suspect list. While he was too big to be the man who'd run out of the dojo, either he or Yoshida could've been the man in the yellow bathrobe she saw in Jade's house.

Her phone buzzed with a text from Mick.

In one more hour, they'd lay the trap to catch a killer. Gilda still wasn't sure they had the right bait. The more she thought, the more doubts nagged at her. While Yoshida was the logical choice for a killer, maybe he was the intended target all along. What if the others were simply in the wrong place at the wrong time?

Mick had kept so many secrets she wasn't sure she could trust him. Using him to lure the killer would only work if Razi wasn't the intended target. If Mick was the killer, was he about to kill his target and end his own life? Death by cop.

Razi had his own reasons for wanting the other black belts dead. As a former soldier, he would've been quick and efficient. What if he planned to kill Mick in front of everyone?

Wary, Gilda made her way to the school. At the front desk, Mick, Thayer, and Fabio glanced up as they went over last-minute instructions. Razi was nowhere in sight. She sighed when the cops went to stake out the best hiding spots.

Alone in the lobby, Mick hugged her. "You okay?"

"This is a bad idea," she whispered,, fighting the urge to tell him what Gary showed her. "Where's Razi?"

He kissed her forehead. "He had things to tie up. He'll be here soon."

Things like dealing with Jade Levy's pregnancy, perhaps? She needed to stop second guessing herself. That part was up to Thayer and Fabio.

Thayer grabbed her arm. "Time for you to go home. Leave the detecting to the police."

"Not a chance." She shrugged him off. "I want to catch this guy as much as you do. Probably more. I won't get in the way."

"I understand that," Mick told her. "We all do. But maybe this isn't the best place for you to be. Anything could happen today."

Gilda huffed. "I've been knocked out, stalked, and found two bodies. I want a front row seat to see how this ends."

"Go home, Gilda," Mick ordered.

She shook her head and glared. "Not. A. Chance."

"I'll take her with me," Fabio said. "She'll be safe there."

Mick grabbed her shoulders. "Whatever happens, don't do anything until Fabio gives you the all clear. Got it?"

Angry and terrified all at once, she threw her arms around his neck. "Please be careful."

"I will," he whispered, his lips brushing her ear. "When this is done, you and I need to spend some time alone to figure things out."

"What things?" Gilda asked.

Her heart beat faster when he gazed into her eyes then leaned his forehead against hers and said, "Like where we go from here. And how we're going to make this work. I vote for a sunny beach and all the margaritas we can drink."

"Time alone on a sunny beach. That sounds good."

Mick glanced to where Thayer and Fabio discussed last minute ideas. When Thayer turned their way, Mick kissed Gilda so hard her body seemed to ignite. Then he whispered, "I do love you."

Unable to speak, she nodded.

Fabio led her to the change room and made sure they had a clear view of the dojo and shrine. A strip of daylight peered through the back door Mick had left ajar. The trap was set and Gilda's heartbeat in her throat.

Mick stripped off his gi top and did the only thing he could to make things appear normal. He trained. Kata after kata, for nearly half an hour. Sweat dripped off his hair and rolled down the curves of his bare back.

Gilda's foot fell asleep. When she shook it, she kicked the wall by accident.

Mick flinched, but didn't stop moving.

"Careful," Fabio whispered from the next stall.

The last thing they wanted to do was give away their hiding spots. The waiting was agonizing, and Gilda's stomach ached from anticipation. Mick was a sitting duck and there was nothing anyone could do if a gunshot rang out.

Luckily—or not—the killer favored more traditional weapons.

Something thumped in the wall down the hallway. After several seconds, the wall vent popped open. Razi would never fit inside such a confined space.

Gilda and Fabio had a clear view as one narrow hand slapped the floor, then another before Yoshida crawled into the school. His dark hair was mussed and dusty. Gilda bit her tongue. Thayer had placed a sensor on the vent. Even though he was in Mick's office, he already knew Yoshida was inside.

Yoshida brushed dust off his clothes, then crept barefoot down the hall. He paused in the doorway with his back to Gilda and Fabio.

Mick ended his kata, then faced his teacher with a bow. "My apologies, Shihan. I didn't hear the door."

"You were oblivious as usual. What is it you wish to discuss?" Brusque and to the point. Mick must've called to lure him in. Then why crawl through the vent?

No witnesses. Just like with all the others.

Gilda held her breath. Could Yoshida sense her heart beating against her ribs?

"The rental agreement for our Toronto school," Mick said, pacing as he spoke. He reminded Gilda of a jaguar with rippling muscles and raw power. He stayed within her sight. "We need to renegotiate. I can't afford that amount. I'll need new equipment for start-up."

In the center of the dojo, Yoshida shook his head. "I cannot do that. I now own the building and need to pay the mortgage. I also need to support my fiancée."

"Your fiancée?" Mick asked. "Don't you mean Walter's widow? Is that why you killed him? I get the katana, but poisoning him seems like overkill. Even for you."

"Perhaps, but as much as his wife no longer wanted to be with him, she did not wish him to suffer. I respected her wishes." Yoshida sank gracefully to his knees and sat with his back at a forty-five-degree angle to Gilda. "I lavish her with gifts and keep up with her in ways her husband never could."

That was one image Gilda didn't need.

Mick continued to pace as he said, "The way I hear it, she's got a lot of boy toys. What makes you think she'll give up her life here to go with you?"

Yoshida's back stiffened. "You are a bad liar."

"Am I?" Mick asked. "You're not her only boyfriend. I guarantee that."

"I have ways to deal with men like you." The Zen calmness was gone in a huff as Yoshida let out a shaky breath. He slid something out of his shirt sleeve.

In the next stall, Fabio made a small noise. Gilda was sure it was all he could do to hold back from running out to tackle Yoshida.

"A blowgun," Mick said, his voice wavering as he continued to pace. "Am I your next victim? Time, right? What exactly does time have to do with me?"

"Ah, you figured it out. Clever, but too late." Yoshida sounded genuinely pleased.

Gilda's entire body tensed. Yoshida was the killer, Mick was about to die, and it was far too late for an "I told you so."

Mick faced Yoshida and glowered. "Walter's past made him dishonorable, plus he was in your way with Jade. Erik was turning his back on you and all his training. Since he showed a lack of integrity, you stabbed him in the back. Xavier's murder has me stumped. What did he ever do to you?"

"He wanted to be your equal with a school of his own. I was reluctant," Yoshida said. "When he poisoned my tea, I lost patience."

A third victim of Xavier's rash of cyanide poisonings.

"Which made him disloyal, so you killed him," Mick said. "The third possession."

"You are smarter than I gave you credit for."

"Actually, Gilda figured it out. She's the smart one. It wasn't wise of you to make her your enemy when you to beat her up in class."

While grateful for the compliments, she wasn't sure Mick giving her credit for solving the mystery was a good idea. If their plan didn't work, Yoshida would come after her and Razi next.

Where was Razi? Why didn't he have Mick's back?

"The receptionist?" Yoshida snorted. "She is weak and not worthy of your loyalty."

"You knew she suspected you all along, didn't you?" Mick went on. "That's why you went after her in the workshop. If she was afraid enough, she'd never tell anyone what she thought."

Yoshida snorted. "You would listen to a silly girl's flights of fancy rather than believe your Sensei. She is nothing."

Gilda held her breath.

Mick smiled and shook his head. "You're wrong. She's the backbone of this school and she was right."

"That is of little consequence." Yoshida raised the blowgun to his mouth.

"I never took you for a coward," Mick said. "A true goju karate master would stand up and fight like a man with his bare hands. Empty hands. Not resort to blowguns and other weapons. Of course, he'd also never kill his students out of jealousy. Not that it matters but, just for the record, what are you using on those? Rat poison?"

Yoshida lowered the blowgun. "Suitable, but too obvious. It is a neurotoxin rarely tested for in North America. Within minutes, you will stop breathing. Then your heart will stop. The poison will spread even after your body dies. No one will know what hit you."

"Cobra venom. The same thing you used on Walter."

Yoshida's back stiffened. When he raised the blowgun once more, Gilda gripped the curtains and forced herself not to burst out of the change room. If he heard her, he'd shoot her instead. Mick and Razi would be safe. Had she become that fearless?

Across the dojo, something clicked. Her blood ran cold.

Had Razi snuck in from the front entrance and who did he have the gun trained on?

The gun appeared first. Then Thayer crept across the mats behind Yoshida with the gun pointed at his head. "Put down the weapon."

Gilda wanted to close her eyes and lay her head against the wall, but couldn't look away until Yoshida handcuffed and defenseless.

Nearly hidden by his baggy top, Yoshida's chest expanded, filling with air. He had too much to lose to quit because of a gun.

As he raised the bamboo reed blowgun to his lips, Gilda shoved the curtain aside. Aware of everything at once, her feet touched the rubber puzzle mats a heartbeat before Yoshida released a sharp puff of air and Thayer yelled for him to drop it.

Her shoulder connected with Yoshida's back, as she bowled him to the mats. Three solid thuds sounded before everything stood still.

"Mick!" Fabio's and Razi's shouts froze Gilda's blood and her breath.

Beneath her, Yoshida lay sprawled face down, the blowgun on the mats two feet in front of them. Gilda pinned him to the floor like she'd seen Razi do in jiu jitsu classes. Yoshida could probably barely breathe, let alone move, yet she had no sympathy.

Yoshida shook, then chuckled before he said, "You are too late, Miss Wright."

Across the room, Mick lay on his side dripping sweat onto the mats. His eyes wide, and mouth agape. His body motionless.

Gilda's vision swam as she started to scream.

CHAPTER 28

G ilda's breath came in short, frantic gasps as she growled, "If
  Mick's dead, you'll never leave this school alive."

"That no longer matters, does it?" Yoshida said, as she dug her
elbow into his back. "I got what I want. Mick Williams will never teach
again."

Razi knelt next to Mick and rolled him onto his back. Beside his
knee, the feathers on the blow dart fluttered from the breeze blowing
in the back door. The tip was embedded in the mat.

"You missed," Gilda said, then laughed as she stood.

"No. No. I never miss." Yoshida cursed for the first time she'd
ever heard. His face tightened to his infamous kabuki mask before an
officer pulled him to his feet.

"Put that creep in a cell before I shoot him," Fabio ordered as he
limped past them toward Mick. "And call an ambulance."

"Gilda, were you trying to get killed?" Thayer asked, giving her a
quick hug. "I could've shot you."

"I'm glad you didn't." She glanced toward Mick but couldn't see him for the officers swarming between he and Yoshida.

"Where's Gilda? Is she okay?" Mick asked as Razi helped him up.

Razi grinned. "She is a hero."

She blinked back tears and stumbled toward Mick. He caught her in a bear hug, nearly knocking them both to the floor. She pressed her head to his bare, sweaty chest in relief. "I thought you were dead."

"Me too, babe." He held her tight.

Fabio gave Gilda a pat on the back. "Lady, you were amazing. Did you see the way she flew out of the change room and saved your sorry neck? Don't ever do that again!"

"No, I kind of had my eyes closed," Mick said. "I was a little worried about dying."

"Miss Wright." Razi flashed a smile. "While I wish you were not here, I am glad to see you are okay."

She willed her hands to stop shaking. "Where you? Why weren't you here?"

"Actually, Razi's the genius who set up the sensors in the vent and wired the doors. No one could get in or out of this place without us knowing."

Gilda clenched her jaw. "Why didn't you do that a month ago and save us a lot of anxiety?"

"Forgive me, Miss Wright," Razi said. "As I told you, Sensei Mick knows all my secrets. I was a secret agent with the Israeli government until I was exiled. I am an expert at surveillance and infiltrating spy networks."

She nodded. "Which is why you walked right into Jade's Levy's house. She thought you were her friend."

"You are very clever. In truth, we have been friends for many years. She gave me the information we needed to catch Yoshida. She recorded every conversation they had since Walter's death. He is one crazy dude."

"Dude?" She never thought she'd hear Razi use that word.

Thayer handed Fabio his phone. "At least we got Yoshida's confession on video. There's no way he's getting away with anything."

As the police trickled out of the school, Gilda's adrenalin surge slowly subsided until she sighed.

"Are you okay, Sherlock?" Mick sat next to her near the shrine.

"I was afraid I'd lost you," she admitted.

"Aww, you do care," he said, then kissed her. "Did you think about what I said earlier?"

"About spending time alone?" she asked. "I'm in."

Thayer snorted. "Oh, please. Everyone knows Mick Williams will never settle down for any woman. He'll dump you as soon as the next princess in distress comes along."

Gilda smirked. "Maybe, but that's a chance I'm ready to take."

Razi threw up his hands. "Thank goodness. It is about time."

She met Mick's gaze. "Time."

"The last kanji was mine all along," Mick grinned. "Guess you just won twenty bucks, Razi."

ABOUT THE AUTHOR

Diane Bator began writing as a kid when she fell in love with storytelling. After ten years with various traditional publishers, she's created her own company, Escape With a Writer Publishing, to relaunch her previous work plus many new titles. She is also a member of Sisters in Crime, Crime Writers of Canada, The Writers Union of Canada, and International Thriller Writers.

A proud mom of three, Diane is also a Reiki Master, a blue belt in goju-ryu karate, and an artist who loves stopping at odd places on road trips and creating new things from old.

Her website is https://dianebator.ca/

Join her newsletter and Escape With a Writer! https://dianebator.substack.com/

Also By

Also from Diane Bator
Published by Escape With a Writer Publishing

Written in Stone, An A.J. Cadell Mystery, Book 1
All That Sparkles, A Glitter Bay Mystery, Book 1